CLOCKWORK CONSTELLATION:

CHRONO CHAOS

PAUL MICHAEL PETERS

CONTENTS

COPYRIGHT

EBOOK: 979-8-9912595-0-7

PAPERBACK: 979-8-9912595-1-4

HARDCOVER: 979-8-9912595-2-1

DEDICATION

For my sister, Anne.
Your laughter and giggles
make the world a brighter place.
Your cat imitations
never fail to bring a smile to my face.

"In a life devoid of
Beauty,
it's easy to become
Obsessed
with seeing it in others."

– Paul Michael Peters

FROM THE AUTHOR

In the summer of 2024, I found myself with an unexpected abundance of free time. Three books were ready to set sail—ideas that had been brewing over the past three years of, well, *let's just say*, unprecedented events (see global pandemic for more details).

Everything I'd been putting on the page seemed deep and serious, the kind of stuff that would have made my high school literature teacher beam. But for a change, I craved something different. Something lighter. Something fun.

"What about an adventure?" I asked myself. "Maybe with a pirate who has the wit of Dorothy Parker?" I could picture it perfectly. "But wait, is there really room for a pirate in an adventure story these days?"

That's when a voice—gruff, charming, and undeniably weathered—piped up inside my head. A man with a face carved by the sea, and a twinkle in his right eye, stolen from a distant star. "Aye," Barnaby Blackwater replied with a roguish grin, "there's *always* room for a pirate on an adventure."

And here we are. Time to leave the dock—*all ashore that's going ashore.* I hope you find this first story in the series, as Barnaby told me, as enjoyable to read as it was to write.

PART I

IT BEGINS

1

TOCK.

TOCK.

TOCK.

Millicent's fingers trembled as she unlatched her grandfather's Pocket Orrery. The clamshell case yielded with a soft click, revealing the Clockwork Constellation in miniature—a ballet of brass and polished nickel, where gems of colorful planets pirouetted around the gleaming Heart Star.

In the hushed expanse of the cosmos, where celestial bodies waltzed to the metronome of time, the Clockwork Constellation stood as a testament to unwavering order. Its nucleus, the planet Gearturn, pulsed with the rhythmic gears and cogs of a conductor, a symphony that had orchestrated the Supercluster's destiny for eons. Her grandfather's Pocket Orrery showed this all in the palm of her hand.

A year had passed since Millicent last watched him cradle

the cherished piece of their shared world. She remembered him always with the stub of a yellow pencil behind his right ear, a smile replacing the concentration on his face when he saw her. Her fingers gently caressed the worn edges of the workbench, each groove a tender echo of the countless hours she spent under his watchful eye. Her gaze softened as it settled on the small divot in the wall—a lasting mark from one of her more daring, nearly disastrous inventions. Like a growth chart, it showed the progress she made building Quark, her robot companion, with her grandfather. The memory tugged at the corners of her mouth, a bittersweet smile forming as she recalled how he had pulled her to safety just in time. A warm, comforting wave spread through her chest, wrapping her in the familiar embrace of those precious moments with her grandfather—moments filled with learning, the thrill of creation, and the occasional spectacular misstep. She smiled at the soft glow of those memories, laughing quietly at the twinge of embarrassment but mostly basking in the deep well of fondness and nostalgia they stirred within her.

Her eyes drifted to the photographs on the wall. There she was, beaming at her graduation, her grandfather's hand resting proudly on her shoulder. It was a day to make him proud, joining the Order of Engineers by his encouragement. Next to it, a faded image of him in his youth with Dr. Kilmoore, their expressions a stark contrast—her grandfather's eyes alight with possibility for the future, while Kilmoore's narrowed with disdain. Then her gaze landed on the final photo: a young couple, their faces eerily familiar yet distant, like characters from a half-remembered dream. "Grandfather's daughter and her husband," she murmured, the words slipping out like a broken cog in her otherwise precise mind.

A chill settled in her chest, the discomfort lingering as she turned her attention to the freshly finished chronometer on her workbench. This was her sanctuary, where every tool and component had its ordained place, where the precise whir of gears brought her solace. Here, she could craft pride for her grandfather.

Millicent ran her hand along the smooth surface of the workbench, feeling the weight of years spent in this room. She knew every millimeter of the woodgrain. This workshop had witnessed her highest triumphs and deepest sorrows, her loves and losses, her successes and challenges. The thought of leaving it behind seemed impossible. What could the world outside possibly offer that would compare to the comfort and familiarity of this sacred space? Stepping outside felt hollow; every sight, every step, would only serve as a reminder of her grandfather's absence, and adventures they could no longer share. She felt a little weepy.

Time was supposed to be predictable. Orderly. Comforting. It wasn't supposed to hiccup. Millicent gave one last look at the etched face of her grandfather inside the caseback of the Pocket Orrery, seeking the reassurance that had always been there. But as she gingerly returned the piece to its home, an odd sensation prickled at the back of her neck. The air started to thicken, charged with an energy that set her nerves on edge. Then, she heard it.

TICK-TOCK.

TICK-TOCK.

TICK-TOCK.

Millicent's breath hitched. The sound was wrong. Terribly, impossibly wrong. The orrery's steady rhythm, once as reliable as the planet's rotation, faltered. Each beat hammered against her ears like a frantic, metallic heartbeat.

On her workbench, the device convulsed violently, gears

gnashing and springs coiling with savage intensity, as if trying to tear themselves free from their precision-crafted prison. A wild, discordant symphony of clicks and whirs filled the air, building to a fevered crescendo.

Then, in a blinding flash, the Pocket Orrery erupted with raw energy, searing across Millicent's vision like a lightning strike condensed into a single, terrifying instant. The light faded, leaving her vision spotted and the acrid scent of ozone hanging in the air.

Forty-two seconds of chaos had undone her carefully calibrated world. When stillness returned, Millicent did what any self-respecting horologist would do in a crisis—she noted the time. Three and a half days since she'd last set foot outside. Her second thought: she needed to report this to the authorities. She strapped on her shoulder pack, clutched her grandfather's Pocket Orrery, and moved toward the exit.

Her hand hesitated on the doorknob, the weight of uncertainty pressing down on her. Stepping outside put her at risk; disorder waited past this doorframe. But her curiosity, that insatiable force, won out. She yanked the door open and stepped into the chaos beyond.

The sky above pulsed like a blistered rainbow, repainted every six seconds. Her neighbor, Mr. Sprocket, was caught in a loop with his corgi, Coggie—entering and exiting his house in an endless, futile waltz. Ms. Meridian's prized lilies bloomed and withered in two-second cycles, never dropping a petal. Millicent's jaw clenched involuntarily as her mind raced faster than the malfunctioning clocks around her. The Premier would know what to do. He had to. He ran the city.

She sprinted toward the center of Celestial City. Her skin tingled with unease, the warm air failing to soothe the creeping sensation. Her gaze locked on to the sky, where stars blinked in and out of existence, like sparks from a dying flame. The hairs on the back of her neck stood on end, and she rubbed her arms, trying to shake off the sense of dread that clung to her like a heavy cloak.

A mob had gathered at the central office, their voices rising in a tumult of confusion and fear. People and objects seemed to flicker in and out of sync, moving forwards and backwards in time. Premier Jasper Horologe stood at the top of the steps, his hand raised in a futile attempt to calm the crowd.

"Amara Epoch cannot pet her cat; it's frozen in time!" a panicked voice shouted, cutting through the chaos.

Millicent furrowed her brow at the odd statement, muttering under her breath, "What an unusual thing to say." But as she looked around, she realized that the bizarre claim was likely true—nothing was functioning as it should.

"Our top scientists are working on it," Premier Horologe called out, his voice trembling with uncertainty. "Please, everyone, try to stay calm. We will find a solution."

As Millicent navigated through the throng, she accidentally bumped into someone. "Oh, excuse me," she apologized, then froze as recognition dawned. There was something familiar in her eyes. "Ivy Equinox? What's happening to you?"

The girl turned, her eyes wide with panic. "Millicent, it's terrible—I am getting younger by the minute! I don't want to be a teenager again; I enjoy retirement too much," Ivy whimpered, continuing to shrink before Millicent's eyes.

"No one *wants* to be a teenager," Millicent consoled, offering a sympathetic smile. "But we all have to go through it."

Premier Horologe's words cut through the air once more. "Citizens, I implore you, remain calm! Panicking will only make things worse." His image flickered, blurring for a moment before solidifying again. "We are doing everything we can to understand this... this anomaly." He flickered again, and when he returned, his voice sounded cracked and desperate. "I hear you. The sky has gone haywire! Ms. Meridian swears her husband has turned into a ghost! And Mr. Mainspring's shower —there is a mermaid in there, and she is not singing lullabies!"

The world was spiraling out of control, a place where time no longer obeyed its natural order. Then, as abruptly as it began, the chaos ceased.

Millicent's nerves crackled like live wires as she surveyed the lingering effects: Ivy Equinox frozen beside her, Premier Horologe babbling incoherently, and the sky itself stuttering like a failing machine. The temporal distortions had left everything fractured, misaligned.

"Good people of Celestial City," she began, her tone shaking despite her efforts to steady it, "I do not have answers, but I will do everything in my power to find out what caused this."

Millicent felt her shoulders tense as she approached the heart of the crowd. Her eyes darted around, searching for a vantage point. The noise was overwhelming, a discordant symphony that made her long for the quiet precision of her workshop. Butterflies danced wildly in her stomach, rising up into her throat. She took a deep breath, forcing herself to focus.

"The light, the sky, the temporal distortions..." she whispered to herself. "Something is fundamentally broken. A malfunction, no doubt. These citizens are exhibiting disparate symptoms—disjointed speech, behaviors out of sync. Time itself was out of joint, with beginnings at the end and endings at the start."

As she turned to leave, Premier Horologe's voice rang out. "Millicent Gearwright is here, and if anyone can help us make sense of this, it is her."

Millicent's mind whirred as she processed the information.

The bizarre changes in people, plants, and the sky all pointed to one thing: time was broken. She had to find the cause and fix it, or nothing would return to normal.

As she hurried past the tabernacle's brick tower, below the belfry where her grandfather's memorial had been held, she paused to allow the key monks to return walking in a line from winding all the public clocks of Celestial City, her eyes catching the Tenets of Time etched into the stone:

Time is fleeting.
Time is subjective.
Time can heal.
Time can be a source of regret.
Time is a force of change.
Time is cyclical.

She lingered on the words, finding comfort in the old ways, in the belief that there was an order to the universe. But what was happening now defied those tenets, disrupting the orderly environment where she was raised. Millicent knew order had to be restored—the fabric of time needed mending. But she could not do it alone.

This was where she first met Orin eight years ago, her dearest friend. Curled up like a lost kitten at the foot of the tower, he seemed so fragile. Millicent had rushed to his side, fearing the worst. But as she knelt beside him, she realized he was from Vaporshade, simply needing a moment to rest—every step on Gearturn a battle against gravity.

As she made her way back to her workshop, her mind was already formulating plans. This was the challenge of a lifetime, a puzzle her grandfather would have relished. The Pocket Orrery in her hand felt heavier than ever, a reminder of the burden she now carried. She needed help from her friends.

2

"*What's the matter?*" Orin asked, his voice a drowsy melody. "*Why do you wake me, Millicent Gearwright, before the dawn has shone? Be gone from here, and let me sleep until the morning light. Return to me when day has broken, and the sun is bright.*"

"Orin, dear," Millicent said, pulling open the drapes. "It is midday, and you are still in bed. Something incredible has happened, and I need your help to investigate," she insisted, her eyes gleaming with a mix of excitement and worry. "My life is dedicated to understanding the clockwork of our exoplanetary system, you know. If time itself is malfunctioning, everything we've worked for could unravel. The fabric of our society could collapse. We have to act now. It might be too late."

> "*Go tinker with your timepieces, let me catch some Z's,*
> *I need my beauty sleep, so off you go now, if you please!*"

"The whole planet is coming unwound, Orin," Millicent

insisted, her words tightening with urgency. "We need you awake."

"My verses flow when I'm at rest,
  Sleep, not adventure, suits me best."

Millicent tugged and strained at the pillows tucked under his brown paws until she freed them from Orin's clutches. The changing colors of the sky bathed his face in flickering light, prompting him to raise a hand to shield his eyes. His movements were sluggish, weighed down by the gravity of Gearturn.

"A million men or more, you say? To rouse me from my bed?
  And embark upon adventures, while cozy dreams still fill my head?
  Nay, I'll stay right here, all snug and warm; at home is where I'll be,
  No quest can tempt me from this spot; I'm quite content, you see!"

Orin's sleepy voice carried a playful rhyme. The stark contrast between his world of Vaporshade, filled with art and whimsy, and Gearturn's rigid, clockwork routines weighed heavily on him. Despite the challenges of adapting to a planet with higher gravity and a faster rotation, Orin had found unexpected recognition here. On Gearturn, he wasn't just another artisan—he was a poet, his words given new weight in this world of gears and springs.

Millicent knew her friend well and whistled loud and true. Her call was to Quark, the handmade robot she had created with her grandfather nearly two decades ago in the workshop. Quark's beryllium copper frame clinked and clanked as he entered Orin's tumbledown cottage, the *tink-tonk* of his footsteps echoing through the room.

"Time to rise and shine, Orin," Millicent said, her tone brightening as Quark approached. "Our beryllium copper friend is here to help you find the rest of the day."

Quark, towering at 1,600.2 millimeters, possessed immense strength—enough to lift Orin's bed, with Orin still in it. Among his many traits, the combination of high strength with non-magnetic and non-sparking qualities made lifting the bed and Orin to the door easy. However, the bed proved too wide to fit through the doorframe.

> *"Oh Quark, my friend, I beg, desist!*
> *This quest, I truly must resist.*
> *Let me dream in peace, I plead,*
> *No adventures do I need!"*

Quark began to shake the bed until Orin tumbled to the floor. "No need for the bed," Quark said, setting it back in place with mechanical precision. Picking up Orin by the nightshirt collar, he added, "Ms. Millicent needs your help. The alarm of opportunity is ringing, and it's time to answer the call. Wake up and let your passion be your guide!"

Sweat beaded on Orin's brow as he straightened his posture, his spine creaking in protest against Gearturn's relentless gravitational pull. Orin dangled from Quark's grip, not for the first time, and said,

> *"Alright, my friend Quark, I'll come along for the ride,*
> *Tell me the trouble, and I'll ponder it with pride."*

Orin's witty rhymes faltered as the gravity of Millicent's

words sank in. He gazed out the window at the flickering sky, memories of his home on Vaporshade flashing through his mind. "If time unravels," he thought, "I'll never see it again." With a deep breath, he looked to Millicent, his eyes shining with resolve.

"Though comfort calls, a siren's song,
Our quest for time can't wait for long.
With you, dear friend, I'll gladly go,
To save our worlds from temporal woe."

"My hypothesis: time is jeopardized," Millicent said, getting straight to the point as she gestured to the sky, the plants, pets, and people they passed along the way to her workshop. Somewhere between the world of dreams and consciousness, Orin drifted back and forth, trying to understand.

Quark set Orin on a swivel chair in the center of Millicent's workspace. She raised the architect's drafting table and turned the surface forward so he could see her calculations. Orin's sleepy eyes opened a crack, following her movements.

"I started tracking something I call 'Chrono Echoes' before I came to get you," Millicent began, her tone serious. "Imagine time as a vast clockwork system, each second a cog turning smoothly. But lately, some of those cogs are out of sync. Something is causing them to misalign, jump, skip, and go in reverse."

She gestured to the map on the table, where faint lines crisscrossed. "These echoes are like the tock of an old clock, bouncing back from the past. They're rippling through space, reverberating off planets and stars. My antenna picks up these disturbances, measuring the distance between the waves—like counting the beats of a clock that's starting to wind down."

Millicent's finger traced a line on the map, leading to the

edge. "And here," she said, tapping a spot just off the map, "this is where the strongest echoes should be coming from. It's as if something at the galaxy's edge is pulling at the threads of time, unraveling the fabric that holds everything together."

"A long way to go, you say? Oh my, oh my!
    But why choose us for this task, and not some other guy?
    In the face of something so grand, what difference can we make?
    Perhaps finding someone else in charge is the path to take!"

"Gearturn is my home, where I grew up, where I learned everything I know from my grandfather. The thought of it being destroyed or fundamentally altered is... unbearable. And if that threat extends beyond Gearturn, to the entire Supercluster, well... how could I, how can we, turn away from that?"

She looked to Quark, then back to Orin. "I went to the city square to check with local authorities. All the good people of Celestial City were affected by this spell cast on them from far away. I know it cannot be magic—instead, science is the root cause. I can tell you when it started and stopped, and what direction it came from. I can show you the evidence of its effects. Without more data..."

She paused to think and reflect for a moment before continuing. "Just like that, it stopped?" Millicent wondered aloud, her brow furrowing as she gazed out the window. Mr. Sprocket had finally made it out the door with Coggie, and the plants stood motionless, their leaves no longer flickering through the seasons in seconds.

Orin yawned, stretching languidly in the swivel chair.

"Well, that's that, my dear. Crisis averted, I'd say.
    Now, if you'll excuse me, I'll be on my—"

A piercing shriek cut through the air, halting Orin mid-sentence. Quark's brass form vibrated, emitting a high-pitched whine that made their teeth ache. Millicent lurched to her instruments, her fingers flying over dials and switches.

"By the gears," she gasped, her face paling. "It's not over."

The air thickened, charged with an energy she couldn't explain. Then, in a heart-stopping moment, a blinding flash erupted from the Pocket Orrery. It was another concentrated burst of raw energy, searing across the three like a condensed lightning strike. The acrid scent of ozone hung in the air.

The potted plant on her desk burst into bloom, withered, and bloomed again in a matter of seconds. Outside, a flock of birds flew backward across the sky. Orin's teacup rattled, its contents switching between steaming hot and ice cold.

Millicent's machines sputtered and died one by one. As their eyes adjusted, an eerie glow became visible through the window—the sky outside rippled with waves of chrono-energy, painting the world in a sickly, pulsating light.

She turned to Orin, her eyes wide with a mixture of fear and excitement. "Time isn't just malfunctioning, Orin. It's unraveling. If my calculations are correct—" Millicent began, but her words were cut short as the room plunged into darkness.

When the lights flickered back on a moment later, Orin found himself on the opposite side of the room, his hair several inches longer. "What—" he sputtered.

Millicent's face was grim. "That is what I have been trying to tell you. Time is not just—" The lights flickered again, and this time when they stabilized, Quark was speaking in Millicent's voice, while Millicent's mouth moved in sync with Orin's poetic cadence.

"—malfunctioning," Quark finished in Millicent's tone. "It is coming apart at the seams."

Lights flickered like a strobe, each flash revealing a change in their positions. When at last the lights returned to normal, they looked at each other, waiting, until they were certain it was over.

"And if my calculations are correct, we have less than fourteen days before Gearturn—and possibly our entire galaxy—ceases to exist."

A deep, ominous rumble shook the foundation of the workshop. Quark's eyes flickered, and in a voice unlike his own, he intoned: "The end of time is nigh."

As the workshop shook, rattling tools and machinery, framed pictures fell, glass shattering on the floor. Quark surveyed the damage.

"The photo of Grandfather and Doctor Julius Kilmoore—this will be difficult to repair. And your grandfather's daughter and her husband, what a pair."

Millicent's hands trembled as she adjusted the dials, a rare crack in her usually steady demeanor. She glanced at the photo of her grandfather, his kind eyes offering silent encouragement. "We cannot let them down," she whispered, straightening her shoulders.

Orin's voice, usually soft, now rose with conviction:

"Millicent, the shadows creep,
    These visions, they no longer sleep,
    What I've seen is not mere fright,
    But a nightmare born to chase the light.
    The time is now, we mustn't wait,
    These disruptions seal our fate,
    For in the dark, truth hides its face,

We must confront it, find our place.
It's you, Millicent, who holds the key,
Your mind, so sharp, can set us free,
You grasp the threads of time's vast weave,
And see what others can't conceive.
For in your hands, our hope does rest,
Millicent, it's you—our very best.
Though Vaporshade calls, my heart does yearn,
I'll stand with you, and save Gearturn."

"The faith you have in me is unequaled. Thank you." Millicent grabbed Orin's hand, pulling him towards the door. "The fate of everything we know depends on us understanding this power source from the Phantom Spires before the last second gets away."

Quark took over, lifting Orin by his collar and keeping pace with Millicent. Rushing out into the chaotic, time-warped streets of Gearturn, Orin found himself swept up by Quark, dangling from his hand. His poetic mind raced, searching for a rhyme to match the gravity of their situation, but for once, words failed him. The adventure he'd so desperately tried to avoid now looked like the only thing standing between existence and oblivion.

3

The Capitol Clocktower loomed ahead, casting its imposing silhouette across Gearturn's skyline. Millicent felt its deep, rhythmic pulse resonate in her bones as she approached, a familiar heartbeat that seemed to synchronize with the breath of every citizen. She glanced at Quark, his metallic frame gleaming in the late afternoon light, Orin securely in his hand.

"We're cutting it close," she muttered, quickening her pace as the shadows lengthened around them.

As if on cue, the clocktower's glockenspiel erupted in a magnificent thirty-five-bell carillon. Three stories above the viewing area, an intricate clockwork theater whirred to life. Millicent paused, transfixed despite herself, as "The Clockmaster's Miracle" began to play out. A show of mechanical wonder telling the story of the Clockmaster saving Gearturn.

Exquisitely crafted figurines danced and twirled in intricate patterns. White mice—symbols of chaos—pirouetted out of rhythm, their tiny gears clicking discordantly, a stark contrast to the harmonious clockwork theater. Then came the Clockmaster, resplendent in blue and gold robes, his miniature face a mask of determination. With each strike of his mallet against the sound bow of the bell, shockwaves rippled outward, driving the mice back.

Millicent's fingers twitched, aching to examine the delicate machinery. But the fractures she'd witnessed in the sky earlier that day flashed in her mind, spurring her forward.

She shouldered through the crowd, ignoring the disgruntled mutters that followed in her wake. The queue snaking from the tower's entrance looked endless, faces etched with a mix of reverence and fatigue.

At the massive maple doors, Millicent reached for the knocker. A nearby woman gasped.

"You can't!" she hissed, eyes wide with alarm. "I've waited three years for my audience. You'll doom us all if you—"

Millicent's knuckles tightened around the brass ring. "If I don't get inside now, there might not be a Gearturn left to save."

The knocker fell, its echo reverberating through the entire city.

Silence fell. Then, a thin voice squeaked from behind the door: "Who dares?"

"Millicent Gearwright," she answered. "I must see the Clockmaster immediately. Time itself is fracturing."

The door creaked open a fraction, revealing a haggard face. "Gearwright, you say? Any relation to old Thaddius?"

Millicent blinked, thrown off guard. "My grandfather. You knew him?"

The doorman's eyes narrowed. "Brilliant man. A real gears and cogs man. Touch mad, though. Always spending time with that odd fellow, something-moore."

"Doctor Kilmoore?"

He peered at Millicent. "Something in your eyes. That same gleam."

"Then you understand the urgency," Millicent pressed. "Please, I would not break protocol if—"

"Rules are rules, Miss Gearwright. Back of the line."

The door slammed shut. The crowd's angry murmur swelled around her.

Millicent's mind raced, gears clicking into place as she scanned the tower's imposing facade. There had to be another way in—the fate of Gearturn depended on it.

She turned to Quark. "We're going up. Can you manage it?"

Quark's optical sensors whirred as he assessed the tower. "Affirmative. It won't be easy."

"When has that stopped us?" Millicent managed a grim smile.

They retreated to the relative privacy of the viewing area of the Clocktower. Orin clasped at the collar in Quark's hand, his luminous eyes fixing on Millicent.

"Though walls stand tall and guards stand stern,
  Our path lies clear, if hard to discern.
  With wit and will, we'll find our way,
  To save our world from time's decay."

Millicent squeezed Orin's hand, drawing strength from his wisdom. "We'll need you with us, old friend. Can you hold on tight?"

Orin nodded, moving to wrap his arms securely around Quark's neck.

With a pneumatic hiss, a metal plate extended from Quark's back. Millicent stepped on, her grip white-knuckled around his shoulder joints.

"Every second counts," Quark intoned, his mechanical limbs extending with precise, deliberate movements.

They began to climb.

Quark's fingers found impossible purchase on the smooth stone, each movement precise and calculated. Millicent's heart thundered in her chest as the ground began to fall away beneath them, the city shrinking to a dizzying distance below. She focused on the warmth of Orin against her, on Quark's unwavering ascent. "Don't look down. Nearly there."

Millicent's gaze instinctively dropped at Quark's warning. The ground swayed dizzyingly far below, the tiny figures of waiting citizens mere specks. She squeezed her eyes shut, willing away the vertigo, but darkness crept in at the edges. "Gearturn," she whispered, the word a talisman against the encroaching void. Then, silence. Feeling Orin's reach was the final thing.

Millicent blinked, the world slowly coming into focus. Quark's metallic face hovered above her, Orin's concerned eyes peering from behind. As she pushed herself up, a glint caught her eye. She was awed—there, mere inches away, stood an army of exquisite figurines. Her fingers traced the air above a tiny mouse, marveling at each perfectly carved whisker. Gears no larger than her fingernail meshed in silent motion, a testament to craftsmanship that made her own skills seem clumsy in comparison.

"These are ancient but look as if they were made this morning. Look at them all. Each mouse, each child's outfit with hand-painted flowers, so much time and care. This is wonderful."

Quark lifted the sleepy companion and gently reminded, "Embrace each tick and tock as a gift. We must find the Timemaster today."

"Yes." She gave a puzzled look, "Tick and tock, my wind-up friend. I could spend my life looking back at these beautiful artifacts without a thought to the future. These are one of the reasons to fix the malfunction."

Orin's eyes glowed with an otherworldly light.

"Through wheels of brass and springs of steel,
The Clockmaster's chamber we must reveal.
Time's heart falters, its rhythm grows weak,
'Tis there our answers we must seek."

"There is a door back here." Quark pointed with his free hand. "It's on the Clocktower wall."

Millicent nodded, squaring her shoulders. "Then let's not waste another second. Gearturn is counting on us."

4

CLICK.
HUM.
WHIR.

uark activated his eye lights, illuminating the hallway. As they traveled the length of the corridor, Orin whispered:

"In darkness deep, I want to sleep,
  But shadows can unsettle and creep.
  Yet fear dissolves when light shines through,
  And understanding quells the haunting hue."

MILLICENT REACHED out her hand and turned the knob slowly. They had no idea what—or who—might be on the other side. Before opening the door, the trio noticed a light from the other side outlining the edges. Muffled sounds came from behind the door, though she couldn't make out what they were saying. Taking a deep breath, she pushed forward.

The three found themselves in the receiving room of the Capitol Clocktower, facing four men. Three men, who looked like brothers, sat on three thrones next to one another, with the center seat slightly higher than the other two. The fourth, standing before them, was a pirate dressed in dark brown twilled fustian over a white puffy shirt, with an elegant panache in his hat.

The pirate smiled and waved, removing his hat and offering a deep and grateful bow. Rising, he said, "I'm Barnaby Blackwater, the scourge of the seven galax-seas and your guide to all treasures—mostly ill-gotten. At your leisure—or peril, depending on your honesty."

"And who is this?" The voice came from the center throne. The man wore robes of blue and gold, as did the two on his left and right. But in the center, the design and cut were somehow more contemporary in a way Millicent could not place.

Millicent stepped forward, her footsteps echoing in the grand receiving room as she crossed the threshold, flanked by Quark and Orin. Having come directly from her workshop, she felt utterly unprepared to meet people of such high standing. Self-consciously, her fingers grazed the clips that held back her auburn red hair, and she tugged at the lapels of her brown jacket, attempting to straighten her appearance. She could feel the flutter of butterflies seeking their escape again. Drawing in a deep breath, Millicent stood tall, her spine erect, and extended her right arm high, her wrist bent and hand turned in a formal gesture of respect. She bowed deeply, facing the thrones, and spoke clearly, "I am Millicent Gearwright. These are my companions, Orin, the esteemed poet of Vaporshade, and Quark, my trusted robot companion. We have come to address the Clockmaster regarding the alarming time malfunction that occurred earlier today."

"Oh, good," said the man on the center throne, a slow, sarcastic smile spreading across his lips. "Another visitor."

"I'm the Clockmaster," chimed in the man on the right throne, his tone equally sardonic, like an echo with a smirk.

"And I," added the man on the left, his voice oozing dry humor, "am the Clockmaster. Gearwright, huh? Daughter of Thaddius?"

Millicent blinked in confusion. "Granddaughter," she corrected. "The three of you are the Clockmaster?"

"In the flesh," they replied in unison, their voices harmonizing—like a barbershop quartet that had practiced just a little too long.

Millicent tilted her head, curiosity piqued but also sensing the absurdity of the situation.

Barnaby chuckled, stepping closer to the thrones, his eyes twinkling with mischief. "Aye, lass, that be the Clockmaster. The one on the left—the youngest—he's from the future. The elder on the right, he's from the past—the very same whose face you saw sculpted on the Clocktower Theater, while the glockenspiel played."

"And the one in the middle? The present?" Millicent asked.

"You've got it," Barnaby replied with a wink. "Three versions of the same Clockmaster, from different, ah, vintages."

The eldest Clockmaster inclined his head with a touch of old-world charm, his eyes twinkling with a mix of nostalgia and dry wit. "A pleasure to make your acquaintance, young Millicent. The honor is mine, truly, though it's been so long, I might have forgotten what honor looks like."

"A delight, truly," added the youngest Clockmaster, his tone breezy but with a sharp edge. "Millicent, your reputation precedes you."

The one in the middle spoke with urgency, "I require your assistance, Millicent. This matter has grown dire. For three years, he has siphoned away precious time, stalling the progress I strive to maintain. No matter how politely I request the next appointment, it never arrives. He is excused but never leaves."

"Endlessly, he regales us with tales of derring-do, stories that stretch on like the years themselves." The eldest Clock-master sighed.

"His presence here has blurred the lines of time; even the reason for his summons eludes me now," admitted the youngest. "Yet here he still is."

Barnaby Blackwater revealed his devilish grin, the sparkle in his right eye captured from a distant star. "Aye, ye've got it wrong. I didn't steal time—I liberated it from the Clockmaster's relentless keeping. Time's a treasure meant for sharing, though I confess, I've been hoarding the whole bounty for myself."

Millicent's brow furrowed in disbelief. "Steal time? That defies all logic. How could such a feat be achieved? And if true, what does that mean for the fabric of our reality?"

"But it's true."

"True."

"True it is!"

"Aye, it's possible," Barnaby added, looking more pleased with himself than ever.

"But why would you steal time?" Millicent pressed.

"Ah, why indeed? Perhaps because time, like treasure, is wasted when locked away. But worry not—I only take what's needed... for now." He continued to explain. "It's a safe port in a storm for me here. This treasure," he said with a roguish grin, gesturing to himself, "be anchored in a calm bubble while storms rage elsewhere, if ye catch my drift. Plenty of old mates out there still keen on finding me."

"What of your arrival, Millicent?"

"Why are you here, Millicent?"

"How can we assist you, Millicent?" The Clockmasters spoke in turn, their attention now fully on her.

She took a deep breath and met their gaze. "Earlier today, there was a malfunction in time. It trapped the people of Celestial City—likely all of Gearturn—in a loop, forcing them to relive the same moment. Some were speaking in a jumbled mix of past, present, and future. Others were frozen, unable to move or be moved. You are wise and knowledgeable, so I came to you for guidance. But your doorman stopped me. A line has formed that stretches back years."

The Clockmasters exchanged glances, their eyebrows raised in unison as they looked at Barnaby.

In turn, Blackwater grinned, then admitted, "The Clockmaster's time? Aye, I've been keeping it safe—in my pocket, you might say." He patted his chest, inferring the inside jacket pocket, kept close and safe.

Millicent ignored the butterflies that had grown in the feeling of escape and spoke loudly to command attention, "Clockmaster, my instruments are tracking the Chrono Echoes. The distance between the waves suggests that this malfunction will happen again. They will continue to grow in strength and potency. Soon, the good people of the whole of Gearturn, not just Celestial City, will start to blur between night and day. Seasons will turn, and chaos will spread as everyone and everything will be lost in time. You need to do something. The people need your help. We only have fourteen days until these forces rip our world apart."

"Fourteen days?"

"Well, thirteen days, six hours, and thirty-four minutes."

"Where is this source?"

"From where?"

"Where is the source from?" the Clockmaster demanded, his voice tinged with urgency.

"The waves are coming from the direction of the Phantom Spires," she answered confidently.

For the first time, Millicent witnessed the trinity look to one another in deep acknowledgment, and in unison, they said with a worried reverence, "The Time Core." Their voices sent a shiver down her spine.

"Time Core?" she asked, confusion evident in her tone.

"It is the origin of time, the beginning, where it was started," the elder replied solemnly.

Millicent's curiosity piqued. "What was started?"

"Everything," the eldest said, his voice heavy with the weight of cosmic knowledge.

Skepticism crept into Millicent's voice. "I thought Gearturn controlled time?"

The elder rose to his feet, raised his arms, and began to orate, his voice filled with awe-inspiring power. "The Time Core is the origin of everything, the singularity where time, space, and matter converge and diverge. It is both a physical entity and an abstract construct, the heart of the Supercluster and the source of all creation."

"It emanates," one Clockmaster whispered reverently.

"Synchronizes," another added, his voice tinged with mysticism.

The third spoke with authority, "But the Time Core originates. We, Gearturn, are the measure; it is the chaos."

Their voices blended as they continued, enchantment in their tones. "Ever shifting, you will know it when you see it.

Light and darkness, a dance of color, shapes that defy description."

Mesmerized, they went on, "An orb, pulsing, vibrant hues from the past and the future. It is both beautiful and terrifying, peaceable and violent."

Their final words carried a sense of enlightenment. "Your mind will blend magic and advanced science, a harmonious balance of arcane forces and quantum mechanics."

Barnaby Blackwater quipped sarcastically, "It's everything and nothing, which means they don't know nothing. A bit of chaos never hurt no one. I make me living on chaos."

"Do not mock, you clockwise corsair." The elder seethed, indignation flashing in his eyes. His voice softened as he turned to Millicent, "Millicent Gearwright, imagine you go to a magical library that makes and houses all the books. This library doesn't just have books about different places and times—it actually contains those places, times, and people. When you enter the library, you can open any book and not only read but actually step inside those moments." His words painted a vivid picture in her mind.

The modern incarnation added, his tone both explanatory and filled with wonder, "Walk into this singularity, it's as if you're entering a library where every book can take you to a different moment in time. It's a doorway to all of time and space at once, giving you the power to visit any moment you want."

"Only enter?" Millicent asked, her voice filled with intrigue and a hint of trepidation.

"You must go," the youngest Clockmaster commanded, his voice brooking no argument. "You must go to the Time Core and right what is wrong." He turned his attention to the pirate, his tone determined. "And you, you must guide her."

Barnaby pointed to himself with question. "Me?"

"Yes, yes—you must go," the three bellowed to Barnaby in harmony.

The youngest said, "Take her and her two companions to the edge of the galaxy and aid in repairing the Time Core."

The middle Clockmaster affirmed, "You know the routes; you've regaled us with tales of knowledge and adventure. You will take them to the edge of all we know and assist her in rectifying this malfunction."

"But my ship, my crew—" Barnaby protested.

Millicent, hoping to avoid this burden, naively asked, "Is there even room on such a journey for a pirate?"

"Aye, lass," Barnaby replied with a roguish grin, "there's always room for a pirate on adventures."

Millicent hesitated and in reflection said, "My expertise lies in clockmaking. How can I help? Wouldn't I serve better by observing the effects from my workshop?"

Quark whirred to life, playing an audio recording of Millicent. The volume increased, allowing all to hear: "Gearturn is my home, where I grew up, where I learned everything I know from my grandfather. The thought of it being destroyed or fundamentally altered is... unbearable. And if the threat extends beyond Gearturn, to the entire Supercluster, well... how could I, how could we, turn away from that?"

Millicent's scowl deepened as Quark played back her own words, the weight of her resolve settling in alongside a pang of embarrassment. "Thank you, Quark," she said, her tone dry and with gritted teeth.

"GO NOW!" the unified sounds of the Clockmasters commanded, resonating with the power of all ages. "BEFORE IT IS TOO LATE!"

Barnaby stroked his beard thoughtfully. "Aye, take them I will, but what's in it for me?"

The eldest Clockmaster leaned forward, his eyes gleaming. "Return once you've been successful, and you will be granted the most precious reward ever to be known. It will be yours, and yours alone."

A slow smile spread across Barnaby's face. "Aye, 'tis a pirate's life for me. Who am I to buccaneer a trend?" He let out a hearty laugh and turned to Millicent and her companions. "Come now, me hearties. Adventure calls, and time waits for no one—except perhaps us."

5

TAP.
CRUNCH.
TAP.
CRUNCH.

Barnaby Blackwater walked briskly along the cobbled streets, with Millicent keeping pace at his side and Quark carrying Orin behind. He glanced to his side, noting they were making good time, and caught a familiar look from his new companion. "Why, yes, this peg leg is made from the finest endangered hardwood. So kind of you to notice."

Millicent was embarrassed, her cheeks flushing a soft pink. "I am sorry. Was I staring? I was staring. I have never met a pirate before," she replied, fumbling with her words. "Where are we going?"

"Arr, the Phantom Spires," Barnaby growled. "Thanks to you."

"No, I mean, at this moment. Where are we going?" Millicent pressed, her curiosity getting the better of her manners.

Without breaking his pace, he replied, "I require three things in a shipmate: a wooden leg, a treasure chest, and no questions. You have none of these."

"I need to know the plan. It helps me to strategize. Anxiety grows in me when there is no plan. Besides, knowing the next steps may help reach our goal," she explained, her fingers fidgeting with the hem of her sleeve.

"Aye, one of those..." Barnaby drawled with sarcasm. "A schemer, a plotter, a planner, a rule maker, and to the point, a rule follower. I've known many of your ilk in me day. But how far has this got you? Here, with me."

"Here, indeed, trying to save the Supercluster with a pirate who does not believe in plans," Millicent retorted with a tinge of exasperation.

"Plans are for the Order of Engineers, lass," Barnaby scoffed, adjusting his tricorn hat. "The Code of the Space Pirate says you live in the moment, embrace the chaos."

Millicent's back straightened, her pride piqued. "I happen to enjoy my membership in the Order. Chaos is the enemy of progress. Without plans, one is just stumbling in the dark, hoping to trip over something useful."

"And yet, I've tripped over more treasure than you've ever mapped out," Barnaby countered, his gold tooth glinting as he smirked. "Aye, maybe it's time you stopped worrying about every cog and gear and learned to trust your instincts."

"Well, do you at least have a plan? A course? A map?" She started to lose step, speaking louder with frustration.

That devilish grin returned, spreading across Barnaby's weathered face like a crack in old leather. "Of course, I have a treasure map... I keep it right next to me stash of bon mots."

And with this, Barnaby Blackwater stopped dead in the street, his peg leg thumping on the cobblestones.

Millicent barely avoided running into him. "What? Why are we stopping?"

"Aye, tell me this true. The talking cat you travel with, or is it a teddy bear who can't walk on his own, why so bold to wear a cape so out of fashion?"

From his dangling perch in Quark's hand, Orin explained:

"My cape, a guise, a mere disguise,
　　A blanket in truth, I must advise.
　　For warmth or shade, for sleep or hide,
　　This cloth of comfort, by my side.
　　A versatile friend, through day and night,
　　Providing solace, blocking light.
　　So let us praise this humble sheet,
　　A blanket's magic, hard to beat!"
Quark added, "It also has pockets."

"Right." Barnaby sighed, assessing this trio. "We are here, me lady Millicent. No need to worry about the plan any longer."

"Here?"

"We will travel the Cosmic Web with the aid of a crystal spider." He pointed to the sign above the shop, which read, *Celestial Spider Travel Terminal.*

A gulp came from Millicent. "Is there another way? Recently, I have discovered that high places do not agree with me."

"Arr, it's not the heights you need to worry about." That sparkle of a distant star returned to his right eye. He ushered them into the terminal and bartered for two tickets, explaining the robot was an accessibility device and the "thing" in his hand a stuffed bear they won at the carnival.

The spider they boarded was much like all Celestial Spiders. With white crystal exteriors nearly transparent, these creatures were larger than most houses, the largest as big as a moatless castle. Attached to the thorax were the passenger quarters, with the wheelhouse on top for the conductor. Its arms scaled the cosmic webs spun by its ancestors at great speed and when needed created its own junction points and lines from the strongest known substance, crystal webbing.

The passenger quarters, oval in shape to match the thorax, were designed in the style of *bayt al-shar*, with curved transparent walls serving as windows to the Supercluster. The walls, outlined by white padded cushions, pillows, and reclined sofa chairs, provided comfortable sleeping space for fifty.

"Oh my, that is an interesting smell."

"Aye, welcome to public transportation. It's not the centuries; it's the musty gigameters on the line."

The first pulls from the Celestial Spider jolted the cabin compartment, sending passengers deep into the cushions of the white leather seats. Once free from the gravity of Gearturn, the ride smoothed. The Celestial Spider started to run at maximum speed, taking great strides and bounds forward along the line. Its mighty eight legs absorbed the bounce and wiggle in the tension of the cosmic webbing, so the passengers felt nothing.

Millicent had never left Gearturn before. From this view, her home looked smaller the farther they went. At first, she could see the continental turn. Seas of smaller sprockets and wheels spun quickly. These spindles turned the larger toothed wheels, ratcheting the countries and cities to connect with one another in a beautiful ballet, synchronizing everything in a wonderful and predictable order.

She liked when things fit. Millicent liked order and predictability. Turning away from the world she knew so well, she looked at her new guide and companion, Barnaby Blackwater, and wondered if this was actually about the promised prize from the Clockmaster, and what that might be.

"Why, Barnaby? Why spend years with the Clockmaster stealing time?"

"Yarr, you know what they say—time be money, and I do so love liberating other people's money."

"I do not believe you. There must be additional reasons. Three years is a long time to stand court with the Clockmaster."

"Three years? Has it been that long already? Time flies when ye're havin' rum—I mean, fun." He smiled.

"If you do not want to tell me... My only concern is fixing this malfunction. Saving the good people of Gearturn from this chaos. If it means finding the Time Core with you, so be it. But you will tell me eventually. Might as well get it over with now."

"I've noticed you don't use contractions when you vocabulate," Barnaby observed, his curiosity piqued. "Might you share that ditty with me, lass?"

Millicent stiffened, her hands fidgeting with the hem of her jacket. "I will tell you, after my question has an answer," she deflected.

Barnaby's eyes narrowed, sensing the sudden tension. "Fair enough," he conceded. Barnaby Blackwater looked around the cabin to make sure they had some privacy and started to explain in full, "You see, me dear, when ye've been piratin' as long as I have, you start to realize that time has value." He leaned in close, "Gold, jewels, rum—they're all well and good, but they're heavy and difficult to carry. Time, on the other hand, be the one thing everyone wants, and it's easy to carry." He patted his breast pocket. "Arr, I decided to take matters into me own hands. The Clockmaster had more time than he knew what to do with, and I had a crew full of scurvy dogs who were always complainin' about not havin' enough hours in the day to properly pillage and plunder."

"How"—her face filled with disbelief—"can you steal time? What would you do with it once you have it?"

He patted his chest pocket, like before. "All here, me dear, all here. Keepin' it close to me heart." He gave a knowing smile. "I spent two months meticulously plannin' and executin' heists on the Clockmaster's temporal vaults below the tower. It wasn't easy—that codger had traps and safeguards aplenty, tighter than a miser's purse. But I was determined. Me escape route was to be the same as your entrance. With the treasure in hand, I tapped through the reception room, the Clockmaster woke, and stopped me in me tracks. I stood there regalin' the audience with a lifetime of escapades of escape and treachery in attempts to send the three to sleep. As the lights went out for one, the other two stayed awake and listened."

"For three full years?"

"It felt like an eternity."

"What will you do with the time you stole?" She was genuinely curious. Millicent felt a pang of unease. Could she really trust this pirate with the fate of Gearturn? But with so much at stake, what choice did she have? "What can be done with stolen time?"

"Aye, lass, if you can't bend time, you'll never break the rules." He gave a wink. "I will use it for my ship and crew. She's the fastest on the seven galax-seas. We could sail from one end of the Supercluster to the other in the blink of an eye, strike our targets before they even knew what hit 'em, and be back at our secret cove sippin' rum before the sunset. It will be glorious to sail her again." His smile grew from ear to ear at the thought of the epic days ahead. "Now, about you? Why can't you vocabu-late like the rest of us?"

"I prefer not to use contractions," Millicent explained. "It requires more thought before speaking, helping me avoid... impulsive decisions."

Blackwater's expression soured. "Well, shave me belly with a rusty razor! That be a right foul maneuver, a true insult to the spirit of sportsmanship." He grimaced. "All that time on me yarn, and you just don't like 'em?" He leaned back in the reclining chair, covering his face with his hat to sleep, mumbling, "Salty swine you be." A muffled, "Nasty bit o' busi-ness unbecomin' of a true pirate," followed.

Millicent said with honest concern, "Who can ever truly trust a pirate?"

PART II

QUILL & WEB

6

AH-OO-GAH
AH-OO-GAH
BEE-DOH
BEE-DOH
BEE-DOH

The alarms blared through the Celestial Spider, shaking Millicent awake with a start. She tumbled off the recliner, barely catching herself. Orin, ever the sleeper, remained blissfully unaware, his makeshift earplugs from tufts of fur doing their job.

Quark started to dance in place, clomping his feet on the deck. "The alarm of opportunity is ringing, and it is time to answer the call!"

"Not an opportunity, a warning. Stay here Quark." Millicent shot to her feet, her eyes scanning the room for Barnaby. *Where was that pirate?* As the ship lurched again, she noticed the pilot house hatch swinging wildly, unlocked. Her mind raced. *What is that scoundrel up to?* Fighting the tilt of the ship, she scrambled toward the ladder, grasping it with both hands as the vessel swayed beneath her. With a grunt, she pulled herself up, popping her head into the pilot house just in time to see Barnaby Blackwater at the helm, his hands flying over the controls with an ease that infuriated her. The conductor, out cold in the corner.

"What—what has happened?" she demanded, speaking over the storm outside.

"Ahoy, lass! We've got ourselves a right nasty gravity tempest!" Barnaby shouted, a wide grin on his face. "Hold on to yer britches! It's about to get rougher than a kraken's mantle!"

Millicent's eyes narrowed, her words sharp. "What can I do to help?"

"You can start by trustin' ol' Barnaby to steer this beastie!" he hollered, yanking the wheel hard to starboard. The Celestial Spider lurched violently, its legs extending to brace against the Cosmic Web, the ship groaning as it fought against the tempest's pull.

Millicent snapped to the open station, her eyes already scanning the navigation panel. "This ship requires precision, not reckless abandon!"

Barnaby let out a hearty laugh, his grip steady on the wheel. "Precision? Lass, we're dancin' with the stars, not calibratin' a pocket watch! Sometimes, ye've got to let the wind take you where it may!"

Millicent shot him a side-eye, her fingers flying over the controls. "There is no such thing as 'letting the wind take you' in a gravity tempest, Barnaby! We must adjust our trajectory by precisely 4.37 degrees to avoid being torn apart!"

The Celestial Spider started to roll to one side, forcing the two to hold fast. Before it could heel over, Barnaby righted the ship.

Barnaby grinned widely. "Ah, Millicent, if I had a nickel for every time precision went out the airlock... well, I wouldn't need to plunder half as much. But where's the thrill in followin' a map when the real treasure's in the journey itself? Besides, it's a tempest, not a tea party. A little chaos is just the spice of life."

Millicent turned cold. She started to remember her blackout on the Clocktower. Butterflies began to tickle at her tummy. "You are confusing spice with poison, Barnaby. The Order of Engineers demands control. We anticipate every variable, every contingency. We do not 'see where it blows us'; we steer. We command."

Fighting the gale, a sheer dropped them hundreds of meters instantly. Her nails started to dig into the underside of the panel. Buoyed by the unseen forces, they returned to a steadier state.

Barnaby raised an eyebrow, his grin never faltering. "Command? That sounds like a bore, darlin'. Command implies somethin' listens to you. The universe is more like a drunken sailor—unpredictable and a bit of a mess, but full of stories if you know how to listen. You can't command it, but ye can charm it into givin' you what you want. And, love, I've got charm to spare."

Millicent glanced at him with a mixture of irritation and reluctant admiration. "Charm does not fix a faulty chronometer, Barnaby. It does not realign the gears or recalibrate the thrusters. I need calculations, not charisma."

Barnaby pretended to be thoughtful. "Ah, but calculations are like promises—easy to make, easier to break. Charm, however, is the real engine, lass. It's the thing that keeps the crew loyal, the stars friendly, and the spiders spinnin' their webs. You keep frettin' over every degree of trajectory, and you'll miss the fact that we're already out of the worst of it."

Millicent blinked, realizing with a start that the readings on her panel had stabilized. "You—did you actually do something right?"

Barnaby gasped theatrically, clutching his chest. "Me? Right? Millicent, you wound me. I simply did what any good pirate would do—I trusted me gut and threw the wheel the way it wanted to go. After all, the stars may not be on our side, but this old pirate knows a trick or two about makin' them think they are."

Millicent rolled her eyes, but a hint of a smile tugged at her lips. "I am beginning to think the real tempest here is you, Barnaby. And like all storms, you are more trouble than you are worth."

Barnaby leaned closer. "Trouble, my dear, is my middle name. But trouble's what makes life worth livin'. And admit it—this ride's been more fun with a pirate at the helm, hasn't it?"

Millicent met his gaze, her expression softening. "Fun? Perhaps. But if we survive this, it will be despite your reckless-ness, not because of it."

Barnaby chuckled, his grin growing even wider. "Fortune favors the bold, not the timid!"

"The bold often find themselves drifting in space with no way home," Millicent retorted, as she turned the three-dimen-sional map on the access. Her eyes locked on to a thin, less-traveled web line. "There! That line—take it! It might just hold."

Barnaby raised an eyebrow, his grin widening. "Might? That doesn't sound like the lass I know. You're usually as sure as a compass pointin' north!"

Millicent's patience frayed as she pointed again, more forcefully this time, her right foot stomped. "Turn left. Port, Barnaby! Port!"

"Ah, port it is, me lady!" Barnaby quipped, turning the wheel with a flourish. The Celestial Spider's limbs reached out, grasping the thin web line with delicate precision, slowing their descent until they hung in a precarious balance.

Breathing heavily, Millicent watched the instruments stabilize, her shoulders relaxing. Barnaby drawled, wiping his brow, "I'd call that a success!"

"What do you think happened?" Millicent asked, gathering her thoughts and reviewing the navigation station.

Barnaby leaned against the wheel, his tone slipping into something more serious. "I climbed up here to stretch me good leg, check our course. Then outta nowhere, a giant black beastie rolls in from the port side. Blinded us all! Pure chaos! But ye can't break the spirit of ol' Barnaby Blackwater. I've been through worse than this on a Sunday stroll."

Millicent crossed her arms, her skepticism evident. "And this 'black beastie'—what did it look like?"

Barnaby's grin faltered for a moment, his eyes distant. "Thick and viscous, like a fog that swallows the light whole. Even the ship's sensors couldn't pierce it. But I swear, lass, it smiled at me like a mermaid callin' me to the deep. It whispered, 'Barnaby Blackwater, stay away.'"

Millicent's analytical mind struggled to process the description. "In all your time as a pirate, have you ever encountered anything like it?"

Barnaby shook his head. "Nay, never."

Millicent turned back to the controls, her mind whirring. "We need to determine our exact location and plot a course to safety. Where were we headed, Barnaby?"

Barnaby shrugged, his usual bravado returning. "Zephyria,

the main hub in the region. Then on to Grablehaven to retrieve me ship and crew."

Millicent scrolled through the map, her fingers pausing on a distant spot. "We are a long way from there," she murmured, tracing their likely current position.

Barnaby leaned in, frowning as he looked over her shoulder. "Phooey, this line only goes to one place before anywhere else—Inkwell."

"Inkwell?" Millicent echoed, unfamiliar with the name. "Have you been there before?"

Barnaby's tone grew mysterious, a touch of the theatrical. "Only in stories. Inkwell is a world where reality is written in ink and dreams are bound in leather. Every thought, every word, every story comes to life. It's a place where the written word bends reality to its whims."

Millicent's rational mind bristled at the notion. "I have never heard of such a place."

Barnaby's eyes gleamed with mischief. "Few have, lass. Few survive to tell the tale. But if you're lookin' for safety, you won't find it there. Danger is just another word for adventure in me lexicon, and Inkwell's got it in spades."

Millicent sighed, the weight of the situation pressing down on her. "We will need all hands on deck to navigate such a place." She watched as Barnaby roused the conductor, helping him back to his feet and explaining their next destination. The conductor's weary eyes widened at the mention of Inkwell, but he nodded in agreement.

"There's a reason we don't have additional lines through Inkwell," the conductor said with caution. "But the terminal should be safe. Every planet and system connected to the Cosmic Web is part of a treaty that makes the Celestial Spider Travel Terminals neutral territory."

"Yar, see, Millicent? The conductor says we'll be safe," Barnaby said, turning back to her with a grin.

Millicent's face remained serious. "Safe," she repeated, though her tone suggested she wasn't convinced. She was tired of the unknown, of the chaos that followed Barnaby wherever he went. Reaching into her tool bag, she touched the cool metal of her grandfather's Pocket Orrery, seeking comfort in its familiarity.

Barnaby noticed her quiet moment, and he softened, almost as if he understood. "Millicent," he began, his words as gentle as a Caribbean breeze, "sometimes the map's wrong and the compass lies. Sometimes you have to sail into the storm, trust the stars, and hope your ship holds. The Code of the Space Pirate isn't about knowin' where ye're goin'. It's about knowin' you'll find somethin' worth findin' when you get there."

Millicent looked up at him. She countered, with a hint of uncertainty, "I am beginning to suspect that control is an illusion."

"Control," Barnaby scoffed, spitting the word out like a mouthful of bad rum, "is a pretty word for a false sense of security. Out here, the Supercluster laughs at your plans."

Millicent paused, her hand closing around the Pocket Orrery. "Perhaps," she allowed, a hint of a smile touching her lips. "But let us try to arrive in one piece, shall we?"

Barnaby's eyes sparkled with mischief. "Aye, Captain Gearwright. To Inkwell, and the stories await us there."

7

As the Celestial Spider docked, the terminal at Inkwell came into view, its towering structure a near-perfect mirror of the one they had left behind on Gearturn. The facility stood ready to accommodate and stabilize up to three of these magnificent arachnid vessels when the need arose. The hiss of hydraulics filled the air as the spider's legs made contact with the terminal's docking platform, announcing their arrival.

The local terminal agent, a figure on the edge of retirement in a dusty uniform, emerged to greet the small party. With practiced efficiency, he slowly maneuvered the stairs into position, aligning them with the spider's door. As the stairs locked into place with a satisfying click, the agent stood at attention to welcome the travelers to Inkwell.

"We weren't expecting an arrival. How are you here?" the frail agent asked.

"Gravity storm knocked us off track," the conductor explained. "She'll need a rest, maybe some food?"

"I'll see what I can scrounge up. Haven't had a visit in years," the agent said, trotting off to the stables, a poof of dust rising with every step.

"I would think," Millicent said to Barnaby Blackwater as they walked down the boarding stairs, "people would travel to a place as magical as this. Just imagine, bringing life to one's writing."

That twinkling star in his right eye glistened again. "Not all are as pure of heart as you, my lady Millicent. Some have darkness docked away in deep and dangerous ports."

Millicent stooped and allowed her fingers to run through the dust on the floor. Thick, fluffy, and dry. "This place is dilapidated."

"Aye, be filthy."

She stood, clapped her hands to swipe away the grime. "What would cause this?" The exit caught her attention, and she approached. She could hear something outside the door. Shadows of movement floated at the frame's lower crack.

"Careful, my dear, curiosity is a real cat killer."

Her hand reached out to turn the knob when she heard, "No! Don't!" from the stables behind her. But it was too late. A mighty wind flung the door open, and the outline of three sizable men came into focus. The Lineman dropped everything from his hands.

"Books, please," a nasal voice, serious and bold, sounded from the inky figure in front. "Data, please."

"Books?" she asked.

"All books, all data, on your persons and in your vessel, must be handed over on arrival. Once copied, they will be returned."

"You want our books?" she clarified. "You must mean our travel documents."

"Books. Data. Hand 'em over. All of them. Anything with writing. Data."

"Data?"

"Yes, your data. And your books, your writing—"

"Writing?"

"You heard me—abstracts, anecdotes, articles, alibis, agreements, ads—"

"Arr, ads?"

"Yes, ads. Autobiographies, ballads, brochures, bylaws—"

"Boring! Yar, boring."

"Covenants, critiques, eulogies, essays—"

"Eulogies?" she asked.

"Even your emails. Everything: manifestos, manuscripts, monologues—"

Her eyebrow raised. "What about my grocery list?"

"Yes. Lists, letters, lyrics—"

"Haikus?"

"Especially haikus."

"And if I refuse?" Millicent asked.

"Well, then we add 'obituary' to the list."

"Yar, that was alpha-magical."

"That is not a word," the inky man replied.

"True, dat be something I crafted on the spot."

Millicent asked, "What do you want with our books? Our data?"

"All will be turned over to the Scribes of Inkwell for duplication and added to the Grand Library for safekeeping."

Millicent thought for a moment. She had a manual on repairs in her bag and a notepad from the triangulation of the Phantom Spires. It occurred to her that she actually had many notes and writings with her, some private and personal. "All of it?"

"All must be turned over to the Scribes of Inkwell."

All of her personal notes, private thoughts, and patents—she realized this was not a harmless request. Millicent looked at Barnaby with wide eyes but spoke to the inky man now behind her. "But what if I don't want to surrender my books? What if they are private? Mine?"

"All must be turned over to the Scribes of Inkwell," he repeated with a serious tone.

"Quark," she whispered to the pirate.

A devilish grin returned to Barnaby's face. "Pardon me, gentlemen. Please allow me to apologize. I have not introduced myself." He removed his flamboyant hat and bowed deeply to gain their trust and attention. "I'm Barnaby Blackwater, the poet of the seven galax-seas and your guide to all treasures—mostly ill-gotten. At your leisure—or peril, depending on your honesty."

Millicent stealthily backed away. She saw the terminal agent gathering the clouds of dead flies from the floor that he had dropped to feed the spider from the stable. Inch by inch, she slowly moved backward to the steps. Watching Barnaby exhaust these men with his tales of grandeur, she moved back into the passenger house and, near the top, turned to sprint inside.

"Quark! Quark! We need to hide you."

Quark's eyes lit, and he started to move, systems starting up. "Hide? Hide? What a twist! What a turn! Who knew I could get wound up like this?"

Millicent searched frantically. Seeing the passenger storage, she decided that might be the first place they'd look. The wheelhouse? Too open, too obvious. Looking Quark over once again, she asked him to put down her sleeping friend Orin. Taking one of the light fixtures, she set it on top of Quark's head, asking him to retract as small as possible. Moving next to the seat on the wall, Quark lowered in height as his legs retracted inside. His arms continued to shrink until only his fingertips remained.

"You are now a lamp, Quark. Don't say another word," she instructed.

Quark nodded his head slowly as the neck retracted and the brass lamp on his head bobbed to a halt as he locked into place.

"I don't care. I don't care. I don't care." The man stomped in frustration up the last step into the passenger compartment. "I don't care, Mr. Blackwater. We are here for the books. Here for the data." He assessed the area. "More of you. I will tell you all, with a warning, and one final time, all books and writing must be turned over to the Scribes of Inkwell." The two large inky men joined him inside.

In protest of privacy, Millicent and Barnaby made their case as the three dark men of Inkwell collected every scrap of paper and writing possible.

"You are removing my sense of safety, taking away my control of my life," Millicent pleaded.

"Yar, how do I know this won't fall into the wrong hands? Or maybe be used against me?" Barnaby inquired while being frisked. "You'll only find scraps of paper with my X at the bottom to make my mark."

"I'll never be able to trust the people of Inkwell if you do this," Millicent said, losing the tug-of-war with the strap on her bag.

His henchmen tore through the other travelers, who trembled in fear. None were so bold or brave as to stand in the way of the search and seizure of documents and data. Their language was empty, their clothes turned inside out, not a pocket left unturned. Frisking the sleeping Orin, they discovered every bit and morsel of poetry he carried in his blanket cape.

The villainous voice dripped with a venomous mix of condescension and malevolent glee as he uttered the words, "Well, well. What do we have here?" The tone was of feigned surprise, as if he'd stumbled upon an unexpected yet delightfully vulnerable prey. Each syllable was enunciated with sinister precision, letting the phrase hang in the air like a coiled serpent ready to strike. The inky man's finger poked at the large, odd, brassy lamp. Quark sprang to life, lights bright, extremities expanding, running in circles around the compartment. "Time to prove that this old clock still has some spring in its step!" He sent the inquisitor falling back on his butt in surprise.

The largest of the three removed a small device from his pocket and watched as Quark's spring unwound. Circling into his reach, the man slapped it on Quark's side. Quark came to an immediate, lifeless stop, falling over from the momentum.

Each of the inky thugs picked a side, feet and head, then lifted Quark, carrying him out the door. Their boss turned to remind them, "We will be back once we're done with the bot to garner anything we missed in this round."

A rare feeling of helplessness swept through Millicent's heart. Watching her companion carried away and out the door she had opened out of pure curiosity left her inconsolable. "I fix problems, not make them."

"It be one of those things in life, my lady Millicent. Some rules can't be beaten."

"A bad rule," she declared. "An unjust rule."

"'Tis knowledge they find be the treasure in this world, no *if*s, *and*s, or *but*s about it."

Millicent raced down the steps.

"Yar, where you going?"

Millicent approached the Lineman and terminal agent in the stable. "Where are they taking my friend? What will happen to him?"

"They are going to the Grand Library, like they said," the agent explained. "The Scribes will make a copy of everything the three seized. But don't worry, they will return it all. And you will get everything back."

"But these are mine. My notes and my thoughts. My Quark. They have no right to them, no right to copy or plagiarize."

The Lineman shrugged. "This is the rule of Inkwell. You shouldn't have come if you didn't want to follow the rules."

Barnaby Blackwater, catching up, stepped up to her side and asked, "Why is this so important?"

"My notes," she explained, "are the directions to the Phantom Spire. My notes include the calculations to get us to your ship. My Quark includes all the information he experiences, including your stolen time, all your stories, and the Clockmaster. These will be in a library. For who knows who to see? What if he saw your treasure maps? You know, the ones you keep with your 'bon mots.'"

"Arr, me tongue be tied tighter than a sailor's knot! What savvy scheme shall we hatch to get out o' this pickle?"

8

S tepping through the terminal door, the world of Inkwell rolled out before them, a vast parchment—a world of off-white. The air was filled with the scent of ink and the rustle of turning pages. The terminal, an obvious foreign body, had landed in the middle of Inkwell.

Millicent and Barnaby Blackwater ventured forward. Reality felt fluid, shaped by the thoughts and stories written down by Inkwell's inhabitants, known as the Scribes. Another step farther into this realm, the pair noticed that the people of Inkwell moved like the images in a flipbook, their actions disjointed and flickering, yet still forming a cohesive narrative. Each step, each gesture, each expression was a brushstroke in the grand tale that unfolded around them.

This monochromatic world explored the expressions of brown, deep in the stroke, bleeding like watercolor in the rain across the parchment, softening into something almost gossamer. Millicent asked a milkmaid at the gate of her country cottage, "Excuse me, we are strangers here looking for the

Grand Library. Three dark fellows took my robot. Maybe you saw them pass?"

The maid's eyelashes fluttered as she looked up into the deep eyes of Barnaby Blackwater, tilting her head in a bashful flirtation. "Never before have I beheld such an enchanting visage, one that speaks of distant lands and untold tales. 'Tis evident that you are but strangers here, wanderers in the land of Inkwell. Pray tell, what twist of fate has guided your steps to the cobblestone streets of the city of Quillton? You are welcome here in the Romance district, a realm where love and mystery intertwine like the tendrils of a blossoming vine."

Millicent's heart fluttered traitorously as she watched the milkmaid's eyes lock on to the handsome pirate, oblivious to her presence. A curious ache blossomed in her chest—jealousy, an emotion as foreign to her as the pirate's far-off lands—while a telltale warmth crept across her cheeks, betraying her inner turmoil. She had never realized that Barnaby Blackwater was handsome and tall. Millicent wanted to know where he got the scar on his cheek and how he lost his leg. At that moment, she wanted to build him a better prosthetic to replace the fine timber that clicked with his every step.

"Millicent?" She heard her name and returned to the moment. "Millicent, what do you think?" Barnaby asked.

"Yes, good," she replied.

Millicent looked at the milkmaid, who was putting her arm through Barnaby's as the two led the way. Inspecting the street closer, it wasn't cobblestone as she thought but love letters—handwritten, signed with big loopy writing, each "i" dotted with a heart. The quaint cottage country, flower-filled and perfect, was inhabited by brawny men in shirts torn open, exposing their chests. Strong arms filled the puffy-sleeved white shirts as they chopped wood, carried maidens over puddles, or lazily enjoyed picnics under fruit trees. The women, beautiful and strong, allowed the men to take control, giving in to the passionate craving glowing from the mixed feelings of confusion —asking, would they? Won't they? Could they, this one time?

Millicent shook her head, attempting to wake from this dream. But it was real. Barnaby and the milkmaid were kissing. Slowly, he removed his arm from around her waist and drew back with a longing look, his strong, rough hand gently wiping a single tear from her cheek.

"Le départ, c'est la partie la plus difficile," murmured the milkmaid, her gaze fixed on the distant horizon. A wistful smile played on her lips as she absently twirled a strand of hair around her finger. "Si tu repasses par ici," she added with a Gallic shrug, "cherche-moi, peut-être." The wind rustled through the fields, carrying with it the delicate scent of lavender and the bittersweet aroma of nostalgia and unfulfilled promises.

Millicent could see just steps ahead that the monochrome world took on a hue of black. The buildings on the other side of this neighborhood were made from every shade of gray, forming dark bricks that stood three stories tall. The streets were wet and rainy, keeping the citizens under umbrellas and turning up the collars of their raincoats and Mackinaws.

Millicent's fingers dug into Barnaby's arm as she yanked him away from the dame. The broad had gams that went on for days and lips that'd make a bishop kick a hole in a stained-glass window, but they had bigger fish to fry. The rain pounded the pavement like a snitch getting a workout from the boys in blue. Millicent's mind raced faster than a cat with its tail on fire. What was Barnaby thinking, swapping spit with some floozy?

He was supposed to be different, but maybe he was just another chump with a wandering eye.

The streets were meaner than a junkyard dog, and the cops walked the beat like they owned the joint. Everyone had a gasper dangling from their mug, lit or not. It was the kind of night that made you want to crawl inside a bottle and pull the cork in after you. But they had a job to do. They needed to find the Grand Library and figure out what those inky goons were up to. The clock was ticking, and the city had more twists than a pretzel factory. They'd have to keep their eyes peeled and their wits sharp if they wanted to come out of this in one piece.

The crack behind them hit like a slug from a .45, sending Millicent's ticker into overdrive.

"Look!" Barnaby's finger stabbed the air, pointing out the shadowy silhouettes of two goons lugging a Quark-shaped tin can. The mugs vanished around the bend, but Barnaby wasn't about to let 'em off the hook. He latched on to Millicent's hand and yanked her forward, the two of them tearing after the snatchers like bats outta hell. Barnaby's phony leg, the one he lost in the big dust-up, clicked and clacked with every step, a morbid metronome keeping time.

The heavens opened up, dumping a biblical deluge on their heads as they pounded the pavement. Ghostly figures lurked in every back alley, haunting the corners like specters from a bad dream.

CRACK! Barnaby's grip went slack. He hit the slick streets like a sack of wet cement.

Millicent was at his side in a flash, cradling his head.

"I'm... I'm done for, doll," he hacked out between coughs. "This is curtains for me. You gotta fly solo on this one, Milli."

"Can the pity party, Blackwater. You ain't checking out on

me yet," she growled. "You're gonna beat this rap, ya hear? You're gonna make it, come hell or high water."

At that moment, a realization came across Millicent's face.

Barnaby sat up. "Aye, you're catching on."

"Yes," she said. "That is not me."

"We're getting caught in this world's trappings."

"Can you walk?"

Barnaby Blackwater smiled and with a little help stood tall. "To err is human, to arr is pirate."

Down the street two additional blocks, and a right turn on the corner, the city of Quillton transformed to blue. Moving walkways, flying cars, and buildings that breached the clouds filled the scene, with population centers crowded with thousands of happy men and women. The men wore tight shorts and large-collared shirts that couldn't close all the way due to their muscles. The women, clad in every shade of blue, sported cleavage, ample and free in a bra-less future, with the cut of their hems just above the knee and a slit in the fabric showing thigh. Bouffant hair styles towered and balanced on their heads, adorned with gold jewelry and large precious gems.

"Amazing!" Millicent commented as they continued to make their way to Quillton's city center.

A slow-building siren ramped to full speed, blaring in the distance. People in the streets began running in every direction. A loud roar echoed in the streets as the head of a blobbed creature rose over the skyline. Opposite, a robot, twenty stories tall, black and chrome, with flashing lights on its chest and a transparent bowl where its head should be, housing swirling mechanics. Citizens frozen in place cowered at the sight of the two creatures, some pointing in disbelief, and the shrill screams of women echoed. Millicent smiled and found it amusing, now understanding the patterns that played out.

Stepping outside the Science Fiction district, the hue changed to green—soft, blazing, spring green—a welcomed feeling that filled them as they reached the center. Acres of green space sprawled in every direction, allowing them to see the outlying neighborhoods butted against the tranquility of the park that surrounded them. Sections, like a color wheel, spoke with shapes and dreams. At the center, a dome of elegantly crafted lines from an engineer's drafting pen laid in ink. Ramps between the canopies exposed the futuristic floors and windows. It was on the nearest ramp that Barnaby spotted, with his good eye, the three inky criminals, with Quark in tow.

9

"Yar, there she blows." Barnaby Blackwater pointed.

Catching sight, Millicent started to run through the grass to close the distance. She looked over her shoulder between strides to check on Barnaby. There he was, limping along at his best speed. He waved. "Go on! Go on! I'll catch up."

Millicent could feel the pounding in her chest, her arms pumping, knees lifting, and her energy draining. Her mind started to wander and pick apart the predicament. Her bag shifted with each stride, CHA-CHING, CHA-CHING, as her tools clattered. She pushed hard to maintain her pace, but the sprint quickly emptied her reserves. Her right foot struck a hard obstacle, and as she tried to recover, she lost her balance, falling and sliding through the cool grass. Rolling over and looking up at the sky, her lungs heaved as she caught her breath.

The familiar face of her pirate companion bent over her, and he said, "Giving up, are we?"

"There," she said between breaths, "has to be a smarter way."

He extended his hand and helped her to her feet.

"This world has us reacting, and we should be thinking through this instead."

"Aye."

Her hands, sticky from the fall, began to rub against her pants, and when she looked down, she saw thick, deep, and fresh grass stains. Her hands, a lighter shade of green, bore the same markings. As if a lightbulb had gone off, an idea came to mind, and she reached into her tool bag, removing a pen and clean paper.

"What be this?" Barnaby asked.

"An experiment," she said, rubbing the clean sheet of paper on her stained pant leg, then taking a handful of grass and rubbing it into the page. With her pen, she began to describe, "An electric cart that seats two adults, speedy and true, fast enough to catch you." The air filled with the sound of rustling pages, and before them, the fluttering of a flipbook brought forth a green, speedy cart for two.

"Hop on," she said with a big, bright smile of satisfaction.

"Arr, using your head."

With a press of the button, the two held tight and shot across the green land, toward the elegant dome. Up, up, up the ramp they went, following a path that circled around the building. WHOOSH, doors opened in front of them, taking them inside the Grand Library. The spiral continued inside, sloping down and around, with each turn of the track taking them lower into the depths, like a racetrack.

"There!" Barnaby pointed, seeing the trio with his good eye as they started to toss Quark onto a dark conveyor belt.

Each of the dark figures emptied their pockets of paper—

sheets, wads, bits, and bobs—all marked items following Quark on the belt.

Millicent released the button, but the cart continued racing down the track at incredible speed. Brakes were not part of her plan, only speed. When the three thugs completed their task, they turned to find themselves face-to-face with Millicent, Barnaby, and the momentum of the sled plowing into them with no recourse. Most dream of flight, wishing to be among the fowl, free to chart their own course. But as these three inky men took flight, they smudged the air, unable to turn or twist, becoming streaks on the floor. Three splatters landed on the concrete.

Millicent recovered first, helping Barnaby Blackwater to his good foot. The two bolted forward, following the automated belt as it hummed along, its destination the mouth of a large machine. A wand of bright light paced back and forth across the entry point, emitting a whiny hum. A copy, a facsimile, a forgery dropped out the other end.

Millicent went first for Quark, but he was heavier than she remembered. With an "UGH" and an "OHHH," she pulled and tugged. With Barnaby's quick aid, the two were able to make Quark roll and drop the three feet to the floor with a ringing *BONG*. Quickly, Barnaby nabbed every scrap within reach. He was fast from a life of trickery, prestidigitation, and sleight of hand, surviving as a pirate. Not a scrap or pinch would get past him. Millicent inspected every inch of her robot friend to find the one misplaced patch. Pulling at it stretched the device like long saltwater taffy until, *SMOCK!*

Quark's lights turned on. His arms and legs moved. Standing on his own, he asked, "Tick-tock, tick-tock, the gears of life never stop. But what makes them turn, and where do they lead? That's the mystery I aim to unwind!"

Millicent started to well up, a thought from deep within bubbling to the surface. "You crazy robot. What if I lost you?"

"No worry, miss. I am here. Safe and sound, don't you fear."

Millicent beamed with joy and wrapped her arms around Quark.

"Ahoy, me buckos! I be no landlubber when it comes to merrymakin', but methinks we ought to weigh anchor and set course for safer waters!"

Up, up, up, and around, round, round the track they went, searching for the exit. As they neared the top, the brightening light with each step fueled their urgency to reach the terminal and leave Inkwell behind.

Mere feet from the automatic door to freedom, someone beckoned. "Checking out?"

They turned to find the source: a wizened woman in a sweater behind a desk, her glasses perched halfway down the bridge of her nose. She repeated, stamp in hand, "Checking out?"

"Yes, please," Millicent replied with military precision. Barnaby noticed her posture stiffen, as if invisible strings had yanked her upright. "May I inquire who you are?"

"I am Calliope, the head librarian. I've been keeping my eye on you since you arrived, and I must admit, I'm highly impressed. Few learn to operate the magic of Inkwell so quickly. Millicent, isn't it?"

Millicent's jaw clenched almost imperceptibly. When she spoke, her words came out sharp and crisp, devoid of her usual thoughtful pauses. "Yes. Millicent, of Gearturn. This is Barnaby Blackwater"—he took the opportunity to bow and remove his hat with panache—"and this is Quark."

Calliope's eyes gleamed with interest. "Ah yes, I'm quite familiar with Quark. My clerks informed me of him right away."

She set down her stamp and approached the trio. "He's a wonder, quite unique. So rich with information. You built him yourself?"

"I did," Millicent replied, her tone clipped. Her right arm moved slowly, almost protectively, in front of Quark. "What is it you want with all this information, Calliope? The writing? The data?" She hardened. "These things are not yours."

Barnaby raised an eyebrow at Millicent's uncharacteristic defiance, exchanging a quick glance with Quark.

Calliope smiled, unperturbed. "Everyone you've met on your journey through Inkwell was unable to resist its magic. But you're different. Not only did you resist, but you controlled it."

Millicent's fingers curled into a fist at her side. "Why take other people's work? Why invade their privacy?" The words tumbled out, tinged with an emotion Barnaby couldn't quite place—anger? Fear?

"Knowledge, my dear," Calliope replied, as if it were obvious. "Inkwell was built on stories, and stories contain meaning and knowledge. It's an intoxicating and addictive ability to control. From ancient times, anyone who arrives must turn over their story so we can continue to copy and grow."

Millicent's eyes flashed. "You never originate. There is no creation. It is only a copy. You are all thieves, plagiarists." She shuddered, and for a moment, Barnaby caught a glimpse of something in her eyes—an old pain, quickly masked.

Quark whirred softly, moving closer to Millicent as if lending silent support.

"I suppose that is one way to look at it," Calliope replied smoothly. "Or, we might be the collectors and keepers of all the Supercluster's knowledge. What we have is nearly safe."

"Nearly?" Millicent was sharp.

"This is why I've stopped you, why I need to ask for your help."

"Yar, that is rich," Barnaby sneered, eyeing Millicent's tense posture. "Wait, are you rich?"

"Tell us," Millicent demanded, her words clipped.

Calliope's eyes narrowed at Millicent's tone before she continued. "You've met my clerks, a relatively powerful group of collectors dedicated to filling the Grand Library. You've met the good citizens of Inkwell, the Scribes who enrich the lives of others with stories, each based in their own quarter. But there are also the troublemakers on Inkwell—a small group who call themselves the Revisionaries."

"Revisionaries?" Millicent's brow furrowed, her curiosity momentarily overriding her wariness.

"Yes, and as it sounds, they are reshaping everything, putting the world of Inkwell at risk. I need you. Inkwell and Quillton need you to help stop them."

Millicent and Barnaby exchanged glances, a silent communication passing between them. They spoke in unison, their questions revealing their differing priorities. Barnaby asked, "Yar, how much will you pay us?" while Millicent demanded, "To what end?"

"Yar." Barnaby quickly recovered, catching Millicent's reproachful look. "That's what I meant."

Calliope's lips curled into a knowing smile. "Millicent, my understanding is that you seek the Phantom Spires—you are seeking the Time Core?"

Millicent stiffened, her eyes widening. "How did you–"

"Your notes," Calliope interrupted, reaching for a notebook on her desk. "I was able to discern this from the journal your fast-fingered pirate friend missed." She offered it to Millicent. "Your original."

Millicent snatched it from her hand, clutching it to her chest. Her entire body trembled, muscles taut as bowstrings, while a hot flush crept up her neck and face. Her eyes flashed dangerously, nostrils flaring with each sharp breath. Through clenched teeth, she hissed, "This is mine. Mine. Private. How dare you."

Quark moved closer to Millicent, his metallic frame humming with tension.

"I could help you get there, a shortcut," Calliope offered casually, unfazed by Millicent's outburst. "Help you understand what the Time Core is, and what it isn't, even confirm who built it. If..."

"If we help you." Millicent's face flushed, a stark contrast to the peaceful green surroundings.

Barnaby stepped forward, placing a steadying hand on Millicent's shoulder. "Let me get this straight, you be wanting us to find these Revisionaries, and then what? Ask them nicely to stop?"

"Help me capture them, bring them to—let's call it justice— or end their misguided ways. Whichever comes first," Calliope replied coolly.

Barnaby was quick on the quip. "Justice? A noble goal, but it doesn't keep the lights on or the ship fueled. Profit and survival —those are real motivators."

Millicent gave a hard look at Barnaby. "You, always chasing after the next score..."

"Lass, the treasure isn't gold—it's the chase." He broke his stare from Millicent, looking back to Calliope. "You get the Revisionaries. We get the map to the Phantom Spires," Barnaby mused. "Yar, and if we don't?"

Calliope's tone hardened. "You'll never make it back to the terminal. It's easy to get lost in Inkwell, get distracted, fall in love, fight criminals, be a hero, save the damsel. No matter how you resist, I will wear you down, point you in the wrong direction, as long as you survive."

Millicent's jaw clenched, her earlier fear giving way to unyielding resolve. "We are attempting to save the Supercluster, the same one in which you reside. Stopping us will eventually destroy your world."

"You'd be surprised how often I hear this," Calliope replied, unimpressed. "'I'm special. I need to save the Supercluster.' Save the Supercluster?" She huffed. "Start here on Inkwell; stop the Revisionaries."

"I'm not special," she whispered, her fingers tracing the blue fabric lining of her recovered journal. She turned to her companions, her eyes searching Barnaby's face and Quark's impassive features, weighing their options. Finally, she faced Calliope, her gaze hardening into a steely, unflinching stare that could freeze fire. "How do we find them?"

10

Barnaby counted twelve regions circling the dome of the Grand Library, a literal color wheel of Quillton fanning out from its center. The vibrant hues stretched out like spokes, each representing a different territory within the magical realm. Calliope led them to the circular tier that wrapped under the dome's canopy, toward the ramp opposite where they had shot up in their speedy cart.

"Orange." Calliope pointed to the section on the color wheel, her voice tinged with a hint of urgency. "Start there, and you'll find the outlaws. There are five of them: Hope Hayes, Kamen Kazi, Grace Garner, Freya Fogg, and the leader, Saoirse Shadow." The last name slipped from her lips like venom, her expression hardening with bitterness. "Bring them to me, dead or alive, it matters not."

"Calliope." Millicent watched as the flipbook flicker of her green post-impressionism olive oil swirls of green wheat surrounded her every step. "I need to know about the magic of your world. How does it work? The ink?" Millicent inquired.

"The color of each district works in that section, just like you used here for your vehicle. Extract the ink from your surroundings and shape them as you need."

"Except?" She paused, waiting for her to fill in the blank. "I feel like you are holding something back."

"Except for green. If it's green, it goes, anywhere." A swirl at the edges of her lips shared a sinister grin. "This was the revelation of the Revisionaries. Once they learned the power of green, they could influence and change at will, forcing others to bend to their wishes, bullying and provoking them into doing what the Revisionaries wanted and thought best."

Millicent removed one of her notebooks from the tool bag on her shoulder. She opened it flat from the metal wire spiral and started to rub a plain sheet of paper on the grass of the center's surroundings. Then, for good measure, Millicent rubbed five additional blank pages with the green stuff. Following in the spirit of the moment, Barnaby removed his handkerchief and started to wipe the grounds clean, sopping the fabric with green before shoving it deep into his exterior jacket pocket.

Looking up at Calliope, Millicent could see the interest swoop up in her eyebrows. It might have been surprise or inspiration for thinking ahead, or jealousy that she had not considered this effort herself.

"Quark," Millicent said, going into her bag. "Whatever happens, you need to go back to the terminal and get Orin home."

"I'm sure he'll sleep the whole trip." He nodded. "I will make sure he gets home."

She opened the hinged mouth of her bag, allowing the clockmaker to see everything inside easily. Reaching into the leather bucket of her everyday carry materials, a flap inside held several writing instruments of all shapes, colors, and sizes. She handed one to Barnaby and attached another to the spiral wire of the notepad for easy access. These two ballpoint pens had baby-blue plastic tips with white tops, where four levers in black, red, blue, and green would extend a matching color to write with. The fine points and variety of colors were the perfect tools for the occasion.

The words Millicent wrote began: *A frame of a door appeared before them. When it opened, they could see deep within the orange territory, the Revisionaries just in sight below in their valley hideout, hatching plans.*

As the words formed on the page, a green magical glow appeared around them, the air filling with the rustling sound of pages turning. The door materialized, its edges glowing faintly with the green Millicent had imbued. When it opened, they were greeted by a world bathed in every tint and tone of orange —a stark contrast to the green that had brought them there.

Millicent's eyes grew as they stepped through the door, her senses heightened by the knowledge that they were entering enemy territory. She glanced back at Calliope, her voice steady but tinged with a warning. "Be ready for our return, Calliope. You *will* make good on your end of the bargain."

11

Millicent led Quark and Barnaby through the portal, arriving in a dusty world filled with boulders stacked high and vast plains between them, creating gullies for the spring rains. Looking out on this western valley below, they had a better view of the ranch. The three ducked behind one of the large boulders, staying low to the ground. The dust settled. They could now see even better: the crew in wide-brimmed hats kept the basking sun at bay, long guns slung over their shoulders, holsters with a six-shooter on each hip, and one, the only male, strapped with explosives, ready to act at a moment's notice.

"Arr, a desert sea before me, the likes of which I'd not think to see. Is that their boat?" Barnaby pointed to a horse-drawn covered wagon being unloaded of supplies at the ranch house.

"Yes, a land boat, called a wagon."

"Yar, I've heard this called a buckboard at port."

"Nearly the same. Quark, what do you see?"

"There are five of them, and eight horses."

"Shiver me timbers, we be surrounded by scallywags and ne'er-do-wells! What's the strategy to outsmart these land-lubbers?"

Millicent pulled out her notebook and said, "I think this might work." She wrote, telling Barnaby every word: *The sun began to set as the gang settled in for the night. One started a campfire to cook from that afternoon's hunt. After a filling meal, the crew talked about the next day's plans, tired from the day, and sleepy.*

"Yar." Barnaby nodded, watching her scribble. "Let's see if that works." Slowly he raised his head above the boulders to get a better view and watched the sun slowly set on the horizon as one of the gang started a large campfire out front. "It's working. We just need a little time. What next?"

"Your jacket."

"Me jacket?" Barnaby looked down at it, his lower lip jutting out and quivering slightly, like a child on the verge of tears. He looked back up at Millicent and explained, "We're nearly insep-arable." He reluctantly began to remove the dark brown twilled fustian, revealing the white silken shirt and blue twelve-button vest, with his sheathed cutlass strapped low.

For all their time together, Millicent hadn't noticed the weapon, as it had been hidden from view under the garment. When he handed her the coat, it brought a unique odor, mixing musk, the sea, and stars into one scent that tricked the senses.

"Yar, dark enough night, and I'd swear it's burnt umber."

Millicent turned her attention back to the notebook and scribbled additional lines. Reaching behind the rock at their rear, she found a wide-brimmed western hat that fit her perfectly.

"Arr, that be a nice trick to pull," Barnaby complimented. He was impressed as rope and handcuffs followed the hat into her shoulder bag. "Nice."

"Quark, dim your lights and make your way to the stable. I am going to introduce myself to the gang."

"And me?"

"Barnaby, you stay here, and if something goes wrong, I will need you to help."

"Aye."

On the edge of night's darkness, Millicent slipped out from their hiding place and moseyed to the wagon trail. She followed it along the line straight up to the campfire, catching the gang just as they finished supper and started to slip into sleep. She put her trust in Quark's hands as he headed to the stable. He could easily be a distraction to save her or the fly in the punch that spoiled the whole plan.

"Howdy," Millicent called out as she raised her hands to the sound of clicking pistols, readying a shot with a cocked hammer prepared to send the bullet through the barrel and into her heart. "Saw your fire." She appeared calm and steady. "I hope I might sit a spell to warm up."

"Who are you?" a woman asked with an Irish lilt.

"My name is Millicent. New here."

"Am I to believe you just stumbled on us from nowhere, Millicent? Or were you sent here?"

"Stumbled, lost, and hoped to find a friendly face," she replied. "Hours ago, it was blazing, and now it's bitter in the night."

"Step a little closer, so we can see you better."

Millicent slowly complied, keeping her arms up. "May I ask your name?"

"I'm Saoirse, rhymes with inertia." She pointed to each person in the circle, calling their names, each a different hue representing a different section of Inkwell's color wheel. "This here's my gang: Hope, Kamen, Grace, and Freya."

"What kind of gang are you?"

"What?"

"I mean, there are all types of gangs out here. What kind are you?"

Hope Hayes stood, her rifle at the ready. "The kind that don't like too many questions," she said, holding the barrel up so her eye could line up on the target, the butt quick to her shoulder to steady.

"You walk all the way from town?" Saoirse asked. "That's a long walk."

"I came from the south, making my way north, and slept in the brush last night. Hope to get some shut-eye by your fire," Millicent explained.

Grace, in her dress and petticoats, bright orange bandanna around her neck, had a much softer smile than the others' gritty grins and looked to be raised indoors. "You don't talk like others around these parts. Where are you from?"

"Off-world. I crashed on Inkwell weeks ago and have tried to make my way to a place called Quillton."

The gang burst into laughter at Millicent's expense.

"What? What is so funny?" she asked, almost insulted.

"Hell, you're in Quillton, have been since everything turned orange," said Hope Hayes. "What were you expecting?"

"I am not sure, to be honest. The last few days have been confusing for me," Millicent told the group, focusing on Saoirse. Saoirse, like Calliope, was green, leading Millicent to suspect some history between them—perhaps an incident at the library, maybe rooted in jealousy. Why else would Calliope seethe at saying her name?

Saoirse Shadow holstered her gun. "Lower 'em. This pale and frail is not a threat to us. You sit there, next to Grace, she'll treat ya good. Cuddle right up next to ya like a cat."

She thought of Orin, curled up and warm, and a grateful smile touched her lips. Millicent inched her way to an open spot around the campfire. Seated with her head bowed, she used her hat to shield her from making eye contact, savoring its warmth against the cold night air.

"I'll ask you this, Millicent. If ya had the chance to go back and change something, to mend it, make it right, would ya?" Saoirse asked.

"Yes, in a heartbeat. I would have changed course to avoid landing here. No offense. Inkwell is beautiful and mysterious, just not my destination."

"Well, that's the kind of gang you're sitting with. The kind that feels fixing the past makes the future better."

"It sounds amazing. That is possible here?"

"Only if ya know how. Which we do. When you walked up, we were talking about how to make tomorrow a better world."

"That is noble. What did you decide?" Millicent tilted her head just enough to see the bright eyes of Saoirse Shadow over the fire. The light flickered on her face, giving her a charm and glow that attracted Millicent.

"There's a witch that runs Quillton. A real meanie. She stole from us, each and every one. She'll want to steal from you too, once she finds you." Saoirse leaned back. "We were just saying how nice it would be if she were never born." The gang, nodding and encouraging that this was the right plan, yipped and yea'ed.

Millicent was torn at the mention of this plan. She was no fan of Calliope. She knew what it felt like for her privacy to be invaded, her personal thoughts exposed. Even if, as Calliope explained, the cause to keep and protect knowledge was a good and just one. Millicent could easily have fallen in with this gang and been one of them if things had been different. Saoirse wasn't that different. But the promise from Calliope—information on the Time Core and the Phantom Spires—appeared greater. Millicent needed to save her home, find what caused this break in time, and bring back order to the Supercluster.

"I am with you," Millicent said. "It would be just awful if this witch were to steal from me. What exactly did she take from you, if you do not mind my asking? I want to be prepared if she arrives."

Kamen gave a guttural grunt, thinking of the pain so real and close. "I have a daughter; she makes me a proud papa. She's smart and funny, has her mother's smile. There is one photograph that I have kept and cherished of her. It was here." He patted his pocket. "On the back, it had the date it was taken. Her birthday, the day she turned ten. Then"—the timbre in his tone changed from a fond memory to seething bitterness—"the witch sent her men after me. They beat me, stripped me, and found this photo. The most important thing I had left in this world, my photo of my daughter. Now"—Kamen touched the straps of explosives covering the pocket that once held the photo of his heart—"I just want to blow them all up and send them to hell."

The circle nodded. Each knew the feeling of pain, holding it tight to fill the void of what they lost.

Grace sat by the crackling fire, the warm glow illuminating her delicate features as she gazed into the dancing flames. The memories of her lost love flooded her mind, and she couldn't help but reminisce about the letters that had once brought her so much joy and hope. "I knew love before arriving at Inkwell," she began, soft and wistful. "I kept letters from that love, and they gave me hope that one day we would see each other again."

Grace told them how the words in those letters were so beautiful, so profound, that they penetrated the essence of her being. The elegant handwriting, the time and care taken to craft each sentence, and the thoughtfulness behind every word were unlike anything she had ever known before or since. It was as if the letters were a secret language, a code that only she and her beloved could decipher, each word a key to unlocking the depths of their love.

For the first time in her life, Grace had felt truly understood, as if someone had finally seen her for who she was. She no longer felt alone in this vast and often unforgiving world. The connection she shared with her love was unbreakable, transcending distance and time.

Now, as she sat there, the weight of her loss bore down upon her like a suffocating blanket. Grace stared into the fire, fighting back the tears that threatened to overflow, her heart aching with a pain that felt all-consuming. "Lost," she exhaled, barely above a whisper. "All my hope for love is lost, forever." The sigh that followed was deep and saddened, resonating through the universe as if the stars themselves shared in her grief.

With a slow, deliberate movement, Grace lifted the edge of her petticoat, revealing a long blade strapped to her thigh. Its razor edge and mirror-polished metal reflected the dancing flames. An eerie glow upon her face overshadowed her exterior beauty as a stubbornness set in her eyes, revealing the ugliness inside. "That witch is going to get her throat cut," she declared.

The hidden weapon, so stealthy and close, sent shivers through Millicent.

Freya Fogg, her skin a mesmerizing shade of lavender, stood tall and unwavering as she faced Millicent. The vibrant hue of her complexion started to shimmer in the firelight, a testament to her otherworldly heritage. With a voice as deep and rumbling as distant thunder, Freya spoke, each word laced with a palpable sense of loss and anger. "She stole my family."

For months, Freya explained, she had traversed the vast expanse of the galaxy, her tenacity fueling her every step. She had searched tirelessly for the history of her family, the lineage and birthright that had been so cruelly taken from her. The ancestral records, centuries of meticulously preserved scrolls, had been housed in a state-of-the-art xenon gas enclosure, designed to prevent deterioration and ensure the survival of her people's legacy.

Freya's hands clenched into fists at her sides, her nails digging into her palms as she fought to control the rage that boiled within her. The urge to lash out, to make the one responsible pay for their heinous actions, was almost overwhelming. Through gritted teeth, she spoke once again, her words dripping with a venomous desire for retribution. "I just want to strangle that witch after her goons carelessly opened that case, turning it all to ash and dust, scattered to the winds."

The air around Freya began to crackle with barely contained energy, her purple aura pulsing with the intensity of her emotions. Millicent, sitting before her, could feel the raw power emanating from Freya over the flames of the fire, a force to be reckoned with. The path ahead for her was clear: Freya would stop at nothing to reclaim what was rightfully hers and ensure that the one who had wronged her family would face the consequences of their actions.

As the night wore on, story after story was shared around the dying fire, its once vibrant flames slowly fading into a soft, warm glow of embers and ash. The crackling of the burning wood grew quieter, replaced by the gentle whispers of the breeze and the occasional chirp of a nocturnal creature. The companions, huddled close to the remnants of the fire, felt the weight of exhaustion gradually overtaking them. Their voices grew softer, their tales sparse, until one by one, they succumbed to the embrace of slumber. The peace of the night enveloped them, their minds drifting off into the realm of dreams, leaving behind the cares and worries of the waking world. In the stillness of the late hour, the embers of the fire continued to glow, a silent guardian watching over the sleeping forms, as the stars above twinkled in the vast expanse of the night sky.

Millicent, her movements as subtle as a whisper, carefully slipped her notebook out from under Barnaby's jacket. The pages felt familiar in her hands, knowing it was open to a green page. With a quick motion, she scribbled a note, her blue and white pen dancing across the paper: *A sleep deeper than they had ever known. Not even the cymbal or drum of a Quatazar marching band could wake them.* A mischievous smile played at the corners of her lips as she tucked the notebook back into its hiding place.

Millicent moved with catlike stealth as she reached into her pocket and retrieved the first set of handcuffs. The metal gleamed in the dim light, reflecting the fading embers of the fire. Slowly, she moved from one gang member to the next, ratcheting the cuffs around each wrist with a satisfying click. The sound echoed in the stillness of the night, a reminder of the power she now held over the slumbering group. As she worked, she linked each person to the one beside them, creating a chain of captives, bound together by the unyielding metal.

With her task complete, Millicent turned toward her hidden companion. "Quark," she called softly, "gather their weapons and stack them over there."

12

The clatter of metal against metal broke the silence, but the gang members, deep in their enchanted slumber, remained oblivious. Millicent watched Quark at work, a quiet satisfaction washing over her. With the gang restrained and their weapons confiscated, she held the upper hand. The ordeal was far from over, but for now, she could breathe easier.

As the dawn's first light brushed the sky with soft orange hues, Millicent stood tall, her silhouette a stark figure against the waking world. There was an unspoken edge in the way she held herself, a quiet hint of the unknown that lingered in the air. With a single, deliberate wave of her hand, she signaled toward the boulder where her trusted companion had taken refuge. Barnaby emerged, the white sleeves of his pirate blouse billowing in the breeze, glowing in the growing light—a symbol of hope amidst the uncertainty.

The gang's weapons, once symbols of their dominance, now lay in a pile, out of reach. The metal gleamed in the early sun, mocking their vulnerability. As the light grew stronger, the gang members stirred, blinking away the haze of sleep. Confusion gave way to horror as the reality of their situation sank in. The handcuffs bit into their wrists, a constant reminder of their captivity.

Anger and disbelief flickered across their faces as they struggled against their bonds, their movements clumsy and uncoordinated—a stark contrast to their usual bravado. Millicent observed with a cool gaze, letting her actions speak louder than words.

Barnaby drew closer, his steps measured and purposeful, a silent declaration of his support. Side by side, they faced the awakening gang, ready for whatever the day might bring. The sun continued its ascent, its rays casting an ethereal glow over the scene, as if the heavens were watching the unfolding drama. Millicent knew with unwavering certainty that the balance of power had shifted.

"By the stars! That was easier than filching a doubloon," Barnaby exclaimed, a mischievous grin spreading across his face. He stumped up to Millicent with a confident swagger, twirling a stray lock of his hair as if the world were his stage.

"The work isn't done. We still need to get them back to Calliope."

The five outlaws—Hope Hayes, Kamen Kazi, Grace Garner, Freya Fogg, and their leader, Saoirse Shadow—strained against their shackles. Cold metal bit into their wrists as their initial cries for freedom echoed through the morning air. Hope yanked at her restraints, teal eyes blazing with indignation. Kamen, his red skin glistening with sweat, gritted his teeth, testing the cuffs' strength with his muscular frame. Grace, her once-pristine orange petticoat now sullied, glared at their captors, her delicate features twisted with fury. Freya, her vibrant purple skin contrasting with the dull metal, cursed in a long-forgotten tongue, her words dripping with venom. Meanwhile, Saoirse sat silently, her piercing green eyes calculating, already weaving a web of plans to turn the tables.

As the reality of their situation sank in, their cries for freedom turned into a chorus of revenge. The air grew heavy with their anger, a palpable force that crackled with each passing moment. United by their shared thirst for vengeance, they silently added Millicent to their list.

"You will comply," Millicent declared, retrieving her notebook and four-color pen—the tools of her trade and her power. As she held the pen aloft, the gang's bravado faltered, their eyes widening as they realized the extent of her abilities. With purposeful strokes, Millicent wrote, and a shimmering green doorframe materialized before them, pulsing with a magical glow. The outlaws gasped, their defiance replaced by stunned silence.

Barnaby moved to assist, lifting the gang members to their feet with surprising gentleness. Quark mirrored his actions, steadying the captives. The outlaws, still reeling from Millicent's display of power, offered no resistance.

With a wave of her hand, Millicent opened the magical door. Beyond the threshold lay a world of green. Fixing the gang with a steely gaze, she commanded, "March."

Their spirits broken, the outlaws had no choice but to obey. In line, they stepped through the shimmering portal, their footsteps echoing in the morning stillness. Barnaby and Quark flanked them, their presence a constant reminder of Millicent's authority.

As the last of the gang crossed the threshold, Millicent allowed herself a fleeting smile of satisfaction. The trio followed, and with a final flourish of her pen, she sealed the door behind them, the green glow fading into nothingness.

"Calliope," Saoirse said, face-to-face with her nemesis, "I should have known you'd put the frail pale up to this."

"I knew she wouldn't have it in her to take you out," Calliope replied, drawing her green quill. "You'll find I have no mercy—in a very slow and agonizing way."

Witnessing the two together made Millicent uneasy.

Barnaby growled, "Arrr, I smell a bilge rat! That whole affair went down smoother than a tot of rum on a still sea."

Without warning, a tremendous gust of wind surged through the group, nearly knocking them off their feet. In that instant, the handcuffs binding the five outlaws fell away, clattering to the ground. As if by magic, each gang member reached beneath their garments, drawing concealed weapons, their deception so clever that even Millicent had been fooled.

Saoirse, the mastermind behind the ruse, stepped forward, a triumphant grin spreading across her face. Her eyes sparkled with wicked glee. "We knew all along," she declared, savoring the victory. "As if I wrote the whole play myself before you arrived."

13

T he words hung in the air, a challenge and a taunt, as the gang members fanned out around Millicent, Barnaby, and Quark, their weapons trained on them with unwavering precision. The once-captured outlaws now stood tall and defiant, their earlier compliance a masterful act, a deception designed to lull their captors into a false sense of security.

Hope pressed the cold steel of her six-shooter against Calliope's neck, her eyes narrowing as she watched her adversary's every move. Calliope took in a shaky breath, her pulse racing beneath the unforgiving metal. A bead of sweat trickled down her temple, betraying the fear she fought to conceal behind a mask of defiance.

Saoirse, her movements swift and precise, snatched the quill from Calliope's trembling hand. She twirled the elegant green feather between her fingers, a wry smile playing across her lips. "Well, well, well," she drawled with sarcasm. "The mighty Calliope, finally at our mercy. How the worm has turned."

She leaned in close, her breath hot against Calliope's ear. "Now, my dear, what would be your fitting last words? Choose carefully."

Calliope's eyes darted between Saoirse and Hope, her mind racing as she sought a way out of her predicament. The weight of her own mortality pressed down upon her, the realization that her once-unassailable power had been stripped away, leaving her vulnerable and exposed.

In that moment, the true nature of the gang's cunning plan became clear. They had orchestrated every move, every deception, with a skill and precision that rivaled even Calliope's own. And now, with the tables turned and the power in their hands, they stood poised to deliver the final, devastating blow.

The air crackled with tension, the silence broken only by the pounding of hearts and the ragged breaths of those who stood on the brink of destiny. The fate of Calliope, and perhaps the entire Inkwell, hung in the balance, waiting for the next move in this deadly game of wits and wills.

14

Calliope glared at the mob, eyes sharp behind half-moon spectacles that had slid down her nose. She stood resolute, every inch of her daring them to act. "Strike me down, and none of you will ever recover your lost belongings," she declared, her voice steely and calm despite the dozens of furious faces before her. "Killing me leaves no way to get them back."

As Calliope spoke, the gun pointed at her face held everyone's attention. Barnaby inched closer to Millicent, moving with the quiet confidence of a seasoned rogue. Slowly, without drawing notice, his left hand slipped into the right pocket of Millicent's jacket. His fingers brushed the squish of his handkerchief. His right hand reached up to his hat, plucking out his panache. With a practiced flick, he dipped its tip into the ink.

Above the group, a neon green *X* blazed into existence. The light seized their attention like moths to a flame, growing brighter, hotter, until it dripped from the sky like molten rock, forcing the gang back a step.

In the chaos, Millicent seized her chance. As the gang's eyes fixated on the dripping X, she swiftly reached into her bag of tricks, her fingers closing around her notebook and pen. Her adrenaline rushed—this was her moment to turn the tide.

Quark, ever alert, sprang into action. His arms stretched with inhuman speed, seizing Hope's wrists and wrenching the gun away. The weapon clattered to the ground, skittering out of reach.

Saoirse, caught off guard, fumbled with her magical quill, which she'd been nervously twirling. Desperately, she tried to write a counter-spell, her thoughts scattered, her words half-formed. But before she could complete a single sentence, Quark's other hand clamped down on her writing hand, locking it in an unbreakable grip. The quill, her last hope, was rendered useless.

Millicent knew she had only seconds. Her pen flew across the notebook's pages, her mind racing as she scribbled a desperate plan. Words flowed from her, fueled by adrenaline and the grim understanding that everything was on the line.

Responding to her will, the ground beneath Kamen Kazi began to shift and churn. A magical slide, born from Millicent's frantic scribbles, opened like a gaping maw, swallowing the bomber whole. His surprised shout echoed as he vanished into the depths.

But triumph was short-lived. The flashing lights on Kamen Kazi's bombs, still strapped to his body, began to quicken, their rhythm growing more insistent. The earth trembled, and a deafening explosion rocked the world around them. Shockwaves rippled outward, quaking the ground and sending everyone stumbling. Smoke and debris erupted from the hole Millicent had created, raining down in a suffocating cloud that obscured the battlefield.

Millicent's realization struck her like a physical blow, the impact of her actions slamming into her heart with anguish. In that moment, she felt as though she had written Kamen Kazi's obituary, her triumph now irrevocably stained by the life she had taken.

15

Through the choking haze, Grace's voice cut through the chaos. "Stop!"

Millicent felt the cold kiss of a blade against her throat, Grace's knife pressing just beneath her skin. Fear surged through her, heart hammering as she realized how precarious her situation had become.

"We're getting out of here," Grace hissed, her breath hot against Millicent's ear. Her eyes, hard and unyielding, locked on to Quark. "Open a gate."

Quark, with a firm grip on Saoirse's captive hand, wrote a glowing command with the green quill: *A gate opened, allowing those to step through passage to their desired location.* The words pulsed with power, and a shimmering doorway erupted into existence, its edges ablaze with otherworldly light.

As Quark released Saoirse and Hope, Freya seized her chance. She scrambled to her feet and dove through the gate, disappearing into its swirling depths. Grace's grip on the knife was firm, her control absolute as she dragged Millicent toward the portal. Desperation sharpened Millicent's thoughts as she searched for a way to break free.

Barnaby, eyes locked on Millicent's terrified face, inched closer, heart pounding. He knew he had only one shot. With a desperate lunge, he threw himself through the gate, hand outstretched, just as the world dissolved around him.

In the Orange West, Grace and Millicent materialized, still locked in their deadly embrace, with Hope close behind, her eyes darting around the unfamiliar terrain, assessing their new surroundings. Barnaby tumbled through, landing at their feet as the portal vanished behind him.

"Get up," Grace snarled, her voice sharp with impatience.

Barnaby, head spinning from the sudden transition, struggled to his feet. His peg leg wobbled, and he stumbled, fighting for balance. With a grunt, he straightened, eyes darting between Grace and Millicent, mind racing for a way to turn the tables.

As Barnaby steadied himself, he noticed Hope circling around, her expression cold and calculating. She moved to flank Millicent, her hand subtly reaching for the knife Grace had dropped. Hope's movements were careful, precise, like a predator closing in on its prey.

"Put the blade down, missy," Barnaby spoke, his voice a calming contrast to the chaos. "You're not here to hurt anyone. You just want revenge on Calliope, not this."

For a brief moment, Grace hesitated, her grip on the knife loosening. It was all Millicent needed. With a burst of adrenaline, she drove her elbow into Grace's solar plexus, feeling the impact reverberate through her own body.

Grace doubled over with a guttural "Omph," the knife clattering to the ground as she gasped for air.

Behind Barnaby, the air crackled with energy, a blinding

flash of green light illuminating the scene as another gate opened, its edges sizzling with power. Millicent darted to Barnaby's side, eyes wide as Saoirse stepped through, the green quill raised like a weapon. Hope stood on Saoirse's left, her hand gripping the knife's hilt, while Freya flanked her right, their faces etched with rage.

The odds had shifted again, and Millicent quickly calculated their chances.

"Outnumbered," she muttered, glancing at Barnaby. "Ready with that penance?"

Barnaby's lips quirked into a grim smile. "Yar, always at the ready. Give the word."

Saoirse's sneer cut through the tension. "You've stalled us long enough, Millicent," she spat. "Grace, get over here. We're leaving these two to rot."

Grace, still reeling, staggered to her feet, her face twisted with pain and fury. The air grew thick with the promise of violence, and Millicent and Barnaby braced themselves for the fight of their lives.

Millicent's gaze stayed locked on her adversaries, but beneath the surface, her mind raced. Her fingers tightened around the four-color pen, the cool metal a stark contrast to the heat of her skin. She knew she had only moments to act. She began to scribe a message on her forearm, each stroke of the pen seeping into her flesh as if the words themselves were alive. The desert air grew heavy, thick with tension, as the dusty orange sky darkened to a foreboding hue. Adrenaline, hot and fierce, raced through Millicent's chest, the ink swirling on her skin like a living thing, its purpose clear only to her. The power she was invoking was ancient, dangerous—but necessary.

"What is that? What are you writing?" Saoirse demanded, her voice edged with fear. Saoirse's eyes widened in horror as realization struck. "What did you do?" she screamed, her voice piercing the eerie stillness.

Millicent's lips curled into a knowing smile as the monstrous spider obeyed her command, but the triumph was fleeting. She watched in grim silence as the spider descended, its vast shadow swallowing Saoirse whole. The scream that tore from Saoirse's throat was muffled, strangled by the webbing that tightened around her as she thrashed in vain, her movements growing weaker until there was nothing left but silence.

Millicent's pulse pounded, not with the thrill of victory, but with a heavy, sickening dread. The weight of what she had done settled over her like a shroud. She had acted out of necessity, to save herself and Barnaby, but the cost was another life—another death by her hand.

She felt the familiar surge of fear and guilt, the same feelings that had haunted her since the first time she had killed. But this time, it was different. This time, the death felt more deliberate, more inescapable. There was no room for doubt or remorse in the heat of battle, yet as the spider dragged Saoirse away, Millicent couldn't help but feel the cold tendrils of regret winding around her heart.

How much more blood would she spill to survive? The growing tally of lives gnawed at her soul, a burden she wasn't sure she could bear much longer.

16

Freya, paralyzed by terror, found herself surrounded by an army of dolls, their lifeless eyes drilling into her soul. The tiny figures, with their empty, malevolent stares, lifted Freya above their heads, their small hands locking together in an unbreakable grip. They carried her off, vanishing over the dune and stone, to a place where her deepest fears awaited, a place from which she would never return.

Grace, once a formidable foe, now stood naked and vulnerable, panic rising in her eyes as the scene around her shifted. She was back in her elementary school assembly, her younger self on display before a sea of judgmental faces. A monstrous teacher loomed over her, screaming, "Grace Gartner, you have failed at public speaking. Failed, failed, failed!" The words echoed in her mind, each syllable a dagger to her soul. Overwhelmed by shame, Grace fled, disappearing into the abyss of her own self-loathing, lost forever in her humiliation.

Millicent and Barnaby stood frozen, their hearts pounding in the eerie silence. Hope was nowhere to be found, but a small, unassuming box caught their attention. From within, soft cries and whimpers escaped, each one laced with the all-consuming fear of the dark and tight spaces—a terror that was a fate worse than death.

Millicent's breath quickened as she watched in horror, the box enclosing around Hope with terrifying speed. "Wait, wait!" she cried, her voice raw with desperation. She lunged forward, her fists pounding against the unyielding surface, her pleas unanswered. The faster she struck, the quicker the box contracted, its walls closing in with alarming swiftness.

From within, Hope's screams tore through the air, each one more bone-chilling than the last. Millicent's blood ran cold as she imagined the sheer terror Hope must be enduring, trapped in a nightmare turned real. The box continued to shrink, the screams rising to a crescendo of agony until, with a sickening **SMUSH** and **CRUNCH**, they were silenced. The box, now too small to see or touch, popped out of existence, leaving a suffocating silence that settled over the orange landscape like a shroud.

"Millicent. Millicent." Barnaby's voice cut through the haze of horror, pulling her back from the brink.

Millicent blinked, her vision clearing to find herself alone with Barnaby, the vast orange expanse stretching out before them, barren and endless. Barnaby extended his hand, a lifeline in the chaos, and helped her to her feet.

His gaze fell on the smudged ink on her hand, the words barely legible: *Face their worst fears*, a grim reminder of the power they had unleashed and the price they had paid.

"It's over, Millicent. You'll be fine," Barnaby reassured her, his voice steady.

Millicent looked up at him, her eyes wide with a mixture of

relief and disbelief. "Nothing happened to you?" she asked, her voice trembling.

Barnaby's expression softened, a flicker of understanding in his eyes. He knew the toll their actions had taken on Millicent, the weight of the lives they had forever changed pressing down on her soul. But he also knew that in this world, where reality and nightmare intertwined, survival meant confronting the darkest corners of one's mind.

"Nay, lass," he said, his voice steady and sure. "I've faced me fears long ago. Buried them deep where they can't reach me. Alone, alone, all, all alone. Alone on a wide, wide sea."

Millicent nodded, a shaky breath escaping her lips. She knew Barnaby was right, but the knowledge did little to quiet the turmoil in her heart. As they stood together in the unforgiving landscape, she couldn't help but wonder at the cost of their victory.

Their eyes met, a flicker of hope sparking in Millicent's gaze. She raised her pen, the instrument an extension of her will, and with a few deft strokes, she wrote the words that would change their fate: *a door to take them to Quark and Calliope.*

As the ink dried on her skin, Barnaby's face softened, a mischievous glint dancing in his eyes. "Yar, before we set sail," he said, his tone laced with longing, "can I have me jacket back? I've missed her something fierce."

Millicent's smile blossomed, spreading across her face like the first rays of dawn breaking through the darkness. She shrugged off the jacket that had been her constant companion, her shield against the horrors they had faced. With a gentle touch, she handed it back to Barnaby, the fabric still warm from her body.

Barnaby accepted the jacket with reverence, his fingers tracing the familiar material before slipping it over his shoulders. It settled on him like a second skin, a piece of himself that had been missing for far too long.

As if on cue, the green door blazed into existence, accompanied by the rustling of book pages turning. The portal shimmered, beckoning them forward, promising reunion with those they sought.

Millicent and Barnaby stepped through the threshold, the world around them shifting and blurring in a kaleidoscope of colors and sensations. When the world solidified, they found themselves on the green side.

Quark and Calliope stood before them, their faces etched with concern and anticipation. "Are they gone?" Calliope asked, her voice a mix of hope and fear.

Millicent met her gaze, her eyes shining with newfound strength. "Yes," she declared, her words resolute. "They'll never bother you again."

Her words hung in the air, a testament to the battles they had fought—both within and without—to emerge victorious.

17

The terminal burst to life with a blinding flash of green light, illuminating the darkness for a fleeting moment. The celestial spider, unfazed by the sudden intrusion, continued to feast upon its prey, its mandibles working with methodical precision. The air crackled with residual energy, a testament to the power that had just been unleashed.

Millicent, Quark, and Barnaby emerged from the depths of the terminal, their hearts pounding with a mixture of adrenaline and anticipation. They ascended the stairwell, their footsteps echoing in the stillness, each step bringing them closer to the passenger compartment.

As they reached the top, they found themselves standing before a sight that was both comical and perplexing. There, nestled in a comfortable chair, was Orin, lost in the depths of slumber. His chest rose and fell with the gentle rhythm of his breaths, a stark contrast to the chaos that had just unfolded.

Millicent and Barnaby exchanged a glance, a silent question hanging between them. How could Orin remain so blissfully unaware, so utterly untouched by the events that had transpired?

"He is from Vaporshade," Millicent explained.

"That makes sense, a month for every day it be?"

"Twenty-eight days and four hours, but yes."

Orin stirred. His eyes fluttered open, blinking. He stretched, a yawn escaping his lips, and then his gaze fell upon the trio standing before him:

"In slumber's sweet embrace, I find repose,
  A world of dreams, where wonder never ends.
  Through visions bright, my weary mind it mends,
  And in this realm, my spirit brightly glows.
  If only I could sleep forevermore,
  And never wake from this enchanted state.
  But as I rise, a question does await:
  Did I miss aught while lost in dreams' sweet lore?
  While I did slumber, lost in visions deep,
  Did anything transpire, secrets to keep?"

"Yar, the saying be, little Orion, you snooze, you lose." Barnaby laughed, and a chuckle came from Millicent.

"We have acquired a dossier about our destination. It was promised to include details about what the Time Core is and how it works, who made it, and also a chart of the local system. And, of course, we recovered Quark."

Orin looked on with the blankness and urgency of someone half in slumber.

"Quark was taken while you slept, and we had an adventure

to retrieve him." She turned her attention back to Barnaby and Quark. "He will catch up in a few minutes. We should spread this out and start to decipher what we can."

18

In the corner of the lounge, the three laid out the materials on a large mapping table once used by navigators to track the stars. The glossy surface, with grains of wood running in long, beautiful lines, invited study, its sheen perfect for the task. Cozy chairs, soft on the bum and supportive on the back, surrounded the table, encouraging hours of deep focus. The table's height allowed them to lean comfortably as they got lost in their work.

Each of them naturally gravitated toward their strengths: Barnaby Blackwater seized the navigational charts and graphs, Millicent immersed herself in the mechanical and scientific findings, and Quark, with his unparalleled speed, began deciphering languages.

"All aboard!" the conductor's voice echoed through the ship, but the trio barely noticed, absorbed in the dossier's secrets.

When the stairs rolled away and the door slammed shut, Barnaby looked up, suddenly aware of their movement. "Yar, where are we going?"

Millicent, startled by the realization, left the table and headed to the pilot house. She rapped on the door with her knuckles.

"Yes?" The door dropped open, revealing the conductor's head poking down from the hatch.

"Where are you taking us?" she asked.

"Zephyria. We have always been charted to go to Zephyria, just got sidetracked by that magnetic storm."

"That might not be where we need to go any longer."

The conductor frowned slightly but remained polite. "Miss, this Celestial Spider is going to Zephyria. This group of passengers bought tickets for Zephyria. I have been watching your group run around, but we are still scheduled for Zephyria."

"Yes, yes, I understand. Thank you." Millicent returned to the pile of papers and her friends. "Zephyria. We are going to Zephyria."

Barnaby grinned. "Arr, Zephyria—a world where cities drift in the clouds, suspended in a gas sea, and the winds whisper prophecies older than time. Nice."

"But that is still a day away," Millicent noted with a frown. "The good people of Gearturn will be suffering."

"Time waits for no one," Quark said, his processors whirring softly. "I am feeling under the clock, tick-tock, to figure out what these mean."

"Yar, Quark is right. It will give us time to decipher these documents, find where X marks the spot. Transport options galore be on Zephyria; we will chart a new course from there."

Millicent allowed herself a brief smile. "Right. If life insists on giving me lemons, I might as well write a five-step plan on lemonade production—complete with footnotes."

Hours passed as they delved into the dossier, exchanging parchments, questioning one another, and chasing down leads.

At one point, they tried to align documents to reveal a larger pattern, only to realize they were misled by a jam stain from one of their snack breaks.

As the hours ticked by and the documents piled up, a nagging thought began to form in Millicent's mind. She could not shake the feeling that they were on the verge of discovering something crucial. Finally, unable to contain her thoughts any longer, she broke the silence. "I think this means something."

19

Orin, who had been quietly observing from his corner, stirred and joined them at the table, his eyes heavy with sleep but his curiosity piqued. Barnaby and Quark leaned in closer as Millicent read aloud:

"In the shadow of the twin moons' light,
Seek the star with a path most bright.
Underneath the ancient oak,
A secret in the roots will poke.
From the oak, a trail unseen,
Leads to where the crystals gleam.
Align them right, the door will show,
The part of the map you need to know."

Quark tilted his head, his eyes narrowing. "What is it that stands out to you? Like a cuckoo clock at half past two?"

Orin chuckled.

"Something about it," Millicent said, her voice soft, "something old, familiar, that I have heard before but I cannot quite place. This feels different—transcribed by a different hand, maybe? Or a different time."

The others nodded thoughtfully but soon returned to their documents. Millicent, however, could not shake the unease growing inside her. Some riddles were never solved. Generations of the brightest minds had tried and failed. Her grandfather's voice echoed in her mind: *"Sometimes, it is about gathering enough data, disproving everything else until the answer becomes clear."* But what if they did not have enough time?

Barnaby's voice cut through the focused silence, filled with a sudden burst of excitement. "Lady, gentlemen, and assorted robots," he declared, his eyes gleaming, "prepare yourselves for a revelation of cosmic proportions. I have unearthed a clue that even the Supercluster could not keep hidden from my brilliant gaze."

Millicent's head snapped up, her thoughts caught in a sudden rush of anticipation. "What? What is it?" she asked, her focus now entirely on Barnaby.

Barnaby carefully unrolled the map on the table and set brass weights on each corner. Removing the magnifying glass from the table's edge, he said, "X marks the spot, just as I thought." He pointed to a planet called "Soma."

"Soma?" Millicent echoed.

"Soma, god of the moon," Quark explained.

"That be a shining moon, my brassy companion."

"Yes, shining," Quark agreed. "Why, oh why does the time fly, a bird, a kite, or even a balloon?"

Orin, who had been quietly listening, suddenly captured their attention with a voice as steady as the stars themselves: "Trials of the Twin Moons."

"Beneath the vast and starlit sky,
    Where twin moons rise and shadows lie,
    A legend speaks of trials old,
    Of secrets lost and tales untold."

Millicent fell backward in her chair. "Trials of the Twin Moons. Of course." With an innocent scold that was not real, she chided, "Orin, you can no longer sleep; you need to participate and give us all the answers."

"Trails of the Twin Moons?" Barnaby asked. "Never heard of it." He nodded to Orin. "Go on."

"When moons align in perfect grace,
    Their silver light reveals a trace.
    Follow then the brightest star,
    To where the ancient secrets are.
    An oak of ages, strong and wise,
    With roots that reach to hidden ties.
    Beneath its boughs, the earth does hold,
    Crystals clear, with light enfold.
    Dig deep within the sacred ground,
    Where whispers of the past are found.
    Unearth the gems, in patterns bright,
    To guide the way, reveal the light.
    Align the crystals, one by one,
    In the dance of moons and sun.
    A hidden door will then appear,
    The path to secrets far and near.
    Legends tell of those who seek,
    The trials of the moons unique.
    Only those with eyes to see,
    Can find the path, unlock the key.

In the twilight's gentle glow,
The ancient oak and crystals show,
The way to wisdom, hidden far,
Beneath the light of the guiding star."

Millicent's eyes widened as Orin finished. "Something is hidden in the poem," she murmured. "A code, perhaps. A location. It must be a location." Her tone gathered Barnaby, Quark, and Orin closer around the table, the glow of the ship's night mode casting soft light on their faces.

"Stories are alive," Millicent began, her voice carrying the weight of her grandfather's lessons. "They grow, they inspire other stories, they evolve, and they can die. My grandfather used to tell me tales that were more than words—they were living, breathing entities. He taught me about the power of standards and how a single decision can shape history."

She paused, letting her words sink in. "Thousands of years ago, a wise emperor decreed that all wheels would have a standardized width. It was not an easy decision—builders argued and fought, but the emperor's decree prevailed. Trails were carved across his empire, and to this day, that standard width influences the design of all vehicles. The impact one person can have on history is remarkable."

Millicent leaned forward, her eyes glistening with passion. "But what about things even older? Life grows, reproduces, and continues to change even after death. Stories are alive—they can live longer than any single being."

She glanced at Orin, whose recitation had stirred their curiosity. "A legend of forbidden love, a love so powerful that the gods punished it. The earth rumbled, black snow fell, and a mountain turned to fire until the woman was cast into the flames. This story has been retold for generations, warning of volcanic eruptions. It teaches us that mountains are not permanent, that the ground can shake, and ash can fall. It is a tale that has carried vital information through the ages."

Millicent's voice grew stronger, more confident. "The poem Orin recited—'Trials of the Twin Moons'—is not just random words. They are part of a living tradition, carrying crucial information hidden within their verses. A location. Soma. It has two moons. My grandfather recited this poem to me. Barnaby, I suspect tales told over 'galax-seas' may have been shared with you. They tell of trials and riddles, guiding us to the Phantom Spire. These stories, as fantastical as they are, hold truths that have survived the passage of time."

She took a deep breath, feeling the weight of her grandfather's wisdom. "We must honor these stories and let them guide us. In their depths lies the path to our destiny, and perhaps the future of time itself."

Her friends nodded, the significance of the poem settling into their minds.

"Arr, the way I heard tell, there were two parts of the poem to guide you home. You needed both clues to find that treasure. Symbiotic, one might say."

Millicent and Barnaby exchanged a glance, eyebrows raised in silent understanding.

Orin cleared his throat, his voice gentler now, as he began to recite the sister poem: "Challenge of the Celestial Map."

"In ancient lore, a tale is told,
    Of secrets hidden, maps of old.
    In the heart where time stands still,
    A challenge set to test the will.
    Amidst the stars, where clocks confound,
    And errant time does circle round,

Seek the tower, tall and grand,
A beacon in the shifting sand.
When the third chime splits the night,
Follow shadows to the light.
In the chamber, grains cascade,
A puzzle in the dust displayed.
Count the sands in prime's embrace,
A sequence set to find the place.
Numbers pure, in order true,
Reveal the path, a hidden clue.
Silent whispers fill the air,
As grains align with patient care.
Each prime a step towards the core,
Unlocking secrets from of yore.
In the stillness, echoes call,
Through the sands, the answers fall.
A hidden door, a silent shift,
Reveals the map, the ancient gift.
Legends speak of those who tried,
To solve the riddle, far and wide.
Only those with patient hand,
Could decode the shifting sand.
So heed this tale, adventurer bold,
In time's embrace, the truth unfold.
Prime sequences your path shall guide,
To the Spire where secrets bide.
The Celestial Map, in parts arrayed,
By ancient hands, with wisdom laid.
A quest for those who seek the core,
To unlock the mysteries evermore."

Quark's sensors glowed as he processed the poem. "Analyzing... the poem appears to reference the creation of the Time Core by the Chronarchs and the Phantom Spire. The repetition of certain words suggests a pattern."

He projected a series of symbols from the dossier onto the navigation table, arranging them in a grid as a hologram overlaid on Barnaby's map. "These symbols correspond to star formations," Quark said. "Look at this constellation."

Barnaby squinted at the projection, recognizing the shape. "That is the Nebula's Grave," he exclaimed. "An old pirate's tale speaks of a hidden trove of knowledge and artifacts in that nebula."

"Two clues. Two goals. But time is running out." Millicent's face filled with worry. "Gearturn, and the Supercluster, will already be suffering from the effects of time malfunction. It will continue to spread; everything will be lost."

"Best we get some rest before Zephyria." Barnaby smiled. "Big days ahead."

Quark gently lifted Orin. "Well done, Orin," he congratulated. "You have all the answers. Millicent is right, no more sleeping on adventures." He took him to the recliner while Millicent and Barnaby stowed the bounty from Inkwell.

20

Barnaby noticed something was bothering Millicent, the way her brow furrowed as she stared at the documents. "Aye, what has got your gears so wound up?" he asked, his tone light but his eyes full of concern.

Millicent hesitated, her thoughts caught in an infuriating loop of dizzying doubt. She had always been careful, cautious, guarding her thoughts as tightly as she did her words. What if sharing this part of herself changed the way Barnaby saw her? What if, after all this time, her secret still had the power to wound her? She drew a deep breath, feeling the knot in her stomach tighten, but then she noticed Barnaby's gaze. There was no judgment in his eyes, only curiosity mixed with a warmth that made her feel as though, just this once, she could let her guard down.

Millicent sighed, pushing a stray lock of hair behind her ear, buying herself a moment longer. "It is... complicated," she began, her words carefully measured as always.

Barnaby raised an eyebrow, his lips twitching in the beginnings of a smile. "Aye, and the sky is blue. Come now, out with it. We haven't got all day, and I'm not getting any younger."

She hesitated again, this time her eyes meeting his directly. Something in his gaze—a mixture of curiosity and genuine care—made her decision for her. "Very well," she said softly. "But you must understand, I have not confided this in anyone."

Barnaby nodded, settling into a nearby chair and leaning forward. "You have my full attention, Miss Gearwright."

Millicent took a deep breath. "My parents," she began, her voice barely above a whisper, "were not model citizens of Gearturn. They questioned authority, challenged rules they believed to be unjust." Her fingers traced the edge of a document absently as she spoke. "In the end, their defiance cost them dearly. They were sentenced to work deep within Gearturn's core, turning the great cranks that keep our world in motion."

Barnaby's eyes widened in genuine shock. "Blimey," he breathed. "That is a right cruel fate."

Millicent nodded, her eyes distant as if she were reliving the pain of that time. "I was raised by my grandfather. He taught me the importance of rules, of careful consideration before action." A wry smile touched her lips as she glanced back at Barnaby. "It is why I speak as I do, weighing each word, avoiding contractions. A constant reminder to think before I act."

Barnaby leaned back, stroking his chin thoughtfully. "So, you're telling me you've broken more rules than a rogue pirate yet still manage to speak like a royal librarian?" he mused, a hint of mischief in his tone. "But you have broken plenty of rules on this adventure of ours. Your gran would not be very happy with you."

Millicent surprised herself with a small, genuine laugh, a

sound that had been rare in recent days. "No, no, he would not," she admitted, feeling a strange mixture of pride and rebellion. "I suppose I have broken many rules."

When the last words left her lips, Millicent felt a strange lightness, as though a heavy weight had been lifted from her chest. She had not realized how much she had been holding back, how deeply the secrets had rooted themselves in her soul. She exhaled slowly, the tension in her shoulders melting away.

Barnaby leaned forward again, his expression serious yet supportive. "You know, lass, sometimes the rules need breaking. Especially when the fate of the Supercluster is at stake."

Millicent's gaze fell on the documents before them, detailing the Phantom Spires. "I am beginning to understand that," she said softly. "But it is... difficult to unlearn a lifetime of caution."

Barnaby's hand found hers, giving it a gentle, reassuring squeeze. "Aye, but you are doing it. Every day, every choice you make to keep going on this mad quest of ours—that is you breaking free of those chains, bit by bit."

Millicent looked down at their joined hands, feeling a warmth spread through her that she hadn't expected. As Barnaby spoke, she realized something had shifted between them. He was no longer just a fellow traveler. He was someone who had seen her scars and hadn't flinched. For the first time in a long while, she felt truly seen, and it filled her with a quiet sense of peace.

A comfortable silence fell between them, but it wasn't the awkward kind that demanded to be filled. It was the kind that spoke of mutual understanding, of shared burdens lightened just by being acknowledged.

Finally, Millicent spoke again, her voice gentle but resolute. "Thank you, Barnaby. For listening and for understanding."

Barnaby grinned, the familiar twinkle of a stolen star returning to his right eye. "Aye, a friend's worth lies in the sharing tales of mutiny and misadventure."

Millicent chuckled softly, the tension that had gripped her now fully dissipated. As they turned their attention back to the documents, she felt a weight lift from her shoulders. She had shared her secret, and the world hadn't ended. In fact, it felt as though a new door had opened—one that led to a future where rules could be bent if the cause was just.

PART III

RELUCTANT ASTRAL DIVERGENCE

21

The large wheels of the dynamos turned at high speed, holding the sky platform cities in place over Zephyria. The elevation of each was a balance between the pull of the rocky planet's gravity below and the centripetal spin as the planet turned. Gas mined from Zephyria fueled the platforms. Pressurized suits protected the cloud farmers harvesting the rare and invaluable Cumulon Crystals growing in the altostratus. The crystals, imbued with an other-worldly energy, harnessed the essence of the planet's volatile and dynamic skies. These same beautiful skies provided the glow of eternal sunsets between the cumulonimbus clouds, creating continuous flashes of lightning. It was here that the Celestial Spider lowered itself and the travelers to the terminal platform for arrival after delays and deviations.

The hatch opened, revealing a nearly identical yet much larger version of the location they had left on Inkwell and origi-nally departed from on Gearturn. Their spider was one of nine and considerably smaller than the others, all in various stages of preparation for departure to another planet. Finding the exit, they entered a transparent tunnel where new arrivals could stare in awe at the beauty and glow among the clouds of Zephyria on their way to departures and ticketing.

Leading the way, Orin dangled cozily from the arm of Quark, while Millicent slowly stepped forward, her eyes sweeping over the radiant clouds. The beauty of Zephyria was almost overwhelming, a stark contrast to the challenges that lay ahead. For a fleeting moment, she allowed herself to get lost in the shimmering horizon, but the weight of their mission soon tugged her back to reality. There was no time to linger, not when the fate of their journey hung in the balance.

"Yar, the universe, me dears, is a magnificent piece of art. Too bad we can't sell it at auction. Believe me, I've tried."

"There is nothing like this on Gearturn. Spectacular."

The ticketing area, a line of tellers circling the edge of a giant transparent dome, provided unmatched views of the Zephyria sky. Bolts of lightning telegraphed charges between the tall towers of clouds, lighting the dark edges with excitement and framing the peppermint, tangerine, and sherbet skies' gloaming, which brought a gentle, dim light that evoked a sense of calm and melancholy.

BRRING! BRRING! Quark sounded. The continued noise broke the moment. "Time to wake up and focus on the task at hand. Each of you beholders is beautiful."

"Yar, those blasted bells need to snooze."

"Two clues. Two goals," Millicent recalled. "Soma and the Nebula's Grave. We should split up, address them in parallel, not in series."

Orin added:

"Adventures unfold,
Math's prime maze or treasure's trap,

Orin dreams his path."

"Appears clear, solving math or following a treasure map," Millicent said.

"Yar, I'm no good at numbers, yet I am familiar with the lore of the Nebula's Grave. And you be sharp with problem-solving but not a map reader like ol' Barnaby."

"I suppose it might be time to grow outside our areas of expertise. There is no obvious answer here."

"Aye, I will follow the twin moons on Soma while you solve maths in the Nebula's Grave."

Millicent started to look at the transportation boards over the heads of agents, scouring the destinations and times for something close to each destination. Soma had a direct route, but, unsurprisingly, nothing was traveling in the vicinity of the Nebula's Grave.

"Barnaby, I fear we have a larger problem to solve. We are in a major hub for the Celestial Spiders, and nothing travels near the Nebula's Grave."

"Might we charter a line? Lay a fresh trail to follow there?"

"It sounds expensive. It sounds time-consuming. If you were to travel the distance to the Nebula's Grave, how would you proceed?"

"Arr, same as I would to Soma. I'd need to get back to me ship and crew. I've got a skeleton in me closet... his name is Johnny, and he's a terrible conversationalist. With me hands back on the rudder, I can take Johnny anywhere."

"Barnaby, as much as you hate 'the maths,' I believe our best plan would be for me to take the Celestial Spider to Soma, while you regain your ship and crew before sailing on to the Nebula's Grave."

"Yar, you be right. I'll make good with the crew of *The Beck*

& Sail and set sail for the Nebula's Grave. She be on the way and will do her best."

"I have every confidence in you, Barnaby. You have proven to be an equal match to anything we have faced together on our journey."

Barnaby, taking her right hand, gracefully removed his hat with panache, bowed, and kissed the back of her hand. "Me lady be too kind. I am then off to Gablehaven, to find passage to *The Beck & Sail*. And you three set sail for Soma."

Millicent smiled. When they first met, she wasn't sure what to expect from the scoundrel. A pirate who steals time, a man so out of place from the life she knew, had been an excellent partner. He did not run in fear or tremble at terror. Yet, despite his proven bravery, could she truly trust a man so adept at bending the rules to suit his needs? Perhaps it was that same unpredictability that now made her hesitate.

Millicent paused, her thoughts caught in an infuriating loop of dizzying doubt. "Barnaby, how do I know you will—"

Barnaby raised an eyebrow, feigning deep offense. "What? Betray you? Steal the treasure and leave you marooned?" His voice was dramatic, though the smile still crinkled the corners of his eyes.

She smiled despite herself. "Follow through. You are, after all, a pirate with a reputation."

He placed a hand over his heart. "Ah, you wound me, Millicent. But fear not," he said, the glimmer of a stolen star returning to his gaze, "even the devil was once an angel." With that, he let go of her hand, gave a mock bow, and jogged backward to the gate for Gablehaven, never breaking eye contact. "Meet me here when your mission is complete."

22

Millicent opted for a private cabin on this leg of the journey, seeking a sanctuary where her thoughts could roam freely. The cabin fit the three of them comfortably, with Orin's peaceful slumber offering a sense of calm, Quark's silent recharging a reminder of their shared resilience, and the porthole a window into the vastness of time and space that mirrored her own turbulent mind. As she stared out, she felt a mix of awe and insignificance, the weight of their mission pressing on her shoulders.

Something inside Quark clicked, and he said, "Time for you to eat."

"Thank you, Quark," she replied and reached into her shoulder pack to retrieve a small brown paper bag. It was functional and had served its purpose for many years, losing its crinkle and becoming soft and fibrous. Inside, she retrieved three large brown pills. One at a time, she swallowed the dry and nutritious pearls, containing the exact amount of calories needed.

A question gnawed at her: what was the cause of the malfunction that sent them off course? It wasn't just a technical glitch; it felt personal, as if the Supercluster itself was testing her resolve. She retrieved her recovered notebook, its pages filled with ideas and half-formed theories, each one a testament to her relentless pursuit of answers. She flipped past the freshly added pages of green ink, each page a reminder of the successes and missteps on Inkwell, and gave herself one extra blank page. Here, she would confront the unknown once again, her tenacity mingled with a lingering dread her home world faced:

Crystalline Celestial Spider on route from Gearturn:

- Described as a magnetic storm (Conductor)
- Described as a tempest, a giant black beastie, thick and viscous fog, smothering all light and suffocating all sound (Barnaby)
- Came from the port side (Barnaby)
- Series of blows to the ship
- Barnaby had never seen anything like it before

"Quark?"

"Yes?"

"When the spider from Gearturn went off course, did you capture any changes prior to the incident?" She hesitated, the memory of the chaotic moment flashing in her mind. "Barnaby said it came from the port side, and the Conductor called it a magnetic storm."

"A cabin pressure change of two millibars. A strong magnetic field that pulled at my back," Quark began, his factual tone doing little to soothe her growing unease. "For the next three hundred and seventy-two seconds, there was a series of abrupt and irregular movements characterized as rapid and unpredictable variations in the vehicle's altitude, attitude, and speed. The encounter involved different masses moving at varying velocities, causing jarring turbulence, pronounced and uncomfortable shaking, with high, almost severe stresses and erratic motions. It was disorienting and led to unsecured objects becoming airborne within the cabin."

Millicent's knees felt weak and wobbly as she absorbed Quark's report. She could almost feel the ship shuddering again, the terrifying sensation of being tossed around like a leaf in a storm. The memory of Barnaby's frantic attempts to stabilize the ship flooded back, making her grip the edge of her notebook tightly. "Thank you," she said softly, with gratitude. "Thank you for always providing so much detail."

"A pleasure to be of service."

"I am more interested in the magnetic field than your description of the physical effects in the cabin. Can you report on this?"

"One moment, please." He began another hum cycle with vibrations. "22 µT, or 0.22 Gauss at its maximum impact on the vessel."

Millicent's face turned pale. "That is the strength of a planet. How could a storm produce that high of a field?"

"Is that a factual or evaluative question?"

"I suppose I was just asking out loud."

"Yes, a planet, large moon, very, very small pulsar, a tiny-tiny, itsy-bitsy magnetar, or likely a solar wind."

"This must be the answer. A solar wind or storm. That is what the Conductor reported, but it differs from Barnaby's description."

"There are three available options, which make a good deal of sense: Barnaby was mistaken, Barnaby overstated and embellished on the facts, or Barnaby was the source."

"Barnaby the source?" Her immediate reaction was, "No! Why would he put us all at risk?" Millicent trailed off in disbelief. "No." She shook her head. "He was by our side all the way through Inkwell. He saved my life. No." The silence that followed was heavy with doubt, her mind racing through every interaction with Barnaby, searching through her memories for signs she might have missed. Her heart ached at the possibility of betrayal, the trust she had placed in him now feeling fragile and uncertain.

"It was only an option, Millicent. There are two others I suggested that are more likely. Especially considering the magnetic forces. Personally, the option where he exaggerates is highly likely."

"Yes, yes, that must be the one," she agreed fully, with vigor. "Still," she almost whispered, "I suppose it was the one blind spot in my thinking."

"We hardly know him." Quark could read the emotional changes in her expressions. "Maybe we could focus on something productive? Let's wake up Orin and concentrate on the 'Trials of the Twin Moons.' You enjoy riddles and problem-solving."

"I do."

Quark turned his attention to Orin, sensing Millicent's need for a distraction from her spiraling thoughts. Attempting an untried tactic, he soaked a washcloth in warm water, his mechanical movements surprisingly gentle. He placed it on Orin's forehead, hoping the warmth would soothe him. Additionally, he focused his eye lights on Orin's face, gradually raising the intensity to replicate a sunrise. Millicent watched, a small smile started, and she stopped worrying. Despite the chaos and uncertainty, these small moments of care and ingenuity reminded her that they were not alone. They had each other. Perhaps that was enough to face whatever lay ahead.

Orin shook awake, sitting up straight:

"In dream's embrace, Orin crawls,
Desert sun and heated thralls.
Water shimmers, just a tease,
Blistering sands, no reprieve.
Turtle whispers, slow and wise,
'Endure the heat, under harsh skies.'
Orin wakes with newfound might,
From desert's grip, into the night."

"Bad dream?" Quark asked.

Orin nodded intensely.

Millicent hid her smile at what continued to transpire between the two as Orin hardly realized he was being tested. "Orin, Quark and I were hoping to spend time solving the poem you recited from memory, 'Trials of the Twin Moons.'"

Orin's gaze turned to the stars outside the porthole window. On his home planet of Vaporshade, this was only one of the seventy-five essential poems each resident was taught and had to memorize. It didn't even make the top twenty list of importance or popularity. It lacked the elegance and grace of their native language, didn't include the assigned steps and dance like so many others, and there weren't any parts to sing. This landed the "Trials of the Twin Moons" in a group saved for historical listings. As Millicent described, an educational story to pass through the ages. Tricks such as throwing a virgin in a volcano or discovering your mother is your wife kept the attention for retelling.

Orin smiled and said:

"Beneath the guiding star so bright,
  Trials forge the brave in night.
  Only the skilled, steadfast, and true,
  Unveil the ancient secrets' view."

"Quark, what is on the planet of Soma that might cause us a challenge?"

Quark started, with his friendly robot mode fully engaged, "On Soma, the planet of the shining moon, where peace and tranquility are the focus of a lifetime's effort to maturity, one might encounter such delightful creatures as the Vorlag serpentine beasts, which are basically the love child of a slinky and a snake, with all the grace of a toddler on a sugar rush. We might meet 'Bubbles,' the Krakenwurm of the deep, whose primary hobbies include scaring tourists and getting tangled in fishing nets."

He paused, his memory banks starting to hum and his body vibrating, "Oh, and don't forget the Shadow Drake, which is as elusive as a bad dream after a spicy meal. And the Gorgonox, those half-lion, part-snake critters that must have taken their design cues from a particularly confused committee meeting."

"There's the Hellhound of Cerberus," Quark continued, leaning in as if sharing a particularly juicy secret, "found in the underworld, where it lounges around in a dimly lit, perpetually smoky room, probably wondering why it never got invited to the glamorous parts of the universe. And let's not overlook the Dire Griffin, which is part lion, part eagle, and fuming like a fire-breathing dragon with hiccups."

His eye lights flashed. "Then there's the Abyssal Chimera, which is basically a teenager going through changes, with all the existential angst of a goth at a family reunion. The Nightmare Basilisk, which is just a snake with an attitude problem, and the Fenris Wolf, which has a very specific vendetta against tall, pale, blonde people who wear fur and horned helmets."

"And let's not forget the Spectral Wraithbeast," Quark concluded with a flourish, "a ghostly creature that sucks the life out of its prey, not because it enjoys it but because it's bad at making small talk at parties."

A rare, vibrant red blossomed across Millicent's face, from chin to forehead. Half of her wanted to break into uncontrollable laughter, while the rational half forced the question, "We may see any of these on Soma, the peace planet?"

Quark extended his arm and gave her a reassuring pat on the shoulder, his metal fingers surprisingly gentle. "You know," he said, his modulator softening, "I've been processing this whole 'king of the jungle' concept. It occurs to me that lions must have quite the demanding social life, what with all these interspecies relations to maintain." He paused, his optical sensors dimming as if in thought. "Perhaps that's the true meaning behind the phrase 'it's good to be the king.'" Quark's head tilted, a subtle whir accompanying the motion, as if the absurdities of nature were just another fascinating dataset for him to analyze.

"Creatures named in lore,
Myths and dreams, are they but air?
Doubt shadows my thoughts," Orin said.

"All of these creatures are cataloged in Myths and Monsters: The Encyclopedia of Soma History," Quark added with a hint of scholarly pride.

"Maybe I should have been more specific with my question," Millicent said as she smiled. "Where should we start our journey? That may be an easier and more direct question."

"Twin moons align, a silver light,
In night's embrace, your path ignites.

Wait for this glow, so pure, so bright,
It marks the start of your new flight.
Follow then the star that gleams,
It guides you forth, through whispered dreams.
To an ancient oak, strong and grand,
Your journey starts on sacred land."

"Once we arrive, we will need to wait for the light. Maybe it will be obvious on arrival to look for the silver light to start." Millicent sighed. "I wish Barnaby were here. Finding treasure and fighting monsters is in his pirate blood."

23

"Falling is fun. Landing is hard," Gideon Highwire remarked, his azure eyes sparkling with mischief. He leaned casually against the tower's cold stone parapet. The gusting wind teased through his dark, wavy hair, painting him against the backdrop of a tumultuous, coal-black sky. Below, the labyrinthine streets of Gablehaven bustled with life. "Up here, the horizon whispers of what might be, don't you think? It's a steeplejack's privilege to dwell among lofty dreams and face fears that tether others to the ground."

Gablehaven, a planet of towering metropolises with impossibly tall spires and needle-like skyscrapers, had their peaks lost in the clouds. The buildings were a maze of intricate stonework, gargoyles, and vertical gardens. Steeplejacks, the lifeblood of this city, scaled the dizzying heights to maintain the structures, repair, and clean, with a few good men like Gideon Highwire using their unique skills to chase criminals across the skyline.

Barnaby Blackwater, standing firm despite his wooden peg

leg, tapped a rhythmic beat against the ancient stone. He adjusted the jaunty angle of his hat, from which the panache danced in the turbulent air. "True enough, Gideon, true enough. Arr, it be your unique vantage that brings me to your doorstep, you savvy? I be needin' a ship, discreet and swift as the wind, not three leagues from here, to reclaim *The Beck & Sail* and 'er scurvy crew, aye."

Gideon's roguish grin broadened, a glint of adventure lighting up his gaze. "Plenty of nimble cutters and schooners for hire around these parts."

"Aye, but there's a snag," Barnaby said, and his tone grew serious as the wind carried away his lighter mood. "She's trapped in a Lagrange Point."

"The Nexilar Lagrange Point?" Gideon raised an eyebrow, surprise etching his rugged features.

"MindShredders," they said together, a blend of awe and dread harmonizing.

Gideon leaned forward, resting his arms on the parapet, his expression turning steely. "I know them well. Ruthless scavengers, preying on the supply lines to our planet. Our people suffer their greed." He dropped to a murmur, carrying the weight of unspoken stories. "It's time someone grounded their flights of terror. I'm all in."

Barnaby chuckled—a sound both amused and tinged with melancholy. "Arr, ever the dreamer, you be, Gideon, a strange fellow. Playin' the blasted hero for a bunch o' scurvy dogs who'd just as soon see you dancin' with the hempen jig at the gallows, you addled swab."

Gideon turned, his eyes intense and unyielding. "It's not about heroics or folly, Barnaby. It's about seeing injustice and not being able to look away. Why stand idle while there's still good in the world desperate for a champion?"

"It's turned you into a blasted outlaw, it has. You've traded your cozy berth and peace o' mind for a life of constantly watchin' your stern. And for what, you addle-brained swab? What treasure be there in such madness?" Barnaby's expression softened, his previous amusement giving way to reluctant admiration. He clapped Gideon on the shoulder, his own resolve firming. "Mayhap there be method in your madness after all."

Gideon's smile returned, gentle and resolute. "The real treasure isn't gold or glory, Barnaby. It's knowing there's still something out there worth fighting for."

Barnaby sighed, his gaze lifting to scan the horizon—a pirate momentarily lost in the dreamer's vision. "Aye, perhaps you're right. But treasure is awfully good."

"Come, I know just the man to help us."

Gideon met Barnaby at the tower's base, leading him through dark, damp cobblestone streets. They paced the lamplighter until reaching the spaceport's edge, where lodgers and taverns found each other. After checking the Kilt & Sporran, Gritty's Grove Gears, The Loaded Cargo, and Cog & Cravat, Gideon found their man at the Quill & Quaff.

Entering the tavern, their eyes adjusted to the dim light. Behind the bar, xenon lights and mirrors illuminated a selection of mid-shelf intoxicants. The lights spelled out, "Quill & Quaff - The Whole Year Inn." Reading the sign a second time, Barnaby chuckled, turning to his friend. "Aye, crafty they be. 'The Hole You're In.' I'd reckon it be the perfect spot for a man of letters, but I fear the only letters 'ere be I.O.U."

Gideon spotted their quarry and gave a slight nod, making direct eye contact. "Stark," he called over the ambient groans of weary workers. The two men took seats with Stark in the secluded corner.

"Gideon," Stark Maddox said with a nod, his weathered face

a map of hard-earned experience. "Didn't think I'd see you here again." He exuded a mix of toughness and intelligence, not large but undeniably imposing. "I'll buy you a round. After that stunt you pulled on *The Crimson Crown*, a wanted man deserves a last drink."

Gideon's eyes flashed with righteous indignation. "Those jewels belong to the national museum, not those thugs and hooligans. Just because you want something doesn't mean you can take it."

"Three more," Stark said to a passing waitress, then turned his attention to Barnaby. "Who's your friend? Not from around here, I take it."

Barnaby's eyes twinkled with mischief from a stolen star in his right eye. "Barnaby Blackwater, scourge of the seven galax-seas and your guide to all treasures—mostly ill-gotten. At your leisure—or peril, depending on your integrity."

The drinks slammed onto the table, splattering liquid across the sticky surface. "Stark Maddox," he said, extending the name like a verbal handshake. "Drink up, me hearty," he teased, mimicking Barnaby's accent.

Barnaby took a swig and grinned. "They say the best ships are friendships; too bad we're all outlaws here."

"You brought me a funny pirate, Gideon. What's the play?"

Gideon leaned in privately close. "We need someone to take us to The Nexilar Lagrange Point to recover what's left of Barnaby's ship and crew."

"Oh, they're all there, intact as a virgin's virtue," Barnaby said with unwavering confidence.

Stark's eyebrows shot up. "With the Brotherhood of the MindShredders in that region?" At his words, the Quill & Quaff fell dead silent. Stark glanced around the room, every eye fixed on him for uttering the name that struck fear into even the bravest souls. "Get back to your drinking, you bilge rats!"

Conversations slowly resumed, some whispering about the unmentionable, others cursing Maddox under their breath.

"What makes you so sure they're still alive, not salvaged, or worse?" Stark pressed.

Barnaby leaned back, a smug smile playing on his lips. "The ship, the crew, and me leg are all in the safekeeping of an Infinity Fold."

Disbelief etched itself across Stark's face. "No way. No how."

"Oh, it be true as the stars are bright," Barnaby continued, dropping to a conspiratorial whisper. "The Infinity Fold traps objects and souls in a never-ending loop of time, layering moment upon moment in a spiral as endless as the cosmos. To those poor devils caught inside, time appears fragmented; they live through the same two minutes over and over, without the means to mend it from within."

"And what's your plan?" Stark asked, intrigued despite himself. "You can't just pop an Infinity Fold like a bubble. You'll get sucked in with them."

"Aye, that's how I know they're still there, intact and whole. Even the Brotherhood of the MindShredders isn't mad enough to try it. I have the fix, trust me on that. What I need is a way to get there without the Brotherhood knowing, and a Second Skin suit."

Stark took another sip of his icy drink. "Well, that's the trick, isn't it? Getting there unnoticed." He studied Barnaby and Gideon, a slow smile spreading across his face. "But I might just have an idea crazy enough to work."

24

As Millicent and Quark stumbled out of the terminal, with Orin dangling from Quark's hand, their senses were instantly overwhelmed by the vibrant world of Soma. The air, a perfect cocktail of fresh oxygen and intoxicating aromas, caressed their faces. A representative from the Soma Tourist Board draped a floral necklace over Millicent's neck, the blossoms humming with an otherworldly vitality.

Millicent inhaled deeply, her eyes widening. "Did you hear that?" she asked in wonder. "It's like... music floating in the breeze."

Quark cocked his head. "Hear what?"

Before Millicent could elaborate, her necklace—a resplendent golden flower lei—cleared its throat. Or whatever the botanical equivalent of a throat was.

"Ahem. Where would you like to go?" it inquired, its voice smoother than rose petals.

Millicent shrieked, her hands instinctively batting at her chest.

"Ow! Ow! Stop that!" the flower protested, its petals ruffling indignantly. "I'll have you know I'm a delicate bloom, not a punching bag!"

Millicent froze, her hands suspended mid-flail. "You... you can talk?"

"No, I'm practicing my ventriloquism," the flower dead-panned. "Of course I can talk! I'm Ruby, your guide to all things Soma. And you are?"

"M-Millicent," she stammered, still gaping at her animated accessory. Her mind raced, trying to reconcile this new reality with everything she'd experienced so far on their journey.

"Pleasure to meet you, Millicent," Ruby replied, her tone softening. "Now, where shall we go? The Water Slide of One Million Tongues is quite popular. I'm told it's one of the most sensual sensations we offer."

Quark, who had been observing the exchange with silent amusement, finally spoke up. "Actually, we're here for the silver light of the two moons. You know, the 'Trials of the Two Moons' riddle?"

Ruby's petals twitched in what might have been the floral equivalent of a raised eyebrow. "Riddle? I'm afraid I'm not familiar with any lunar riddles. Though I can certainly guide you to the best spot for tonight's Silver Light Spectacle. It's quite the show—imagine a cosmic ballet performed by moon-beams, with occasional guest appearances by shooting stars."

Orin recited the poem "Trials of the Twin Moons" with a dramatic flair that would have made even the most pretentious of space bards cringe.

Ruby listened intently, her golden petals swaying thought-fully. "Well, I'll be pollinated," she mused. "I've never heard of this poem or any of these references. Ancient oak? Sacred lands? Sounds like someone's been reading too many intergalactic fantasy novels. But never mind that—shall we head to the viewing area? I promise it's more comfortable than trying to solve cryptic space poetry."

Millicent nodded, a sheepish smile crossing her face. "Yes, please. And... I'm sorry for the, um, physical misunderstanding earlier."

"Water under the bridge, dear," Ruby chirped. "Or should I say, nectar under the stigma? We're all one here on Soma. Well, except for that one carnivorous shrub who insists he's a lone wolf. But we don't talk about him."

As they set off, Ruby added, "Oh, and another thing. If you think you're going to take me off and go running off on your own, you should know that all the fauna of Soma is sentient. Most of my conversations with the natives are basically, 'Don't eat this one. It'll spoil all our marketing efforts on tourism and blow the budget.'"

The group followed a winding path through lush foothills. As they crested a ridge, a strange, loud noise reached their ears.

"Flock of birds?" Millicent asked, her eyes widening in surprise.

A few more steps revealed an enormous amphitheater built into the natural curve of the hillside.

"That's the Salad Bowl," Ruby explained. "Seats 150,000 at maximum capacity. Must be a slow night; it looks only two-thirds full. On big nights, this place is bursting at the seams."

"Are we going to sit down there?" Millicent asked, marveling at the structure.

"No, no. We're staying up here, honey. You're going to see the show from the best seats, the cheap seats."

They settled into a secluded spot just off the path. As Soma's local star set, painting the sky in hues of red and orange, Millicent felt a mix of anticipation and unease. The hard, dark line where Soma's horizon met the fading glow was punctuated by a single star, flashing emerald green before darkness enveloped them.

Then, as if by magic, the galaxy awakened above—a million pinpricks of light, each a whispered promise of eternal devotion. Millicent was in awe as she noticed the first moon, full and bright, rising on her right. Its twin soon followed on the left, both racing along mirrored paths.

"Watch carefully," Ruby warned as the celestial bodies approached one another.

The curved edges of the moons illuminated against the dark night, slowly inching closer until they finally met from Soma's perspective. A shaft of bright, focused silver light burst into being, cutting straight through the sky to a point not far behind them.

Simultaneously, something inside Millicent's shoulder pack began to hum and buzz. Millicent's hand trembled as she unzipped the side pocket of her pack, retrieving her grandfather's Pocket Orrery. The small brass device pulsed with a strange energy, vibrating against her palm as if alive with urgency. She clicked it open, revealing the Clockwork Constellation with Gearturn at its center. To her shock, the miniature solar system began to glow an ominous red. The planets spun backward, their paths erratic and breaking apart as if the very fabric of time was unraveling before her eyes.

"We've got to move," Millicent called out. "This is what we've been looking for!"

She sprang to her feet, her earlier fatigue forgotten in the rush of discovery. Millicent broke into a sprint, her legs pumping furiously against the uneven ground. The silver shaft of light beckoned her, cutting through the night like a beacon. Breath coming in short bursts, she glanced over her shoulder to check on Quark and shouted, "Ruby, where is that light point-ing?" Each step brought her closer, but the growing distance from her companions heightened her sense of isolation, the world around her narrowing to the urgent path ahead.

"That looks like the Soma Intergalactic Botanical Garden," Ruby replied, her petals trembling.

"Can you lead us there?"

"Hell no!" Ruby protested. "The Botanical Garden holds the harshest and worst criminals in the system. Those plants are killers!"

"Then get us close," Millicent insisted, her pace quickening.

As they approached the garden's edge, Millicent stopped, bent over and gasping for breath. She looked up to see Quark moving at full speed on his extended legs, making huge strides with Orin dangling from his pinched fingertips, bouncing and thrashing like a subatomic particle in the universe's most chaotic mosh pit.

"Had... to find... where it... pointed," Millicent explained between breaths.

Orin, his face red with frustration, burst out:

"In the shadows, anger flares,
   Treated like a toy, who cares?
   Bouncing ball on string and paddle,
   I'm no pawn in endless battle."

"I apologize, Orin," Quark said, gently setting him down. "I was merely trying to keep pace with Millicent."

Millicent's eyes were drawn to the garden's center. "I swear I could see a giant tree in there," she mused. "It must be the 'ancient oak' from the poem."

Quark ratcheted his legs to their maximum extension,

towering over their position. His eye lights illuminated, capturing and analyzing images of the garden's layout. After his scan, he retracted back down.

"The Pocket Orrery's behavior has changed," Millicent observed, holding it open in her palm as it continued to flash and vibrate.

Quark studied it for a moment. "It's a pattern," he declared.

"A pattern?" Millicent asked. "Can you decipher what it means?"

Quark began to match the hum and vibration of the hand piece. "It's your grandfather's code. Gearturn and the Clockwork Constellation are caught in the same time malfunction we experienced earlier. It's worsening, impacting the whole system now." Quark began to hum and vibrate in calculation again. "Hypothesis: your grandfather's Pocket Orrery protected you from the initial malfunction on Gearturn. It created a safe bubble of normal time around the workshop during the initial attack."

"Attack?"

"Yes. This malfunction is by design, not by error."

"If we find this piece of the puzzle here, and Barnaby gets the detailed map to the Time Core in the Phantom Spire, the Pocket Orrery might be able to confirm, or validate, if we are on the right path."

Quark buzzed with analysis. "Yes. I believe the answer is yes. Tick-tock. Tick-tock, we're on the clock."

"Tick-tock?" Feeling the growing importance of their success, Millicent felt the weight of her people's safety. But she was tired. Tired from travel, unable to sleep in transit, and exhausted from the adventures on Inkwell. Her sprint down the hill only added to that fatigue. She was a bit jealous of Orin, who was fast asleep where Quark had laid him down.

"What did you see up there?" she asked Quark.

"The Botanical Garden is surrounded by a labyrinth," he replied. "Hedges, shrubs, and other plants form the walls along the path."

"Yes, that's them!" Ruby cried out. "The group of the worst killers in the system. Please, I beg you, don't go in there!"

"We have to go in," Millicent said firmly. "The fate of Gearturn—maybe the entire Clockwork Constellation, the Supercluster—depends on it."

25

"She's called *The Tern*," Stark explained, patting the sleek, swept wings. "You will not find anything faster in this system. Oh, and she is one hell of a bird—outmaneuvering most pilots in seconds. The good ones who can keep up will find a surprise or two."

"Yar, she's a beauty, I give you that." Barnaby smiled. "But rather small."

"She has to be," Gideon replied. "*The Tern* carries a customized Troxler generator for escapes."

The three climbed aboard and made themselves comfortable. Getting to The Nexilar Lagrange Point was not something they could approach head-on. It involved finding a specific plane of orbit around Gablehaven. This elliptical path would pull them faster on each pass, gaining speed and distance, mimicking debris or a stray satellite on most scopes until they were within range of *The Beck & Sail* at The Nexilar Lagrange Point.

"It will take us a day to reach her, which is long, but we will not be disturbed," Stark assured them during takeoff.

After making the third pass around the planet, Stark put the bird on automatic and swiveled his chair to face the other two.

"What's your plan?" Gideon asked.

"We have a few hours," Stark explained, "and I suggest we spend that time working on our mental strengths."

Barnaby raised an eyebrow. "What do you mean by 'mental strengths'?"

"The Brotherhood of MindShredders recruits people with certain talents and skills. They are not an army of brutes and beasts, as the barmaids might tell you from the horror stories they hear. They are highly skilled mentalists. Most have a large forehead, a globular braincase that gives them an odd appearance, but the bone shields them from external brainwave attacks. From the front, the face is flat with a gracile brow ridge, but from the side, a weak chin and these angular attributes make them appear to have a sloped face—small at the bottom and large at the top, like a triangle. With the proper training and techniques, the Brotherhood of MindShredders uses these brainwaves and the inherent genetic protection in the skull to attack and defend themselves. They force thoughts on their prey, manipulate what they see, think, and feel, making them playthings."

"Ah, so they're mind readers," Barnaby simplified.

"They spread fear, make victims hurt each other or themselves. But with a little work over the next few hours, we can build some walls around your mind that will keep you safe on the first, perhaps the second, attack."

"But eventually?" Gideon asked.

"They will find a way in. They always find a way in. They

find a weakness, a seam, a small hole. I have seen them crack a mind like a nut, forcing the prey to face things, feel things no one ever should. Rumor has it that they know the self-destruct code for every mind and can end their enemy's life in the most horrible ways imaginable." An eerie silence fell over the cabin at Stark's warning. "So, let us try to prevent your brains from becoming fried eggs."

At first, the exercises were silent meditation. The goal was to find calm and peace. In that tranquility, the organization of thoughts proceeded. Placing the most sensitive areas in safer locations of memory, they built up walls and defenses to hold fast. A layer of camouflage to hide these thoughts and memories was added. The trappings of empty, easy concepts that the MindShredders could attack without injury to the prey were set as decoys. Sophisticated exercises caused severe headaches that would torture the attacker. The practice allowed each of the three to know how to activate and deactivate these things in themselves, control them, and limit the long-term harm that might follow.

With the end of each exercise came rest. The mind needed to stay fresh and alert, and there was nothing better for it than rest. Nourishment followed. The number of calories the well-trained mind started to burn through was immense.

Stark, who had been a practitioner of these ways, was powerful, hiding his talents under the appearance of a gruff middle-aged man.

"Aye, I feel smarter," Barnaby replied when Stark asked how he felt.

"Me too," Gideon answered. "I feel I could take on the whole Brotherhood on my own."

"Good, you might still get that chance. So be ready." Stark

returned to the pilot's chair and took over the controls. He activated the only purple switch on the panel, which turned the lights in the cabin plum and gave an odd feeling of increased cabin pressure. Stark had activated the Troxler generator, creating a visual illusion around *The Tern* through a plasma-generated field across the skin of the bird. In this mode, refraction of light waves made *The Tern* appear invisible.

"Yar, there she be!" Barnaby got excited seeing his ship again. In anticipation of the reunion and success, he moved forward in his seat to get a better view. "Looks like not a day's gone by."

A blue glow from the Infinity Fold surrounded her. *The Beck & Sail* was a sleek, menacing vessel built for sailing through the cosmos, complete with a gray metallic hull like a shark's skin, energy sails flying from three long masts, glowing windows, and cannons extending from the front and aft. Once *The Tern's* orbit brought them closer, Barnaby could make out members of the crew cycling through the same two minutes as when he had escaped. Gone were the marauder attack ships of the Brotherhood of MindShredders that had encircled them years ago. Those had given up and left once the Infinity Fold activated.

"Well, I got you here. What now?"

Barnaby moved towards the aft, near the hatch. "Yar, it be time for the Second Skin suit." He placed a snug-fitting white belt around his waist and checked that the power pack read full. The hatch was protected by an airlock, which he would need to pass through to reach the exterior door. "This be where faith takes the helm. Faith in our fancy gadgets, trust in me fellow spacers. Once I'm out in the black void, I gotta get close enough to release the plundered time. It needs to follow me into the blasted Infinity Fold as I tumble to fire up and set things right in the cosmos."

"What happens if you're wrong, or it doesn't follow you?"

Barnaby smiled, the glint of that stolen star in his eye shining brighter than ever. "The same two ticks o' the clock forever with me vessel and me buccaneer crew. Not a shabby way to while away the rest of the cosmic ages." With a press of the button on his belt, a yellow-orange glow covered his body, moving with his step to the airlock.

Pressure from the airlock hissed, giving Stark and Gideon a strange sensation in their ears. That same pressure pushed Barnaby Blackwater out of the hatch, swimming through space to the blue haze bubble circling *The Beck & Sail*. As the ship appeared to grow in size the closer he approached, he caught a flash in his peripheral view. Six Mindshredder ships had entered the system, powering up weapons and coming into range. This moment was familiar to Barnaby, but the way he remembered it, the last time this happened, he was heading away from his ship while it was being fired upon.

There was no way for Barnaby to speed up or slow down; the best he could do was contort his body and, through sheer willpower, alter his course to where on the main deck he was going to land.

Looking over, he could see that the MindShredders were coming for him. None of the six had altered course. He clung to the hope that *The Tern* was still cloaked. He started the mental exercise they had practiced throughout the trip. He cleared his mind, found peace, and began to organize his thoughts. The order of the process: remove the stolen time from his breast pocket, release it, and fall into the ship's bubble. With the MindShredders now on approach, they would find themselves in the same spot as when he escaped. All Barnaby would have done was delay the inevitable by years. Once the Infinity Fold collapsed, the ship and crew were sunk.

A sudden, sharp pressure pressed against the edges of his consciousness—an unmistakable sign that the MindShredders had begun their assault. A flicker of panic brushed the edge of his thoughts, but Barnaby crushed it under the weight of his resolve. "MindShredders be targeting me brain treasure!" he thought, steeling himself as a cold sweat broke out on his brow. His mind quickly shifted into defense mode, but the gnawing fear of what might happen if they broke through lingered, sharpening his focus.

Barnaby visualized the mental walls Stark had taught him to build—strong, impenetrable barriers designed to shield his most vulnerable thoughts. He layered each wall with false memories and decoys, traps set to ensnare any intruder. With each breath, he reinforced the walls, his mind now a fortress ready to repel any attack. "Nothing's gettin' inside," he muttered, steadying himself.

The MindShredders' assault came as a series of subtle taps, probing the edges of his defenses for any weakness. Each was followed by a pause, as if they were evaluating the structure of his mental walls. Then, the pressure increased—sharp and insistent, like a relentless battering ram. They began to cycle through mental "keys," searching for the one that would unlock the treasure hidden within his mind. Barnaby could feel them testing the barriers, applying different pressures, trying to pry open his defenses bit by bit. As the pressure intensified, a wave of dread washed over him as the MindShredders zeroed in on a weakness—a slight crack in his defenses. Was this the end? No, he could not afford to think like that. Gritting his teeth, Barnaby marshaled his last reserves of strength, determined not to let them see his fear. Just as the final lock clicked open, Barnaby triggered the trap he had set. A surge of mental energy burst forth, a controlled explosion of raw force that ripped through the MindShredders' consciousness, vaporizing them before they could react.

"Yar, pretty good trap," Barnaby delighted. As the last of the MindShredders' presence dissipated, Barnaby let out a slow, shaky breath, his body trembling with the aftershocks of the battle. Relief flooded through him, but it was quickly replaced by a sharp, pulsing headache that shot through his temples. Something had shifted in his mind during the battle—a lingering shadow of their presence. The unease grew as he wondered what they had managed to do before being destroyed. His fear gnawed at him, but he forced it down. There was still work to be done, and he could not afford to falter now. "Yar, such freedom in the chaos of free fall," he mused, the words feeling strangely right as he hurtled through space, unmoored in both body and mind.

Floating closer to the bubble's edge, he calculated the speed to the target and prepared to deploy the stolen time. Reaching for his breast pocket to retrieve the stolen goods, Barnaby could see that five of the Brotherhood's ships were still on approach. One in the lead started to drift away from the other vessels as if it were no longer in control.

"Those must have been the scurvy dogs that tried to break in," Barnaby thought.

Removing the stolen time from his pocket, he readied its release. It needed to follow him to the ship. Too much force and it would find its own path. Too little and it might get ahead of him, spoiling the opportunity. As he released the stolen time with the lightest touch, a sudden, forceful assault hit his mind —stronger than before. The distraction caused a misfire, sending Barnaby and the stolen time floating side by side. He hadn't anticipated this. As the stolen time began to unfold like a sail, he realized the situation was spiraling out of control.

Barnaby froze, his body immobilized. The space pirate found himself drifting parallel to the packet of stolen time, speeding toward the ship, while monsters began taking over his mind. The MindShredders had discovered the real treasure.

26

"I should go first," Quark explained. "It's most unlikely anything in the garden will be able to damage me."

"Don't count on that, honey. These are vicious killers. Stepping inside, you'll find venomous thorns and spines," Ruby warned, her tone as sharp as the dangers she described.

"But I'm made of the toughest metals."

"Carnivore killers," Ruby said from around the neck of Millicent. "That'll seduce and trap you to digest."

"I'll refer you to my first point."

"Spores!" Ruby proclaimed. "Toxic spores will fill the air, suffocating you, planting seeds in your lungs."

"I don't have lungs. I don't breathe."

"Explosive seeds." She wiggled a warning. "They'll shoot seeds."

Quark stood, saying nothing in reply, growing bored.

"Grab roots, pitfall traps will snare and snag you, dragging you to your doom," Ruby warned again.

Quark looked Millicent in the eyes. "I'll be fine."

Quark started down the path inside the Intergalactic Botanical Garden, cautious with his steps, and carefully made his way to the center. The map from initial scans guided him through the hedge maze, passing sections both ominous and menacing. Vines recoiled as Quark approached. Something unseen slithered in the underbrush. Whispers and rustling of branches sounded just out of reach. Something loomed and watched Quark. All this would drive humans mad with fear.

Illuminated by the light of the full moons, in the center of it all, stood a tree that looked withered, ancient, bearing the face of a witness to a millennium if not two.

"Hoo," an owl called from its lowest branch. "Its bark is worse than its bite."

Coos of laughter rattled the branches and brush all around Quark.

The clicking of a beak from another branch started. "Caw, best you leaf it alone."

Additional coos of laughter filled the center from all around him.

From the first branch, Quark heard, "We're going swimming tonight, look at those trunks."

An eruption of laughter filled the surrounding forest.

"Excuse me?" Quark said politely. "Excuse me." The laughter faded.

"Hoo?"

"You."

Quark watched as two owls landed in sight on a nearby tree. One was large, with feathered pointed horns on his head and a foul expression. Next to it was a small gray-feathered friend, eyes black and lifeless like a doll, face white and heart-shaped.

"My name is Quark. I am seeking the ancient oak tree. Is this it?"

"This oak's been through more seasons than you've had system reboots, and it's still more reliable than your faulty programming!" the horned owl squawked.

An eruption of laughter and shaking encircled Quark.

"Why? Why would you say something so mean and targeted?" Quark asked.

The barn owl replied, "Hey, Quark, I've seen toasters with better personality than you! At least they know how to get things hot—unlike your cold, lifeless circuits."

"Oh great, the Tin Man's less charismatic cousin. Tell me, Quark, did you leave your heart in the same place you left your common sense?"

Quark wasn't sure what to make of all the laughter and pointed comments. So, politely, he said, "Greetings, fellow sentient beings."

The two joined the chorus of laughter surrounding him.

"Listen here, you feathered fossil." Quark turned up the volume to overcome the cackles. "While you're busy hooting insults from your tree, I'm calculating solutions to save the very timeline you're perched in."

"Congratulations, Quark! You've single-handedly lowered the bar for artificial intelligence. Even a magic 8 ball gives more insightful responses than you."

Quark started to retrace his steps through the maze. Following the shortest route, there were no encounters from the deadly garden Ruby, the Soma guide, had warned about. Just pointed jabs.

Millicent waited by the entrance while Orin slept. "It's scary," Quark told Millicent and Ruby. "But the worst thing in that garden is two cantankerous wise guys with a bad sense of humor. I've found the oak."

"Grab Orin, let's get on with this."

"Just leave me here." Ruby tugged at Millicent's neck. "I'll be fine, find my own way back."

Millicent ignored the struggle and moved forward with Orin, Quark, and Ruby. The path twisted like a serpent through the undergrowth, each turn revealing more of the garden's secrets. The stones beneath her feet were uneven and treacherous, shifting slightly with her weight as if they were resisting her passage. The air was thick with the scent of damp earth and decaying foliage, a faint rustling echoing from somewhere deep within the maze—as though the garden whispered ancient secrets to itself. Millicent felt the prick of cold air against her neck, as though the shadows themselves were drawing closer with every step. She drew in a sharp breath—not from fear, but from the eerie feeling that the garden was a living entity, observing her every move. The subtle rustle of leaves sounded almost like whispers, and a brush against her leg from a creeping vine made her instinctively recoil, her mind calculating the odds of danger.

At the center of the garden, where the light of twin moons still created a spotlight, Quark said, "This is Millicent. We're here to solve the 'Trial of the Twin Moons.'" Quark jostled his arm a bit to wake Orin. "I said, to solve the 'Trial of the Twin Moons.'"

Orin heard his cue and started to recite the poem.

Before ending the second verse, the horned owl hooted, "'Trials of the Twin Moons'? More like 'Trials of the Audience's Patience'! How about a verse on making a quick exit?"

The owls' audience shimmered and shook with laughter and delight at the expense of the poet.

"'Twin Moons,' eh?" the barn owl hooted. "Is that what you call those two brain cells bouncing around in that empty head of yours?"

"See? See? Monsters!" Ruby tugged at Millicent's neck. "Ruthless killers! Cut you to the quick!"

Millicent, ever logical, said, "Ruby, they are bad jokes. Words from birds. Shake it off. Toughen up."

"Hey, folks, watch out! Red's got a wrench and she's not afraid to use it... probably 'cause it's the only way she can get a date!"

"What?" Millicent said in great surprise. "I can get a date if I want. I just have little time to—"

"I've seen less grease on a potato chip than on your face, kiddo. Ever heard of soap, or is that too 'girly' for ya?"

The owls fed off the laughter and the insults, silencing the four visitors.

"Look at you, all covered in grease and grime. You know, most girls your age are discovering makeup, not motor oil!"

The laughter rose to a crescendo all around the four. Like the back of a wave, the laughter's roar fell, allowing Millicent the opportunity to reply, "Wow, for a birdbrain, you sure know a lot of words! Did you swallow a thesaurus, or is that just yesterday's worm talking?" A crash from the new wave of laughter came down from the forest, this time landing on the owls.

"You know, they say owls are wise," Millicent continued, "but I'm starting to think that is just a myth. Keep hooting, Grandpa —the closest you could ever get to making music!"

Guffaws and cackles of nature's audience mixed with gasps for air and cracks of timber swaying. An acorn dropped from above, landing right in front of Millicent. She looked up to see that it wasn't just the birds and woodland creatures in the audience; the oak she had been seeking was the biggest fan.

She spoke louder for all to hear, "I might challenge you to a battle of wits but see you came unarmed. How about we call it a day before you hurt yourself thinking up another zinger?"

Acorns began to rain down in a deluge from the oak trembling in laughter. A roar of belly laughs, chirps, and squeaks in the woods echoed up the hillside and back as the owls spun their heads, looking around and bobbing at the insults. With no comeback, no follow-up, and having lost the audience, both owls took flight.

Quark looked to Millicent and asked, "Now what?"

She shrugged. "Not sure I trust Ruby's definition of scary places. So, Ruby, where to now?"

Before anyone could answer, the ground started to shake. All around them, the tremor rattled cobblestones, leaves fell, and acorns danced on the ground in rhythm. At the base of the mighty ancient oak, a hole began to open. Roots began to separate, the bark split and cracked, as a cavern opened at the base of the trunk.

"I guess we go in there," Millicent said, stepping forward.

The soil hardened as she moved forward, creating a descending path. With each step lower into the ground, darkness encroached, where the light of the twin moons could no longer follow.

tark and Gideon stood transfixed at the viewport, watching their pirate companion shoot across the void. Barnaby's form, illuminated by the eerie glow of his Second Skin suit, grew smaller against the backdrop of stars and the looming *Beck & Sail*.

A clangor of alarms shattered the tense silence. The control panel erupted in flashing lights and urgent beeps.

"What's happening?" Gideon shouted over the noise.

Stark's fingers danced across the console, his face bathed in the glow of warning indicators. "Trouble," he growled. "Big trouble. MindShredders just dropped into the system. Six heavy ships. They must have been monitoring us."

"What's on Barnaby's ship that they want so desperately?" Gideon mused aloud.

Stark's eyes narrowed as he studied the tactical display. "I don't know, but they're on an intercept course with Barnaby. And they're moving fast."

"They're after him?" Gideon's eyebrows shot up in surprise. "I guess we know your cloak works."

"Exactly," Stark replied, his tone grim. "We're invisible, but he's exposed out there."

Gideon's jaw clenched. "There has to be something we can do to help."

Stark hesitated for a moment, then nodded decisively. He rose from the pilot's seat and strode purposefully to the center of the cabin. There, set into the floor, was a circular pad ringed with soft lights.

Stark lowered himself onto the pad, crossing his legs in a meditative pose. "Whatever happens, don't break my concentration."

From a nearby compartment, he retrieved a wired headset. With practiced ease, Stark settled the device over his temples, adjusting it until it sat just so.

The moment Stark's eyelids shut, the atmosphere in the cabin changed. The air grew heavy, charged with an unseen energy that made the hairs on Gideon's arms stand on end. He watched in awe as Stark's breathing slowed, becoming deep and rhythmic.

Through his psychic senses, Stark's consciousness expanded beyond the confines of *The Tern*. The ship's hull became as insubstantial as gossamer, allowing his awareness to stretch out into the star-studded expanse. He saw Barnaby, a tiny figure hurtling through the void, his trajectory locked on to the shimmering bubble of the Infinity Fold surrounding *The Beck & Sail*.

But he wasn't alone.

The Mindshredder ships loomed in Stark's mental landscape like predatory beasts, their hulls bristling with weapons.

From the lead vessel, tendrils of psychic energy lashed out, probing and grasping at Barnaby's mind.

Stark watched, impressed, as Barnaby's constructed mental defenses flared to life. A dazzling blossom of protective energy erupted from the pirate's consciousness, scattering the first wave of MindShredder attacks like leaves in a full-force gale.

"Impressive work for a first try," Stark thought, allowing himself a small smile.

But the victory was short-lived. The lead MindShredder ship, its crew vaporized by the backlash of Barnaby's defense, drifted lifelessly. The others, learning from their fallen comrades, adopted a new strategy.

The second ship surged forward, its crew projecting a battering ram of pure thought. They slammed into Barnaby's mind with reckless abandon, heedless of the danger.

In that moment of impact, Stark's awareness zeroed in on something clutched in Barnaby's grasp. It pulsed with an other-worldly radiance—vibrant, electric, and unmistakably power-ful. As Stark's consciousness drew closer, his amazement grew.

"By the stars," he breathed, scarcely believing what he was seeing. "Time itself. Barnaby wasn't speaking in riddles—he's literally carrying stolen time."

The paradoxical substance began to unfurl, freed from whatever containment had held it in check. In the vacuum of space, unbound by conventional physics, it expanded at an alarming rate.

Stark's attention snapped back to Barnaby. The pirate floated motionless, paralyzed by the MindShredders' assault. The stolen time, now a billowing sheet of temporal energy, amplified to envelop everything in its path—including *The Beck & Sail*.

With a Herculean effort of will, Stark extended his psychic

grasp. He seized hold of the escaping time, its otherworldly texture slippery and resistant in his mental grip. Gritting his teeth against the strain, he began to pull it back, guiding it towards its intended destination.

The MindShredders, sensing the shift in the cosmic balance, recoiled. Their psychic tendrils withdrew from Barnaby's mind as they realized the true nature of what they faced. The attackers fled back to their ships.

"There's depth to you beyond what meets the eye, Barnaby Blackwater," Stark thought with both admiration and concern.

The effort was monumental. Sweat beaded on Stark's physical brow as he poured every ounce of his considerable mental strength into controlling the stolen time. It bucked and writhed in his grasp, slipping at the edges as his power began to wane.

With one final push, Stark guided Barnaby and his impossible cargo into the shimmering expanse of the Infinity Fold, just as he had planned. As the pirate's form merged with the scintillating energy field of the Infinity Fold, the glow of the Second Skin suit switched off, and stolen time wrapped around the blurred barrier. Inside *The Tern*, Stark allowed his consciousness to snap back to his body.

28

Quark's eye lights flickered to life, cutting through the oppressive darkness. The cavern walls writhed with subterranean life, glistening roots dripping with moisture. A rich mix of fresh soil and damp decay filled their senses, reminding Millicent of the world above—a world that now felt impossibly far away.

She shivered. "I wish Barnaby was here with his sharpened cutlass," she whispered, barely audible over the distant drip of water. "He would know how to make light of these situations."

A glint caught her eye—something bright and wonderful reflecting in Quark's illumination. She almost missed it, hidden as it was beneath layers of grime. As they approached, Millicent's pulse raced. A crystal pendant dangled from its chain, snagged on a gnarled root.

With trembling fingers, she reached out and grasped the pendant. As she brushed away the muck, intricate details emerged, forming a perfect triangle on its face. The crystal hummed with an unnatural energy, feeling unbreakable and ancient in her palm.

"I think this is what we came for," Millicent breathed with a mix of relief and trepidation. She turned towards the entrance, eager to leave the suffocating darkness behind. But fate had other plans. The roots around them began to shift, the soil softening underfoot. To her horror, Millicent watched as their exit slowly, inexorably, closed. "No!" she cried, lunging forward, but it was too late. The way back was sealed.

Orin's lyrical tone cut through the despair:

"In dark caves where shadows creep,
    Danger lurks in caverns deep.
    Twisting paths and turns unknown,
    Fearful whispers, chills to bone.
    Creepy crawlies slither near,
    Every sound ignites our fear.
    Yet through the gloom, we press on tight,
    Facing dread with heart and might."

Millicent squared her shoulders. "Fine, we keep going," she said, overriding her fear.

They pressed on, deeper into the stygian blackness. Even Quark's formidable illumination struggled to penetrate more than a few feet ahead. The smooth crystal turned in Millicent's hand as her fingertips traced its surface, an anxious habit. Her instincts screamed that there was more to this pendant than met the eye.

"Quark," she asked, "can you still see the path?"

"Affirmative, but—" Quark's response cut off abruptly. "Stop. The path ends. A pit begins."

Millicent gasped as Quark increased his power output, his

frame humming with the strain. The extra light revealed the razor's edge where solid ground gave way to a yawning chasm.

She stepped back slowly. "Orin," Millicent began, her mind racing, "let's review. We found the spot where the twin moons rise, traced the silver light, followed the bright light, got the oak of ages, and now we have this crystal. What's next in the prophecy?"

Orin's voice filled the cavern once again:

> "Dig deep within the sacred ground,
>> Where whispers of the past are found.
>> Unearth the gems, in patterns bright,
>> To guide the way, reveal the light.
>> Align the crystals, one by one,
>> In the dance of moons and sun.
>> A hidden door will then appear,
>> The path to secrets far and near.
>> Legends tell of those who seek,
>> The trials of the moons unique.
>> Only those with eyes to see,
>> Can find the path, unlock the key.
>> In the twilight's gentle glow,
>> The ancient oak and crystals show,
>> The way to wisdom, hidden far,
>> Beneath the light of the guiding star."

A wave of dread washed over Millicent. "Crystals? Plural? How many? Two? A mine?" Frustration was evident in every line of her body. "We should have taken the other trial. Let Barnaby chase this down."

"Millicent," Orin said, gentle but firm, "you've led us through,

With strength and heart so pure and true.
You've brought us far on this long quest,
With every step, you've done your best.
We're so close, just another stride,
Your courage, Millicent, our guide.
Don't give up, we're almost there,
With you, we conquer every snare."

She felt a lump form in her throat, touched by Orin's unwavering faith. "Thank you, my friend. You're right, of course." Millicent took a deep breath, steeling herself. "Now, where could the other crystals be?"

Quark's ocular sensors swiveled, scanning their surroundings. "Logic suggests we may have missed them in our haste. Perhaps they lie behind us?"

Millicent nodded, a grim smile playing on her lips. "I hope you're right, Quark. Because the alternative..." She peered into the bottomless pit before them, its depths promising only darkness and danger.

29

"Ready the cannons," Barnaby barked. "Mister O'Malley, steady our course." Barnaby turned to the aft. "Mister Wren, we need full power. Kick whoever you must to make us move." The excitement and scurry on the deck were intense. Each man focused on the task at hand, saving the ship from the attack and preparing for return fire.

"Cannons at the ready, Cap'n!" Mister Marlowe called from below.

Barnaby Blackwater looked over the targeting scope Mister Rook manned, seeing the sweep showing ten blips on the screen. "Which one is the command ship, Mister Rook?" He pointed to the flicker just behind the lead.

"Aye, that's the one, Rook. Send coordinates to Marlowe and set all cannons to fire at maximum effect," Barnaby growled out the command.

He reached for his cutlass and pointed to the target. "Show no mercy, give no quarter, you scurvy dogs!"

Looking up, the blue dome that shrouded them started to flicker. There was something about this moment that was highly reminiscent. A strong sense of déjà vu overwhelmed his senses. For the first time, Barnaby Blackwater, scourge of the seven galax-seas, doubted himself. An urge to run away and flee the fight overtook him. He wanted to know where the dinghy was to escape. It wasn't fear. Barnaby wasn't scared. He just had the sense to run. If he didn't, all would be lost.

Before Barnaby could delay the order, all cannons fired at the attacking ships from the marauders. As the powerful blasts left the barrels, the concussion echoed. A bright blue wall pulsed in front of them, sending all the shots back to the ships. The impacts tore the hulls to shreds. Each of the three masts crumpled like twisted straw. Barnaby watched as the horror and gore of his loyal men melted and broke from the fire sweeping across the decks.

"Infinity Fold," Barnaby remembered. He had kept one in his pocket for just such an occasion when there was no way to win, all hope was lost, and the only glimmer of a chance was to try again in some future he could improve. Barnaby's right hand dug deep into his jacket pocket and removed the glowing blue cube. At the same time, Barnaby was sprinting to the aft, where the dinghy was secured and ready. Each step felt like it was landing on a plank in motion. The ship melted under his feet, and his footing required speed. Jumping for the craft, he grabbed the release mechanism. Looking back to where he had just been, Barnaby threw the blue cube at the ship and grabbed the edge of the dinghy as it launched.

The blue cube exploded. Its shaft shot power up into a mushroom and turned into a full ball of energy surrounding the mighty war vessel. As it closed, Barnaby clung to the dinghy by his pinky. The bubble wrapped around his leg, severing it completely from the rest of his body.

There was a brilliant flash of light. The actions started over.

"Ready the cannons," Barnaby barked. "Mister O'Malley, steady our course." Barnaby turned to the aft. "Mister Wren, we need full power. Kick whoever you must to make us move."

30

BUZZ
BUZZ
BUZZ

It was unavoidable. The vibrations from her pack were growing stronger.

"Hold up, Quark, I need light over here."

The brassy robot turned, bringing light to Millicent as she dug into her shoulder pack. It was the Pocket Orrery again. In the clamshell seam, around the unopened clasp, lights from inside were dancing and flashing. Removing it from her pocket to hold out, it leapt from her hand and landed in the muck and soil. A pulse of energy radiated from it in waves like a droplet hitting the water's surface. On its own, the clasp came undone, and a powerful beam of light shot out, filling the cavern. Above the internal etched face of her grandfather, a hologram appeared, growing into a life-sized version of him.

Millicent was in awe of the moment. "It can do that?" She

was so happy to see him again that tears started to form. "Grandpa?" she gasped. "I've missed you so much. You wouldn't believe what's happened in the year since you've gone. I've got so much to say."

The beam from the Pocket Orrery flickered in an inverted triangular shape, making it evident that it wasn't sentient but a recording. Thaddius Gearwright III cleared his throat from a little over a year ago, in the safety of the workshop on Gearturn, and said, "Millicent, I love you. You are the most important thing to me in the universe, which is why I am leaving you this digital chronicle... there is still hope, a chance to redeem myself. A chance to save the Supercluster."

"What?" Millicent asked. "He knew a year ago? Quark, were you aware of this?"

"News to me."

"As a young man," the recording continued, with a note of rushed desperation in his voice, "I worked under the instruction of Doctor Julius Kilmoore. You know him from the photo in the workshop. He was a scientist on Gearturn who showed great promise. I learned about time from him—its nature, its balance, and fantastical theories. It was beyond just gears and springs. He discovered that there was a balance in the Supercluster. The Time Core created time, but Gearturn controlled and regulated it. Without Gearturn, time would bounce, skip, and jump, creating confusion and chaos. When he discovered this and took the information to the Clockmaster, he became a laughingstock. He was ridiculed. The good people of Gearturn told him that time was invented by the ancients; there was nothing left to discover. But his experiments, ones that I witnessed and took part in, proved them wrong."

"By the cogs of the Clocktower! What happened?" Quark blurted.

"Doctor Kilmoore was able to send himself back in time, forward in time, and to any location he wanted. But with each trip, he returned less the man I knew and increasingly obsessed with the Time Core itself. He came back changed, hating the control and order that Gearturn brought to the Supercluster. He craved chaos and disorder, breaking controls, destroying what had been built through the eons. Each return transformed him further. Fixated on destruction, he became a monster, consumed by his insatiable desire. When I realized what he was doing—seeking out the Time Core to destroy Gearturn—I burned his lab to the ground, preventing him from ever returning.

"If you are seeing this digital chronicle, I have failed," he said.

"Failed?" Millicent was confused. Her grandfather had never failed, never done wrong. He was a good man.

"You must continue this effort without me. Recently, I have been tracking changes in the Time Core. Changes that may impact Gearturn. Changes that only Kilmoore could achieve. I don't know how," he said in frustration. "He has found the Time Core, hidden in the Phantom Spire. This digital chronicle was made to activate in close proximity to the Temporal Locket. Look for a pendant; you will think it is a crystal, but it's not alone, not a single crystal. You will need to make a triangle, a tetrahedron." The image changed from her grandfather to the schematics of a crystal pyramid, with the initial pendant at the base and the others attached to it. The image floated above them, rotating slowly to show the form from all sides clearly. "If you are seeing this digital chronicle, you are near the crystal shards, and you will need to assemble them into one piece. This design is how I believe it should look. From here, you will need to find the Time Core hidden in the Phantom Spire. These digital chronicles have been pre-recorded and will activate when you are near the places and items you need. But these are my best guesses. I hope that this information can help you right your grandfather's wrongs. I let Kilmoore go too far and escape instead of stopping him." Her grandfather turned in the recording to a sound at the door of his workshop. It was Millicent.

"That was recorded the day before he... I remember that day."

The recording of Millicent asked what her grandfather was doing before he deactivated the device. Then the recording started over again: "Millicent, I love you. You are the most important thing to me in the universe..."

Millicent stepped forward, snapping the Pocket Orrery closed once more. The cavern was plunged into darkness. Looking across the wall, near where the initial crystal had hung, she noticed four spots, deeper in the soil, glowing softly. As she brought the Pocket Orrery closer, the crystals grew brighter.

"Quark, put down Orin and help me with these."

"You're lazy, you shed too much, and are a burden on Millicent," Quark said to Orin.

"Quark, set down Orin and help me," she repeated with exasperation.

31

"Ready the cannons," Barnaby barked. "Mister O'Malley, steady our course." Barnaby turned to the aft. "Mister Wren, we need full power. Kick whoever you need to make us move." Barnaby felt the heat of the flash sending him back. The coldness from a powerful vacuum sapped the heat of the moment. The attack ships were now distant MindShredders in formation. Barnaby blinked from the position of his backside planted on the deck. The groans and moans of the men's awakening senses were a dull chorus in the background.

Barnaby got to his feet. He was whole. A young man again. He could remember it all: falling in space, the attack on his mind, and why he was here.

"Millicent," was the first word he spoke, with the spell now broken. "How long have I been here?"

Barnaby helped the men to their feet, starting with, "Mister Rook, check the scope. Who's out there?" Moving forward, he ordered, "Mister Marlow, ready the guns." Speaking into the communicator, he continued, "Mister Wren, full power, get those engines ready."

He looked over the deck to see that his men looked the same as the day he left, although they were bewildered by the moment. They were alive, the ship in nearly perfect condition, and they had a future to fulfill.

"Engines at the ready, sir."

"Cannons ready, sir."

"Five, no, make that four ships in range."

"Yar, choose your target, Mister Rook, and let loose," Barnaby instructed.

"Calloway," he called.

"Aye," came the reply from behind.

"I need you on the lookout. Right over here." Barnaby pointed to empty space. "Let me know when you see—"

From the empty point in space where Mister Calloway was being instructed, a wave of energy blasted as a bird-shaped ship came into focus.

"Hold that order." He turned to Marlow. "Fire at the enemy ships."

The Beck & Sail shuddered with the mighty blow. The bolts fired from the cannons glowed against the backdrop of space on their trajectory. They honed in on the same targets as the mysterious energy wave and struck true.

The Tern made its agile adjustments, gliding close and softly landing on *The Beck & Sail's* top deck. As they exited from the door, Barnaby greeted the men, "Gideon, Stark, so good of you to join us. How long did you have to wait?"

"Only a moment or two," Stark explained. "I saw you deploy the time sail—time chute? Whatever it was you stole. I was able to hold it for a moment while you landed."

"I'm deeply indebted to you, my friends. You've saved me,

you saved the crew, and my ship. I may never be able to repay you for this deed." Barnaby was gracious and humble.

"There are still many fights ahead of us, Barnaby. I hope you join our cause on your next trip to Gablehaven. There is much justice to dispense." Gideon shook his hand. "Are you taller?"

"Less need to lean."

"Good to see you, old friend." He smiled and returned to *The Tern*.

"Thank you, Stark Maddox. Yours is not a name I'll soon forget."

"What you've learned in this short time is impressive. Stay practiced. I see a great deal of potential in you." Stark nodded and returned to his captain's chair. *The Tern* lifted off to return to its home world to right wrongs and deliver justice to save the good people of Gablehaven.

"Mister Rook," Barnaby called.

"Aye."

"Set course for the Nebula's Grave."

"Sir?"

"We've got treasure to find. Mister Wren, we're in for rough waters. Ready the ship. Mister O'Malley, when you're ready."

32

"I don't know how it's supposed to fit," Millicent said, frustration evident in her tone. Butterflies fluttered in her stomach. "We've been sitting on the ground for hours trying to piece it together. Quark, can you scan it again? Maybe you missed something."

Quark began to hum and vibrate, his eye lights cycling through a spectrum of colors as he examined the pieces. "Your grandfather's estimates must have been pure conjecture. I don't think he knew what the crystals would look like." Then he added, "I noticed you've been using contractions since your grandfather's appearance."

"Just tired. Rattled. I lack focus and control." She sighed.

"It's not breaking the rules. You're allowed to use them."

"Yes, I know. But the control it takes not to use them, the required thought before speaking, means that I avoid superciliousness. There is less damage to others' feelings."

"I suppose."

"But?"

"But, you also lose authenticity. Things don't just fly out of your mouth, or brain."

"Are you implying I am not fun?"

Quark started to buzz and hum, turning his attention back to the crystals.

"Oh, I see." It was one more thing on the pile. Her confidence was in free fall—learning her grandfather, a man she idolized, was not who she thought he was, being trapped underground by a sentient oak, and being unable to complete this ancient relic mystery. "Ruby."

"Yeah?"

"I think I might be allergic to you." She started to itch.

"Wouldn't be the first."

Millicent wanted to cry, just let it all out, break down, and sob. But she didn't. She remained somewhat composed, closed her eyes, and took a deep breath.

Opening her eyes, she screamed and shook her fists above. "Oak tree! Let us out!"

The soil began to move, the ground trembled, and the ramp where they had entered reappeared.

Quickly, Millicent picked up the crystals and got to her feet. "Grab Orin, let's go. Quick."

Quark scooped up Orin, and the four of them hurried up the ramp and out to the cobbled path again.

"Well, well, well! Look what the cat dragged in—or should I say, what the cave spat out! Here comes Millicent, looking like she just lost a wrestling match with a mud monster!" The familiar caw came from above. It was the owls.

"Hey, Red, did you mistake that cave for a beauty salon? Because that mud mask is doing wonders for your complexion —it's the first time you've looked better!"

"Well, well, the gang's all here! Quark, Orin, Ruby, and what appears to be a sentient mud puddle—oh wait, that's just Millicent!"

"Shut up!" she commanded. "Shut up, shut up! I am in no mood."

"Hoo-hoo, sorry, Red. Just trying to lighten the moment."

Millicent looked down at herself. Angry and frustrated, she refused to break down in front of these birdbrains. Then, she noticed the crystals. They looked different under the twin moons.

"How long were we in there?" she asked everyone.

"Half an hour." Quark reported.

"Thirty minutes? It felt far longer. Hours without end." She looked up. "How long will the moons stay out like this?"

Ruby said, "Another few minutes, maybe. They come out like this every night."

"I'm not sticking around another night here." Millicent rubbed the grime from the crystals that had built up from the muddy slog out of the cavern. Markings that were previously invisible inside the crystals were now clear under the moon-light. "Quark, see the lines. They look built inside the crystals."

The pendant crystal was the base, and each of the other four crystals locked together, aligning in only one pattern. The pattern was only visible under the twin moons of Soma, then placed on top of the pendant base.

"Temporal Locket! Done. I did it." She held it high up. "I beat the trial. Not you owls, not the oak—me. Millicent Gear-wright of Celestial City." She stood and did a little dance. "Woo!"

She took a deep, satisfying breath. "Thank you, oak tree, for your help. Owls, you can suck it. Time to get back to the terminal."

"That wasn't nice," the barn owl screeched as the four went back up the stone path. "We were just having a laugh."

"Maybe we were a bit hard on her," the horned owl replied.

A low moan and creak followed from the oak tree. "I think you're hilarious."

It wasn't until they were in the private cabin on the *Celestial Spider*, after a shower and a change of clothes, that Millicent felt better. The muddy things all had a good soak and hung over the line while she sipped her tea by the porthole window, admiring the Temporal Locket.

"A locket often implies that there would be a keepsake or memento inside," Millicent mused. "I wonder if there is something in there now? Or if something needs to go inside?"

"Do you think Barnaby will be back at Zephyria when we arrive?" Quark asked.

Millicent answered, "I hope so."

"I wonder how big and grand his tale will be?"

"His stories are grand."

"I like him."

"I like him too," Millicent confirmed.

knock came at the door.

"Enter."

"Captain, we're passing the edge of the Nebula's Grave."

Barnaby Blackwater sat in the center of his cabin, legs crossed and eyes closed, practicing his meditation, building the safety around his mind.

"Aye, thank you." His eyes opened, and he started to rise. "Life is so much easier with both legs."

"Sir?"

"Lead the way, Mister Marlowe. Lead the way." He buckled the cutlass, exited the door, and headed to the bridge.

At these unbelievable speeds, the Supercluster felt different as they entered the nebula.

"Mister O'Malley, standard speed, please," Barnaby asked the bridge.

The Nebula's Grave was a dark nebula; the gas and dust blocked light reflections inside from getting out. Safely inside, stellar nurseries were protected from outsiders. Clusters of stars were being born in a dazzling display of light and color after millions of years of incubation.

"Mister Rook, activate the radiation shields. Keep me abreast of any changes to the shields or spikes in gravity."

Mister Marlowe, in awe of the moment, said, "It's... it's beautiful."

"Aye, it is. If we survive this day, Mister Marlowe, you'll want to share this memory with everyone—the price of admission, a ration of rum." Barnaby winked and smiled.

Marlowe gulped. "If?"

"Captain's made this run before, Marlowe. No need to worry," O'Malley encouraged.

"Rook, set course for near the center."

"Near?"

"Aye, there's a supermassive black hole. Get us close, but don't let us fall in."

Concern and worry were now on the brow of every man on the bridge. It was one thing to go to the Nebula's Grave, but entirely another to tempt the fates of a supermassive black hole.

"Mister Wren," Barnaby spoke into the bridge communicator, "we're gonna need those engines at the ready. Full radiation shields are running, and we might need breakaway speeds."

"Aye-aye, Captain," came the reply from the speaker.

Sailing closer to the center, Rook reported the supermassive black hole coming onto the scope, taking up most of the real estate; there would be little else to see.

"Time dilations ahead, sir," Marlowe called out.

"Steady as she goes. Mister O'Malley, straight through the pocket, please."

"Aye," O'Malley responded.

"Energy jet spotted, Captain," Rook called.

"Aye, steer clear of her, O'Malley."

"Aye."

Rook took time to adjust the scope with the assistance of Marlowe. The reconfiguration allowed for better precision, with the interference of electromagnetic fields from the super-massive black hole taking its toll.

The Beck & Sail traversed the distance in far less time than anticipated by cutting through the time dilations, taking days off the whole trip. Approaching the black hole, the ship slipped into a plane of orbit, keeping them from the event horizon and the shockwaves of supernova remnants.

"Wren, how's our girl holding up?"

"Captain, she's holding steady. Power is nominal, radiation is just above the green into the yellow. Try to avoid any surprises, and she'll be fine."

"Aye, that'll do," Barnaby replied. He turned the communication switch. "Mister Little, Mister Jenkins, join me on the bridge."

A few moments later, two bookish pirates came onto the bridge. Scholarly, in the sense that they were the best at reading, writing, and arithmetic on the ship, they mostly spent time in the workshop crafting munitions, explosives, and inventions. The way the two smiled and studied the bridge, it must have been a rare sight, if not the first time.

"Yar, I'm told the two of you are the smartest of the crew. Is that true?"

"Aye, we are fair by these means," Little said.

"Aye, that'll do," Barnaby replied. "We're seeking treasure. A map, or something that will point us to the right spot in the Phantom Spire. The only way to find it is to follow the poem, 'Challenge of the Celestial Map.' Sabe?"

"Aye," the men said in unison.

"You know the poem?"

Jenkins replied, "Aye, I have it memorized."

"But sir," Little added, "you know it's a myth, a poem, some-thing made of fiction? It's not likely we'll find anything for all our risks."

"Safe harbors never filled a pirate's coffers, Mister Little." Barnaby gave a dreadful stare. "I'm not a fan of mutiny, but I do encourage feedback." Barnaby smiled at the two, who were starting to shake in their boots.

"Captain, maybe you could tell us where we stand," said Jenkins with caution.

"Gentlemen, we stand inside the Nebula's Grave. On port, we orbit the Galactic Maw."

"Where time stands still, we fight gravity's forces," Jenkins said with serious thought.

"Aye."

"And we're looking for a tall tower, a beacon of shifting sand?"

"Aye, I'll point your attention in the direction of the star-board." Barnaby raised his finger and pointed to an arm of gas and rock above the stellar nurseries they passed on entry.

"It's beautiful," Little added.

Jenkins thought again, reciting the poem in a low mumble, "The third chime, that splits the night?"

"Aye, and that's where you two come in," Barnaby said, satis-fied with the pair so far. "We'll need to work together on the rest."

"So we go to the beacon, the trail end of the tower."

"Yeah, but the next stanza is 'follow shadows to the light.' It's pointing to the nurseries. We can't just go to the nurseries. Sailing through the tower of gas and rock will wreck the shields, and I guarantee those nurseries are filled with deadly radiation. Deadly."

"You skipped a part. What's 'the third chime?' It needs to 'split the night.'"

"Captain, are you sure the tower in question is that one? I mean, how can you know?"

"Mister O'Malley."

"Sir?"

"Take us to the top of that tower, best speed."

Clicking the switch on the communications panel, "Mister Wren," he said.

"Sir?"

"I need you to be true to your name—be ready for activity, hopping and climbing, through the thicket."

Wren snickered. "Aye, Captain, on the ready to be true to my name."

Pilot O'Malley set *The Beck & Sail* on a starboard course, climbing to the top of the tower of gas, dust, and particles that had formed over eons. Closing in on the tower, those particulates were the size of moons, between rubble and rocks of crashed and crushed debris. The explosion that created this tower shattered its origins into a vast field of rubble. O'Malley used his quick hands to steer the wheel around anything sizable in the way, while the shields took the impact, pushing the smaller pieces safely away.

"Almost there, Captain," Mister Rook notified.

"Jenkins, Little, what are we seeing now? Anything new or outstanding?"

"You know, a chime could be a ping."

"Or, the edge, like on a cask or a barrel."

"But it's a sound, right? The sound of the third chime?"

"Third barrel?"

"Maybe we make three pings? What harm could three bells do?"

"Gentlemen?"

"Mister Rook?" Jenkins asked, "Do you see anything on the scope shaped like a barrel?"

"Three?" said Little.

"Yes, three barrels," Jenkins corrected. "It would be between us and the nursery."

The captain joined Rook at his navigation station. Over each shoulder, Jenkins and Little loomed, worried about what might happen if they were unable to find the answers.

"This be the easy one," Barnaby said low. "They only get tougher from here."

The strain of a gulp came from Jenkins and Little, feeling highly motivated. Barrels started to appear on the scope that weren't there, created and imagined by hope.

"Try the ping?"

Jenkins shrugged.

Little asked, "Mister Rook, could you please sound three pings, three pings only, please, with a three-second gap between them?"

Rook looked up to the captain, who smiled and nodded in the affirmative.

"Aye, Mister Little, three pings coming your way," Rook said, flipping the safety cover on the metal switch of his panel up and turning the switch to the right. The loud ping inside *The Beck & Sail* got every crew member's attention. A device so rarely used on the ship created a sound wave that sounded as described: *PING*. The energy of the echo rippled forward through the nebula, cascading like a stone on water, but in three dimensions.

PING. The second sound went out, grating on the pirates' nerves like nails on a chalkboard.

"How is this supposed to work? We're just making random guesses here! There's no need for the plank," Jenkins pleaded with Barnaby.

"Plank? Nobody mentioned walking the plank."

PING! The third wave began to open space at the center of the tower like a straw, the energy ripple pushing aside the rocky debris, opening a passage.

"Mister O'Malley, follow that ping, please," Barnaby called out.

"Aye."

The nose of *The Beck & Sail* pointed down, accelerating to catch up with the wave created by the pings. It continued to pick up speed to pace the wave. The ship bounced and thrashed between the obstacles, challenging the strength of the shields. The tunnel grew bigger and faster ahead of them, pulling away.

Barnaby called out, "Do not go gentle into that good night, Mister O'Malley."

The struggle and strain of the wheel prevented the pilot from acknowledging.

At the base of the tower, the tunnel opened into the unknown, unseen space of the stellar nurseries, filled with light, and the gravitational forces pulling one another in equal balance, creating a calm, buoyant chamber between the infant clusters of dazzling lights.

"Yar, good work, good work, the lot of you. We might just yet survive this day," Barnaby praised.

"Captain," Mister Rook called. "There's a planet on my scope."

"That's impossible," said Jenkins.

"Ready the skiffs," Barnaby called into the communicator, "assemble the shore party."

34

"It was just there, Captain, but now it's gone," Rook called out.

"Set 'er down just before the last reading," Barnaby instructed.

The smaller craft and its sister ship behind it set down in a clearing in the sand. The crew and captain looked at one another. For many, it was the first time in a long while that they had been on land. Clicks of gears and the whirring of automated instruments filled the air as they worked.

"Green light, sir. Pressure and atmosphere are in range. Except..."

Stepping down the ramp to the planet's surface, Barnaby led his party forward. "Keep your flints dry and cutlasses ready," Barnaby ordered. "Arr, this be ridiculous," he added, his voice three times higher than normal.

"It's a helium-rich atmosphere," Rook explained in a higher pitch. "It won't hurt us, just make us sound funny."

"Aye." The men stifled their laughter under Barnaby's leadership. "Could be worse. Little, Jenkins, stay close, keep your eyes peeled."

The crew moved forward across the sand, following their captain. The wind picked up every speck light enough to carry and placed it directly in each man's eye. With a bit of whimpering and bellyaching, nearly all of them had put on their protective eyewear. A brief break in the breeze revealed eruptions of light and color from beneath the planet's surface, creating spectacular displays. A giant cloaked creature appeared before them, as if some dark power had willed it. On its right flank, thirty soldiers, and an equal number on its left. Sixty intimidating soldiers, each carrying a single large, flat slab of rock on their back.

"Ahoy there," Barnaby said in a friendly tone. "I'm Barnaby Blackwater, the scourge of the seven galax-seas, and your guide to all treasures—mostly ill-gotten. At your leisure—or peril, depending on your honesty. This be my fearless and faithful crew. And you be?"

The cloaked figure rose five feet above the flat stretch of sand, its eyes began to glow, and it raised its arms, saying in a deep, bellowing tone, "Prepare yourself."

"Yar, must be a deep bass without the helium," Barnaby quipped. "Ready for a fight, men." The rattle of each pirate putting his hand on a cutlass filled the air.

With a motion of its arms, the cloaked creature looked to the thirty soldiers on its right and pointed. The soldiers marched under orders in a straight line. The large flat stones on their backs, peeking above their heads with a pointy side facing down, dug into the sands and created a line. Once complete, the second set of thirty soldiers, each fierce and frightening, carrying similar flat-faced slabs, wide at the tops above the head, and pointy protrusions dragging in the sands, created a horizontal set of lines. Once complete, Barnaby and his crew faced a thirty-by-thirty grid of columns and rows.

Barnaby looked down to Jenkins and Little, saying, "This 'ere looks right up your alley with the maths."

Jenkins started to repeat the poem, picking up the focus where they left off:

"Count the sands in prime's embrace,
   A sequence set to find the place.
   Numbers pure, in order true,
   Reveal the path, a hidden clue.
   Silent whispers fill the air,
   As grains align with patient care.
   Each prime a step towards the core,
   Unlocking secrets from of yore.
   In the stillness, echoes call,
   Through the sands, the answers fall.
   A hidden door, a silent shift,
   Reveals the map, the ancient gift.
   Legends speak of those who tried,
   To solve the riddle, far and wide.
   Only those with patient hand,
   Could decode the shifting sand.
   So heed this tale, adventurer bold,
   In time's embrace, the truth unfold.
   Prime sequences your path shall guide,
   To the Spire where secrets bide.
   The Celestial Map, in parts arrayed,
   By ancient hands, with wisdom laid.

A quest for those who seek the core,
To unlock the mysteries evermore."

"It's the grid to a map. That's plain to see," Little said, studying the outlines in the sand.

"Count the sands in prime's embrace." Jenkins nodded, his mind already racing. "Prime numbers—those that can only be divided by one and themselves—are often seen as pure and unique. In the context of the poem, they likely represent the foundation of the map's coordinates, guiding us to the core."

Little added, "Numbers pure, in order true, like 2, 3, 5, 7... they stand apart from other numbers, just like these squares should stand out from the rest of the grid. They're the key to unlocking the pattern we need."

Jenkins paused, staring at the numbers they had circled. "Prime numbers are like the backbone of the universe—indivisible, unchangeable. In a place like this, where everything is built on ancient wisdom, it makes sense that they would be the key." Jenkins drew his cutlass and began to walk to the farthest left top corner. "I'll take the rows, you start the columns."

Thoughtfully, the two started to work in unison, filling in each box with a number between one and thirty. In the end, the two finished in the lower right corner with an odd-looking chart. One started the upper left corner of both row and column, thirty the last number in the upper right and bottom left. For each of the numbers 2, 3, 5, 7, 11, 13, 17, 19, 23, and 29, they made a circle in the square, setting them apart from the rest.

Having worked up a thirst, the two were back at Barnaby's side, drinking from a flask.

"Impressive." Barnaby nodded. "What's it mean?"

"From the poem, we've identified the possible numbers that would plot out the map," Little said.

"Yes, yes, the map coordinates, so to say, based on the clues in the verse."

"Aye, ye've done that." Barnaby scratched his head. "But nothing's happened. Maybe, and I don't know much about maths like you or navigation like Mister Rook, but for me, we fly in three dimensions, not flat lines."

Little smacked his forehead with the palm of his hand, while Jenkins shook his head in foolishness. Each took another swig of water and retraced the identified numbers into pairs: $(2,3)$, $(5,7)$, $(11,13)$, and so on. This effort removed the majority of options and made an interesting design. Graphing the course, based on what Barnaby called "Fancy Maths" involving x, y, and numbers, the two returned with three numbers of importance, which they had solved for by writing in the sand with their cutlasses: 5, 8.41, and 129.

Before they could explain their findings to the captain, the spectacle resumed. Eruptions of light and color burst from beneath the chart etched in the desert sands. The cloaked creature pivoted to face Barnaby and his crew, its right arm extended downward, indicating the scrawled calculations.

The ground beneath them trembled as grains of sand began to shift, moving as if guided by an unseen hand. Pebbles clattered together, tumbling in cascading streams that caught the light in a dazzling display of color. The steady, rhythmic *whoosh* of sand pouring away filled the air, growing louder as the hidden passageway emerged from the depths. It was as if the desert itself had taken a breath and was exhaling, revealing its long-guarded secret. The first glimpse of the passage was dark and narrow, with walls that glistened faintly in the dim light, promising both mystery and danger below.

As the last grains of sand slipped away, a cool, musty draft wafted up from the passage below, contrasting with the dry, heated air of the desert. The dim light from above cast long shadows, making the walls of the passage seem to shift and shimmer as if alive with hidden energy.

With a nod to his men, Barnaby took the lead, guiding them down into the newly uncovered passage.

35

"You are our first visitors," the ragged, dry man said in an unexpectedly clear tone. "Welcome to Mirage."

"Aye, a name that fits," Barnaby replied, his smile widening as he regained his usual composure. "I must say, I like the atmosphere down here."

The wise and ancient man chuckled softly. "Yes, yes."

"How rude of me. I haven't asked your name, my friend," Barnaby continued. "I am—"

"Barnaby Blackwater, yes, yes, we overheard your introduction. I am Prince Illuviar Veilweaver of the planet Mirage."

"Prince? How old is your father?"

The air around them began to shimmer and glow as the prince transformed into a youthful figure. "He is ancient, regaling us with tales from epochs past. Would this appearance suit your preference?" The atmosphere shifted again, light refracting differently, now presenting the prince as a beautiful woman reminiscent of fairy tales and mischief. "Or perhaps this?"

"Aye, I may not be a gentleman, but I do have a fondness for blondes."

With a wry shake of his head, Veilweaver morphed into a fiery redhead. "Let us find a compromise."

This shade of red reminded Barnaby of Millicent. Adventuring with her was both exhilarating and less burdensome than he anticipated. She challenged him yet also shared in the weight of their journey.

"On Mirage, we oversee the birth of stars, nurturing them until they are ready to shine on their own. To travel so far, to unravel these mysteries, there must be purpose. You seek places that shun discovery, individuals who prefer obscurity. Tell me, why?"

"Aye, the most noble cause—save the Supercluster. My good prince, we've discovered strange and abnormal patterns, caused by the malfunctioning Time Core within the Phantom Spire. My crew and I aim to locate it and set it right."

"Ah, indeed, a lofty goal," Veilweaver mused. "Yet, it's uncommonly altruistic for a pirate. You can understand my skepticism."

"True, true, pirates be known for deceit, plunder, and disarray. But what I speak here is true. We seek to correct the wrongs caused by the Time Core. The Clock Master himself tasked me with aiding a maiden named Millicent Gearwright."

"And where is she, if you are her guide and guardian?"

"She's on Soma. Time is of the essence as we race against it. She is seeking an artifact that will aid us. Er, we seek any artifacts that may help on this noble quest, not just the one. Anything to help us find and stop this disturbance."

"So, the missing artifact you seek lies there?" Veilweaver affirmed.

"Well," Barnaby repeated his intent, "we seek any artifacts that may help on this noble quest. Any at all."

Veilweaver loosened his collar and revealed a magnificent metal device secured around his neck by an elegant chain. He removed it, approached Barnaby, and placed it gently in his cupped hands. "You are now the keeper of the Whispering Astrolabe." The prince guided Barnaby to hold it close to his heart, then to his right ear. "Listen carefully. It will whisper the direction and location of your quest." He paused, gentle yet firm. "To locate the Time Core within the Phantom Spire, overlay your course with the solution to the riddle you've unraveled on your charts."

Barnaby's expression turned contemplative as he grasped the weight and warmth of the Astrolabe, understanding its significance in an instant. Barnaby felt the weight of the Astrolabe in his hands, physical and importance. The fate of Mirage, even the Supercluster, rested on the choices he would make with this. "This is a gift."

"Yes."

"The course and setting—they be the treasure map. Why gift me this?"

"Mirage faces a fate intertwined with the Supercluster's own. Mend the Time Core, and you save our world. Save the stars."

Veilweaver's gaze turned distant, as if looking through time itself. "Mirage has nurtured the birth of countless stars, guiding their light into the Supercluster. But if the Time Core fails, all our efforts will be for naught, and the stars we've birthed will wink out before their time."

Barnaby nodded solemnly. "Thank you." He smiled, and the twinkle of that distant star in his right eye gleamed. With resolve, he turned and strode purposefully back towards the surface. "No time to waste. Back to *The Beck & Sail*. Once we clear the Nebula, open a communication to the good doctor."

PART IV

IMPENDING GLORIOUS DISASTER

36

L anding never felt so good. After a jolting ride of leaps and bounds across the Cosmic Web, Millicent and her friends, Quark and Orin, landed safely on Zephyria. Gathering their things and making their way to the exit of the passenger car, Millicent thought aloud, "I hope we see Barnaby again soon. The time malfunction must be growing and spreading at a terrifying rate."

"I do not suppose we will see him for a while. Tick-tock, never stop, world of pirating, who can tell?" Quark replied, a sleeping Orin dangling from his hand.

She shook her head in frustration. "We need to act soon. And what is this 'tick-tock' you keep saying?"

It was a wave. She could see it crashing through the solid walls of the terminal. It existed on another plane, washing through the air and sparkling and rippling like sunlight reflecting off the morning surf. White foam rode the crest as it fell over everything. A bubble emitted from the Pocket Orrery in her pack, protecting her like a thick shell.

Millicent watched as her companions, the exiting passengers, and the crew were all affected. Just like on Gearturn, they moved forward and back, stopping, starting, and repeating the act. She was protected—safe, shielded by her grandfather's invention. It was not scary; it was a surprise. She thought she had time. "Time is fleeting," as stated in the Tenets of Time. And she felt that now. If this was happening on Zephyria, the systems in the Clockwork Constellation must also be under the impact.

As the time malfunction continued, her patience waned. She started to look for exits and options. The conductor, caught in a loop, thanked each person for being a patron and riding the stars. Nearly all had made the trip to Soma just for the nightly show and now wore t-shirts, funny hats, or magnetic characters clinging to their outfits or luggage. For them, it was a destination of family fun and memories of the spectacle. For Millicent, it certainly would be unforgettable. Her chest swelled with pride as she recalled Quark's solitary venture into the deadly Botanical Garden, his unyielding spirit reflected in every careful step he took. She looked forward to sharing these stories, and other moments, with Barnaby. Without Barnaby, the adventure lacked its usual spark, each moment tinged with a sense of incompleteness.

From the top of the terminal wall, she could see the wave subside. It pulled back with a rush of force, dragging moments with it, and disappeared. Once it left, the bubble around her melted away.

"Millicent?" Quark checked on her. "Millicent?"

"Did you see that?"

"See what?"

"The time malfunction. It just swept through Zephyria." She

was filled with energy, worry, and excitement. "What did you perceive?"

Quark started to hum in thought, considering and playing back the last thirty seconds, his head tilted. "A large magnetic shift, like the one recorded on Gearturn and the one on the Celestial Spider before Inkwell, has just taken place. My instruments show it rippled with waves of chrono-energy."

"What did you perceive of me?"

"You became a blue frozen blur, a copy of yourself."

Walking out to the ramp and down the first step, she looked up again to see the terminal dome still shared the amazing vistas of the sky she remembered. "I would hate it if this beauty ever became common."

"Move on, move along," someone from behind her called. "Some of us have another spider to catch."

The rude person pushed through the line and made their way down the stairs, quickly walking to the terminal exit.

"They have places to be, it would appear," Quark noted.

"We need to find Barnaby. Time is running short," Millicent said.

Working their way through the transparent tunnel into the ticketing center dome, Millicent caught sight of a strange ship. She continued her quick steps to keep her eyes locked on it, attempting to figure it out. It was unlike any other ship she had seen. There was no spider driving it or any other creature on board. It had three large flagpoles, each holding up screens on two opposite sides. Large circular windows glowed on the sides. Tubes ran along it, stuck out the front, and looked like they had the ability to extend. It almost looked like a tricorn hat from this vantage.

Fixed on the ship, she could see it was docked and ported to the terminal. "It is beautiful. What is it?"

"Arr, that be *The Beck & Sail*," Barnaby called out, opening his arms wide and placing his hands on his hips. With his left hand shooting up, he pointed. "She outpaces a Mindshredder's fleeting thought and leaves Gearturn's continental shifts looking like a leisurely stroll."

"Barnaby?" The name tumbled from her lips, carried on a breath she hadn't realized she was holding. "Is, is that you?"

"Aye, it be me, Barnaby Blackwater. The scourge of the seven galax-seas and your guide to all treasures—mostly ill-gotten. At your leisure—or peril, depending on your honesty."

Millicent's feet danced across the floor as if she were weightless, but her heart was anything but. The moment she fell into Barnaby's arms, a storm of emotions surged through her—relief, joy, disbelief, and a fear that clung like a shadow. His embrace was warm, familiar, yet it felt like a memory she couldn't fully grasp. As his strong arms wrapped around her, she wanted to lose herself in the comfort they provided, to believe that everything was as it should be. But the gnawing questions remained. What had happened to him? And why did she feel a pang of sadness amidst her joy, as if this reunion were too good to be true?

"Barnaby! I am so glad to see you." She pulled back. "But, how?" Her voice was barely a whisper as her gaze dropped to his leg, expecting the familiar peg but finding nothing amiss. "I mean, how?" The question hung between them, heavy with confusion and a tinge of fear. When she looked up, the sight of his clean-shaven face—a decade younger, ruggedly handsome—stirred a mix of emotions. She couldn't deny the comfort of seeing him as she remembered from stories, yet it unnerved her. Was this truly Barnaby, or had time altered him into someone she no longer knew? Her chest tightened as she struggled to reconcile the man before her with the one who had shared in their countless dangers.

"Yar, I'll take it as a compliment." A sly smile flashed on his face. "I cannot wait to tell you all about it. But let us get you on board first. We need to set sail and make way." Barnaby ushered them through the boarding tube, up the plank to *The Beck & Sail*. In the pilot house, he introduced each of the senior crew to her, all on their best behavior. She was shown her private quarters as Quark took Orin to his room to sleep.

While they settled in, Barnaby cast off and made best speed for the Phantom Spires. "No time to waste, Mister O'Malley."

Finally, with a moment to themselves in the briefing room, Millicent marveled, "So this is a real-life pirate ship."

"Aye, it be. Masts, guns, crew, and all," Barnaby replied timidly. "I must admit, Milady Millicent, there were many times I turned to tell you something on this adventure, only to remember you were not there."

"I am here now. I want to hear all about it," she replied. "I want to know how you have a leg, missing your scar, why you look so much younger, what happened? How did you return to Zephyria before me?"

"Aye, that last one is the easiest. We actually arrived before we left. You see, we passed through several time dilations on our travels, taking days off our trip," he explained.

Skepticism etched itself in the corners of her eyes as they tightened, her mind rebelling against the impossibility of his words. "That does not appear logically possible, but..." She trailed off, her thoughts spinning in an ever-widening loop of disbelief and reluctant acceptance. She had always trusted in the certainty of logic, the unbreakable laws that governed their Supercluster, but here was Barnaby, standing before her, living proof that some rules were meant to be broken. It unnerved her, this shaking of her foundations. What did it mean if time itself could be twisted and bent at will? And more troubling, what did it mean for her place in this ever-shifting world?

"It worked," he explained with a calm voice. "That's all you need to know." He rang a small bell, and one of the crew rolled a cart to the table, filled with meats, cheese, vegetables, and baked goods. "I imagine you're starvin' after such a bold journey."

Two plates dropped onto the table between them, spinning to a stop before flopping flat, followed by silverware and napkins.

"Water only for me, please," she said when the bottle of wine came around.

Barnaby's plate was piled high with hearty servings that he dug into with knife and fork. His teeth chomped, and his fingers pulled and picked at his favorite parts.

Nonchalantly, without making a fuss, she removed her three brown pills from the brown paper bag and took them with water.

"You're not diggin' in? No appetite?" His big smile revealed evidence of what he aimed for his mouth, but a bit fell, staining his shirt.

Skepticism turned to a smile, and she glowed as he started to talk about his visit to Gideon Highwire and meeting Stark Maddox on Gablehaven. There was a dreaminess to the way he told stories of his adventures.

As the plates were removed and the table cleaned, Barnaby waved off the dessert tray before it even entered the room, noticing his guest's highly disciplined, efficient focus on practicality over pleasure.

Then, Millicent asked, as if waking from a daydream, "Am I staring? I am staring. I am staring. Sorry, sorry."

Barnaby smiled, the twinkle of a stolen star in his right eye glistening. "Aye, my dear, if you are looking for a piece of meat, I suggest the galley. Even as a younger man, whole and fit, I might be too salty for you."

A sudden warmth spread across Millicent's skin, the sensation akin to the precise gears of her internal chronometer abruptly shifting into a higher gear as her heart quickened unexpectedly. These sensations cascaded through her, each one a delightful shock to her precisely calibrated system. Her meticulous calculations and logic wavered, leaving her breathless as an unquantifiable emotion surged within her—a feeling she instinctively understood.

With the Supercluster hanging in the balance, Millicent knew she must focus. She pulled out her notebook, the familiar act of jotting down observations anchoring her scattered thoughts.

Barnaby's eyes gleamed as he recounted the mental exercises, the stolen time, and their wild descent through space into the fold, each word painting a vivid picture of their daring escapades. He went on to tell the tale of the dark nebula and solving the riddles laid out in the poem. It was his crew that won the day and outsmarted the cloaked stranger.

"It is called the Whispering Astrolabe. It is powerful ancient magic. It tells me where to go when I ask sweetly." He handed it to her. "The course is set according to the coordinates, but when we get close, this will tell us where to go."

The Whispering Astrolabe rested in Millicent's hands, its weight and substance palpable. It pulsed with a life of its own, whispering secrets she felt compelled to uncover. Carefully, she raised it to her right ear and listened. "Right in front of you."

"What did it say?" Barnaby asked.

Millicent looked at it in her hands and smiled. "It told me a secret."

"Yar, that is nice." He sat back in his chair comfortably. "Now, tell me your tale. What did you learn?"

She recounted the glow of the twin moons, the bizarre conversations with the talking plants, and Quark's fearless steps into the "deadly" Botanical Garden, each word a testament to their harrowing journey. "I could not help but think how much you would have appreciated these two owls we met in the garden. I certainly did not like them."

As she spoke, Millicent found herself sharing beyond facts. She revealed her moments of self-doubt, her wavering confidence, and the unexpected joy of seeing her grandfather's recording. Her fingers traced the Temporal Locket as she explained its significance, her renewed confidence after assembling it. "This should help us fix the malfunction."

"Aye, you did good. Good indeed, Millicent," he said. "But you're worried still. I can see it in your eyes."

Millicent's voice dropped to a near whisper, the weight of her emotions finally breaking through her carefully maintained composure. "There is more."

37

The Pocket Orrery landed on the briefing table with a muted thud, its polished surface reflecting the dim light of the room. It sat there, deceptively still, nestled between the enigmatic Temporal Locket and the cryptic Whispering Astrolabe. The trio of artifacts, now united, seemed to hold their breath in silent anticipation.

Seconds ticked by in a tense silence. Then, almost imperceptibly, the Pocket Orrery quivered—a subtle vibration at first, barely noticeable to the watchful eyes surrounding the table. But the tremors quickly escalated, transforming into a violent shudder that sent ripples of unease through Millicent and Barnaby.

The device's erratic dance became frantic—a mechanical seizure that defied explanation. Just as the tension in the room reached a breaking point, a sharp click echoed in the air. The Orrery's latch sprung open on its own, the lid snapping back to reveal its mysterious innards.

But it wasn't the intricate gears, nor the precise pulse of the

Clockwork Constellation, that drew their attention. Instead, all eyes were fixed on the glittering apparition materializing above the open device. Blurry and indistinct at first, the image slowly coalesced, reminiscent of that fateful day in the caverns of Soma.

"Grandfather?" The word escaped her, more a breath than a voice, as if saying it aloud might shatter the fragile image before her. The atmosphere thickened, as though time itself had slowed to bear the weight of this revelation.

The apparition pulsed in response, and a voice both familiar and ethereal—elderly, gentle, yet tinged with a mystical echo—filled the room. As it spoke, flickering scenes materialized within the projection, each one a vivid tableau pulled from the depths of memory. The images danced and shifted, playing out as if the past had become the present.

"They were different times on Gearturn," the voice began. "The world was less automated. Manual power was needed, and that is where his mother worked—in the sub-level, turning a crank. Without leaving her station, she hoisted herself up on the production table, pushed through the pain of giving birth without stopping the turn of her crank, and used the gears to sever the umbilical cord before returning to her duties. He lay in a warm grease box those first three hours, hidden under the operations table until her shift ended. Then, she carried him to the fire station. Those few minutes were the longest time he would ever spend with his mother. She left him at Fire Station 129 in the underworld, knowing someone else could offer him a better life. That is where the firefighter who discovered him entered the name Julius Kilmoore in the drop-off diary, using block writing in ink the color of ash."

Millicent's fingers pressed hard into her palms, her nails leaving faint imprints as she absorbed the story of Julius's life.

The isolation of his childhood, the shadow of abandonment, the relentless fight to find his place in an indifferent world—these were struggles she knew all too well. Tears welled up, but she blinked them back, determined not to let them fall. It was as if she were hearing echoes of her own life. Was this the path she was destined to follow, or could she forge a different future? She turned to Barnaby, their eyes locking in a moment of shared understanding. The parallels were unmistakable—the absence of parents, the mystery surrounding her own origins.

"Barnaby," she whispered, her voice tinged with trepidation, "I... I never knew. My parents, the underworld..." She trailed off, unable to articulate the storm of emotions swirling within her.

Barnaby nodded, his expression somber. "Aye, lass."

Millicent nodded mechanically, her thoughts spiraling. Had she, too, been named by an underworld firefighter? Her name scrawled in some forgotten logbook, inked in ash? The question echoed in her mind, each repetition a sharp stab of uncertainty. What if everything she thought she knew about herself was a lie? Was her identity nothing more than a series of chance encounters, like Julius's? The possibility that her origins might be as obscure and hidden as his loomed over her, casting shadows across the carefully ordered world she had built. Her stomach turned with unease—had she been living in a sheltered world, blind to the truths that had been lurking just beneath the surface?

"When I first saw him, he was small. He looked two years younger than his actual age, at least. I wasn't that old myself. The local ruffians—three older boys—had him on the ground, curled in a ball. I knew I wouldn't make a difference in the fight, but my twin brother Ethan ran in without thinking, and I followed. I always followed. Ethan taking on the leader slowed them down, but eventually, we found ourselves curled in balls next to Julius, taking a beating. That's all we proved—that we could take a licking. The three of us stuck together after that, knowing we might not win the fight, but we were in it together.

"School was easy for Julius. While I applied maximum effort, he knew everything. Ethan was smarter than me, but we both struggled. And when they tried to move Julius to a higher grade, he continued to show up to our class every day, sitting between Ethan and me.

"It was a girl on a surface playground who first showed him kindness and sparked the idea. He explained it as a simple, random act that planted the seed in his mind—randomness, outside of order, had a greater chance of changing the world. He replayed that morning to us several times over the next year:

"A six-year-old girl is playing in a park. She is picking solaris florets. She notices an old man sitting alone on a bench, looking sad. On impulse, she gathers her solaris florets and approaches him. 'These are wish-flowers,' she says, offering him the bouquet. 'You blow on them and make a wish!'

"The old man, touched by her innocence, smiles for the first time in months. He takes a solaris floret and blows, sending seeds floating into the air.

"'What did you wish for?' the girl asks excitedly.

"'For someone to talk to,' he replies softly.

"The girl beams and sits next to him. 'I can talk to you!'

"Julius later told us the results that sparked this interest. This chance encounter broke the old man out of his depression. He started visiting the park regularly, eventually becoming a beloved storyteller for local children. His renewed engagement with the community led to the creation of an intergenerational program that enriched the lives of both elderly residents and young families in the neighborhood.

"Watching this initial scene unfold, Julius was struck by

how this small, spontaneous act of kindness from the little girl set off a chain of events that could positively impact so many lives. This moment planted the seed of Julius's belief in the power of unpredictability and random acts to create significant change—something that carried forward for the rest of his life.

"The year before university, everything changed. Julius got the three of us summer apprenticeships working on Gearturn's revolutionary Tidal Resonance Regulator—a massive clockwork mechanism designed to find harmony between natural and artificial systems. The device was built on a colossal offshore platform, merging Gearturn's advanced timekeeping technology with nature's rhythms.

"We had been on-site for six weeks. During a critical calibration process, Ethan noticed a microscopic flaw in the central gear. I glanced at Ethan, a knot of unease tightening within me. He looked calm, focused. But I couldn't shake the feeling that something was about to go terribly wrong. 'Be careful,' I found myself whispering, barely audible over the hum of the machinery. As he moved to address it, the flaw triggered an unexpected interaction between the machine's intricate temporal mechanics and the natural tidal forces. It created a catastrophic temporal feedback loop. The result was what they called a 'temporal tsunami'—a massive wave that existed simultaneously across multiple timelines.

"All we could do was watch. Ethan, up in the tower, desperately attempted to fix it while the adults held us back. We were unable to run in and save him. I remember it all clearly—the approach, its flicker in and out of existence, its size and speed fluctuating unpredictably. The wave defied conventional physics, its water infused with visible strands of temporal energy.

"Despite the platform's advanced safety systems, the

temporal nature of the tsunami rendered them useless. Ethan, trapped on deck and struggling to make corrections, turned to watch in awe and terror as the wave swelled. He knew he was witnessing something never seen before.

"My body felt like stone, weighed down by the sheer help-lessness of the moment. Ethan's face twisted from determina-tion to fear as the wave approached. I wanted to scream, to rush to him, but my feet felt as though they were nailed to the ground. All I could do was watch as my brother was consumed by the impossible. Whatever it was that he did up there saved the whole of Celestial City, focusing all the energy on the tower, isolating the impact to that spot.

"When the temporal tsunami hit and Ethan was swept away, it was unlike any normal drowning. His experiences fractured across multiple timelines, and I watched in horror as my brother died hundreds, maybe thousands of different times and ways, all in a matter of seconds.

"Search efforts were complicated by the fact that Ethan now existed fractured across time—parts of him washing up on shores in the past, present, and future. Even when they found him, it wasn't him; it was a ghost, a specter, a fading memory.

"In the days that followed, I wandered through our home in a daze. Ethan's absence was a gaping void, a black hole that swallowed all light and joy. I found myself sitting by his empty bed, clutching his favorite book, the pages worn and familiar. The memories of his laughter, his stubborn determination, haunted me. How could he be gone?

"Lost, I followed Julius to university but couldn't keep up. He was infinitely smarter. We shared similar interests and studied the same fields. I became his assistant. I watched up close as Ethan's death impacted his work. It twisted him over time. The same people who cheered and encouraged his accelerated efforts, placing his name on the lips of every professor on campus and at the top of every list in post-graduate recruitment, were the same ones who laughed and ridiculed him for releasing his first paper, 'Chaos as a Catalyst for Universal Betterment.' Gearturn, as great as it was, wanted order and control. There was no place for chaos, no need for the randomness of nature.

"He fought through the process; he was a survivor. No child born in the underworld and pulled from the trash and hot grease as a newborn would ever give up so easily. He became a doctor and continued his private work and tests. I followed him, supported him, and stayed his assistant. We were in it together. I didn't see the madness growing; it was a blind spot formed by our years together.

"At thirty-three, I was married, a father of two children, and was called in front of the Clockmaster with him. Julius discovered that there was a balance in the Supercluster—the Time Core created time, but Gearturn controlled and regulated it. Without Gearturn, time would bounce, skip, and jump, creating confusion and chaos. We were labeled 'loose springs,' sprung gears, crackpots, a danger to Gearturn. We were blamed for destabilizing Gearturn's power grid through recent experiments, leaving people in the dark for almost a week. Julius was changing, morphing into something bigger, uglier, less compliant, less compromising. No one would listen. They just referred to him as Kilmoore, making him sound villainous.

"The good people of Gearturn told my friend Julius that time was invented by the ancients; there was nothing left to discover. But his experiments, ones that I witnessed and took part in, proved them wrong.

"I was late to the lab that last day. He had started an experiment without me. He wanted to test the bounds of chaos, to find the Time Core. On a planet of control and order, this idea was radical. He claimed that chaos fosters adaptability, that chaos is the birthplace of innovation, that chaos introduces a sense of wonder and excitement. Chaos and order, he said, were not mutually exclusive but interdependent. Chaos teaches us humility. Chaos is not the enemy of order but its essential counterpart.

"In the chaos field Julius created, I realized I could not follow him where Kilmoore was taking him. Kilmoore slipped away from the lab, somewhere in time, determined to bring change to the Supercluster through chaos with the Time Core. I turned off the machine. My lifelong friend Julius was gone. I focused on raising a family and built a reputation for myself in the old ways—a gears and sprockets man.

"Always watching and hoping, my instruments in my lab stretched out in observation, looking for that hope to find Julius Kilmoore. I taught Millicent, my granddaughter, everything I could—to a point. Educating her in the lab after class, advancing her knowledge beyond what was taught in school, she eventually out-mastered me in ideas and accelerated past my capabilities. Hopefully, equal to Kilmoore.

"I record this message because I believe I have found Kilmoore—or perhaps, he has found me. Time is..." His expression grew tense, a flicker of worry crossing his face. "It's not blasphemy to say it—time is not working as it should. The readings on my workshop instruments show something unnatural, something incredible. I have updated this Pocket Orrery to help locate him, but it will need assistance." His attention shifted suddenly as something off camera caught his eye— Millicent, entering the workshop a year ago. "If Kilmoore..." His voice faltered, the pause stretching into silence, as if the weight of his words could never be fully measured. "If he finds me again, and I cannot stop him...

"I leave this record," the hologram concluded, "Thaddius Gearwright, of sound mind, that maybe one day it will help in understanding my eternal friend Julius." The man turned to his granddaughter. "Welcome back, Millicent. I need your help with the Pocket Orrery now that you're here."

The room went dark as the projection ended. With a small click, the Pocket Orrery snapped shut.

"Last year," Millicent said. "Right before..."

38

"Captain, we've arrived at the coordinates discovered on Mirage," Mister Rook reported through the communication center.

It stirred Barnaby from his meditation, something he found refreshing, better than restless attempts at sleep filled with guilt and remorse. Returning from the depths of his mind, he reached for the switch to reply, "Aye. Please inform Miss Millicent."

Five minutes later, the two reunited to see the swirls of strata and storms across a gas supergiant before them against the black void of space.

"What are we looking at?" Barnaby asked.

"Strong magnetic fields, composed mainly of hydrogen and helium, deep atmosphere, lack of a well-defined solid surface," Mister Rook explained. "It's the destination from the coordinates we found on Mirage."

"Aye, could it be another Mirage?" Barnaby asked aloud, looking to gauge Millicent's reaction. "Any chance of life?"

"Negative, Captain. Negative," Rook replied.

Millicent and Barnaby's eyes locked, knowing what they had to attempt. Barnaby reached under his shirt and pulled out the Whispering Astrolabe. He cupped it in his hands, rough from swordplay and pulling mainsails. The smooth surface warmed in his hands as he thought hard about Julius Kilmoore and let the name whisper out of his lips, "Kilmoore." He brought the Astrolabe to his right ear, like a shell sharing the sweet sounds of the oceans he sailed in youth. He listened. Carefully, quietly, he listened for anything. And there it was, the most angelic voice, spun honey on the breeze, seducing him to a rendezvous, which he knew to be true.

Closing his eyes, he broke the enchanted siren's whisper spell and reconnected with Millicent. A few small steps and an extended hand, Barnaby hovered over Rook and pointed to a spot on the scope with the calm of a coming storm, saying, "There, Mister Rook, there. Best speed, please, shields up, batten the hatches, guns at the ready."

The eerie stillness crept through the bridge, every eye on Barnaby. "Action stations," he said with a firm command. "You scallywags waiting for an invitation? You can lead a crew to plunder, but you can't make them think." He gave Millicent a wink and a smile to let her know that he was just motivating the crew.

Barnaby's command set The Beck & Sail into motion. The ship veered sharply, its course shifting as the crew sprang into action, their voices steady despite the tension. With a calculated maneuver, the ship arced around the swirling layers of the gas supergiant, the planet's turbulent atmosphere casting deep shadows across the deck. As the ship broke free of the gas giant's pull, the second of the Phantom Spires loomed ahead, and beyond it, the silhouette of a habitable planet emerged from the darkness, its surface dotted with mysterious formations.

A brilliant orange beam shot up from the planet's surface, arcing toward *The Beck & Sail* with startling speed. As it neared the ship, the Pocket Orrery in Millicent's pack flared to life, casting a protective bubble around the entire vessel. The energy from the Orrery radiated outward, merging with the beam's light. Before their eyes, ghostly images of *The Beck & Sail* began to materialize, stretching out in a widening circle around the planet, each one a near-perfect replica of the original, as if time itself was fracturing into possible futures.

"Set an orbit, Mister O'Malley," Barnaby called out. He sounded as steady as the rudder of reality, calming the crew.

Fearful of crashing into the ship ahead of them, Mister O'Malley followed the orders, and as the beak of the ship turned under his hand, the line of ships in front of them aligned to perfectly match speed, yaw, and pitch.

"Captain?"

"It's an illusion of time, Mister O'Malley," Millicent assured. "Just an illusion. There is no possible way for you to crash into ourselves of the possible future," she explained.

As the strength of the blue beam from the surface intensified, the straight line of ships, in front and behind them, began to play out what might be and what could be, in ways that were unimaginable.

"The Orrery, it will not last long."

"Aye, you three are with me," Barnaby ordered, his voice cutting through the tense atmosphere. Without missing a beat, he took Millicent's hand and led her towards the skiff, with Quark following closely behind, Orin cradled in his arms. The shift from the controlled chaos of the bridge to the confined space of the skiff was sudden, the urgency of their mission pressing down on them as they prepared for the descent.

Making their way down a deck, Millicent said, "Once we board the skiff, the Orrery won't protect *The Beck & Sail*."

"Yar, won't need to, it'll follow us to the surface, of that I'm sure," Barnaby answered.

The skiff took them on a bumpy ride to the planet's surface under the piloting skills of Blackwater, with the distractions of chaos and what might be casting doubt and confidence in wave after wave of uncertainty.

Entering the planet's atmosphere, the beam broke contact.

"We're too low for it to target us," Barnaby explained.

Even with the beam gone, they shot towards the location of emanation, tracing just above the surface.

"It's not much of a planet," Millicent mused, her gaze scanning the barren landscape. The gray, rocky surface stretched endlessly, the kind of desolation that seeped into your bones. Even from the skiff, she could feel the cold creeping in, as if the planet itself had long since given up on warmth.

"Aye, there she blows." Barnaby pointed to an opening in the planet's surface, surrounded by high ridges of unnatural rock formations in rings around it. "Let's take her inside." He pushed the wheel forward.

The effects of the planet's gravity could be felt as the nose of the skiff turned down and followed the hole. Blackwater pulled back hard, bringing the skiff to a hovering halt just above the cavernous opening.

"You three are with me." He pointed to Millicent, Quark, and Orin. "Brace yourself for the great unknown."

39

"It's cold," Millicent said, shivering as she stepped off the skiff, the frigid air biting at her exposed skin. Orin tightened his blanket cape around himself, his breath visible in the frosty air. The click of Quark's internal heater kicking in provided a welcome hum against the silence. Barnaby grabbed a fur coat from the rack by the portal and draped it over Millicent's shoulders, giving them an extra rub. "Try this on."

Millicent smiled as the warmth enveloped her. "Thanks."

Before them lay the underground lair, a labyrinth of ruins and abandoned workshops from a lost civilization. At its center, a towering cannon barrel glowed orange, still cooling from recent use.

Millicent pointed. "There?"

"Yes, that is logical," Quark replied.

"Can you map this place, Quark?" Millicent asked.

Quark set Orin down, extended his legs, and scanned the cavern with glowing eyes before ratcheting back down.

"Aye, neat trick," Barnaby said. "Darker than a coal mine at midnight. Time to light a candle or go mole."

Quark's eye lights illuminated the way ahead. "This way, this way, no time to delay." They followed Quark through the crumbling outer ring of the workshop to the inner ring, leading to the building housing the cannon.

Millicent wiped the grime from a window with her coat sleeve and peered inside. The sight was unsettling: the cannon loomed large, and beside it, a strange machine pulsed with an intense light. It rose and fell like a breath, and at each peak, the light became so bright that the walls holding it started to tremble, threatening to shatter. The pulsing light from the Time Core cast alternating shadows across the room, making everything seem to shift and dance.

A nasal voice echoed through the cavern, slicing through the stillness. "I call it a Pandemonium Paradox Pulse. A pure beam of unpredictability from a non-linearity device I've invented."

The sounds echoed off the cavern walls, each word reverberating through Millicent's bones. She couldn't see the speaker, but the slurping of spittle and the occasional deep chest cough—"Moore, Moore"—sent a chill down her spine.

"That is an impressive creation," Millicent called out. "It must have taken a long time to build."

"Time is relative, my dear Millicent. Especially break time and lunchtime."

"You know my name?"

"I do know you. Thaddius's little protégé. I've been watching, waiting, planning, pulling strings."

"The Time Core. Is that your power source?" she asked, recognizing the structure's glow, masking her dread.

"Thaddius taught you well."

"He told me about you, Julius Kilmoore." Millicent stiffened her spine, digging deep past the butterflies to find her strength. "You're smart, maybe the smartest. Why create such harm? Destroy Gearturn?"

"Please, call me Moore. It fits so much better." He breathed heavily through an open mouth. "Destroy Gearturn? No, no, save Gearturn, my dear." Tremors rumbled through the cavern floor. "Gearturn is wrong about time, wrong about time's origins, and especially wrong about me." He turned upbeat, with a note of deranged glee. "They need a little chaos. Isn't that right, Captain Blackwater?"

Millicent's blood ran cold as she turned and froze at the familiar click of Quark's power switch. She gasped as his lights went out. Barnaby had turned off her robot. Orin dangled helplessly from Quark's frozen clutches, twisted and turned, struggling in vain. The sight shattered her.

"Barnaby, what are you doing?" she pleaded, disbelief and betrayal crashing over her like a wave.

Barnaby met her gaze, his eyes devoid of warmth. "Aye, Mister Moore. Chaos is a space pirate's ally. Bountiful treasure, its prize."

"No, Barnaby, not you," Millicent whispered. She took a step back, feeling the walls of her world closing in, the weight of betrayal pressing down on her chest. Tears welled up in her eyes, blurring her vision. "We trusted you. I trusted you."

"Aye, Miss Millicent, that you did. But see, the Brotherhood of the MindShredders had this deal. Flip my loyalty switch, and Moore would expand their membership to a much bigger slice on the map. They were waitin' for me." He revealed the three artifacts dangling from their chains. "Got a good deal. I swapped 'em for a fur coat."

Millicent's rage simmered beneath the surface, her hands

trembling with the intensity of her anger. She stepped forward, eyes narrowing with a cold, vengeful fire. Her voice was low and dangerous, each word dripping with venom. "Know this—hell hath no fury like a woman scorned. I will make you pay for this betrayal. You go to hell, Barnaby Blackwater."

"Yes, ma'am, I'm on my way. But first—" He grabbed her arm tightly, his grip like iron near the shoulder, digging into her pit.

"Get your hand off me, you brute! Let me go!" Millicent struggled, raw with fury and pain, but Barnaby's hold was unyielding, a vice that only tightened as she fought against him.

40

"No violence, please," his voice beckoned. "Ah, Millicent Gearwright. You look so much like your mother."

Millicent faltered, caught off guard by the mention of her mother. Her heart skipped a beat, and she felt the blood drain from her face. "You... you knew my parents?"

Moore let out a low, rasping chuckle. "Knew them? My dear, I worked alongside them. Brilliant minds, both of them."

Millicent let out a small gasp. She had spent years trying to piece together fragments of her parents' past, but those pieces never formed a clear picture. "But they were just... turning cranks," she stammered with uncertainty. "That's what Thaddius told me."

Moore's chuckle deepened, a sound that sent chills down her spine. "Turning cranks? Is that what he told you? Oh, Millicent, your grandfather was always good at controlling the narrative."

Millicent's mind raced. Her grandfather had always been a

stern, unyielding figure, insisting on precision and order, warning her of the dangers of chaos. "If they weren't turning cranks, then what were they doing?" she demanded, her voice a mixture of fear and desperation.

Moore paused, letting the tension hang in the air. "Your parents were revolutionaries, Millicent. They were part of an experiment—a time manipulation device. They were trying to free Gearturn from its rigid temporal structure."

Millicent's world tilted, the ground beneath her feeling unstable. She had always believed her parents were victims of the system, punished for rebellion. Now, everything she knew was being upended. "No," she whispered, shaking her head as if she could dispel the words. "That can't be true."

Moore softened, sounding almost sympathetic. "I know it's difficult to accept, but think about it, Millicent. Why would two of the brightest minds in Gearturn be relegated to mere manual labor? They weren't prisoners—they were continuing my work. Work that your grandfather tried to stop."

Millicent's adrenaline surged through her veins, her thoughts swirling in a storm of confusion and disbelief. Her grandfather had always spoken of the dangers of chaos, the importance of maintaining order, but never had he mentioned this. "Why wouldn't he tell me?" she asked, more to herself than to Moore.

"Guilt? Fear? Both powerful allies. Who knows what went through Thaddius's mind? Maybe he feared you would follow in their footsteps. Or maybe he wanted to protect you from the truth." Moore's tone was gentle, but the words cut deep. "But in doing so, he denied you your heritage, your true potential."

Tears welled up in Millicent's eyes as memories of her grandfather's stern lessons flooded back. Had his insistence on precision and order been a shield, protecting her from a truth too terrible to bear? Or had it been a cage, keeping her from becoming who she was meant to be?

"Your parents understood that true progress requires a degree of chaos," Moore continued, his voice growing more intense. "They sacrificed everything—even their relationship with you—to create a better future. And now, you have the chance to complete their work."

Millicent trembled, her mind reeling from the weight of the revelations. Her entire life had been built on a foundation of lies—lies meant to protect her, or perhaps to control her. But now, those lies were crumbling, leaving her standing on the precipice of an unknown future. "Even if what you're saying is true," she said, shaking, "it doesn't justify destroying the Supercluster."

"Destroy?" Moore sounded almost offended. "No, no, Millicent. We're not destroying—we're liberating. Freeing time itself from the shackles of order. It's what your parents dreamed of. What they died for."

The words hit Millicent like a physical blow. She staggered back, the air thick with grief and disbelief. "Died?" she echoed. "But I thought—"

"Another of Thaddius's lies," Moore said, his tone softer now, almost regretful. "They didn't abandon you, Millicent. They died in an accident with the time manipulation device. Thaddius couldn't bear to tell you the truth, so he invented a story of rebellion and punishment."

Millicent's mind was a whirlwind of emotions—grief, anger, confusion, betrayal. She felt as though the ground beneath her had been ripped away, leaving her to tumble into an abyss of uncertainty.

"You have a choice now," Moore said, extending his hand toward her, his voice calm and persuasive. "Continue believing the comfortable lies, or embrace the complex truth. Join me. Finish what your parents started. Let's free the Supercluster from the tyranny of rigid time."

For a long moment, Millicent wavered, the weight of her newly discovered heritage pressing down on her. She could see the path before her, a path of uncertainty and danger, but also of potential and power.

She spoke steadily, stronger now. "What happened to you, Kilmoore? You left Gearturn a man, not a monster."

The ground shook. From the shadows, a large presence appeared, dragging colossal feet. As he stepped into the light, Millicent could see the way his misshapen skin appeared to shift and ripple with each movement, like clay poorly molded.

"More is what I am after. More power, more chaos, more of everything," he moaned. "Do you know what it's like to lose everything, Millicent? Everything? I need more power to make this right. To bring him back."

"Him?"

"Ethan. Bring Ethan back."

He stepped closer, now in the light, revealing his distorted form. His body was a grotesque combination of stretched limbs and hunched shoulders, as if he had been torn apart and crudely stitched back together.

"My crossings of the universe, coming here, going there, made me what you see," he continued. "Every molecule stretched and resized, the spaces between atoms extended and reassembled across time and space. But I am here. I found it, the Time Core. The absolute power to conduct my experiments away from the fools and disbelievers of Gearturn."

"What are you talking about?"

"Don't you see?" His lips quivered as he attempted to spit out the sentence. "Ethan is still out there. I can bring him back.

I need more power to find him. Tick-tock was just the start. Just a test."

"What is this 'tick-tock' people speak about?"

Moore's eyes glinted with a sinister grin. "Tell me, Millicent, what is the sound of a clock?"

"Tock-tock. What else would it be?"

"You were protected by your grandfather's Pocket Orrery during the test. Captain, what's the sound of a clock?"

"Aye, it be tick-tock," Barnaby said.

Millicent looked to Orin for confirmation.

Orin replied,

"It's true, it's true, I never lie to you.
   Tick-tock, says the clock,
   not tock-tock, you see.
   In every tick, a moment flees;
   in every tock, a new one frees."

Millicent's mouth went dry, her tongue feeling like sandpaper as she tried to form words. She cracked with anguish as she whispered, "Tock-tock... it was always tock-tock." She clenched her fists, her knuckles white, as tears streamed down her face. "You've destroyed everything I knew. Everything I believed in."

Her body shook with sobs, the weight of betrayal and loss pressing down on her. Yet, amidst the chaos of her emotions, a flicker of resolve ignited deep within her. She wiped her tears, straightened her back, and lifted her head, her eyes like granite.

"No," she murmured, more to herself than anyone else. "I won't let it end like this. You may have changed the sound of time, but you won't change its course."

"That was only a small test, child. I can bring Ethan back,"

Moore obsessed. "Bring him back. Bring Ethan back." He turned to his workshop.

"Yar, he gets like this at times," Barnaby said.

Millicent turned away. "I am not talking to you."

"I need more to stretch my capabilities," Moore muttered, eyes fixed on the Pandemonium Paradox Pulse. "More tests to introduce the right amount of chaos."

Millicent glanced around desperately, her eyes landing on the artifacts dangling from Barnaby's hand. The click of Quark's power switch echoed in her ears, drowning out all other sounds for a moment. His startup was a soft hum of reassurance in the chaos. She turned her head and saw that Orin had slipped out of his cape and switched Quark back on.

"You never saw what your test did to Gearturn, how it destroyed lives, trapped people in infinite loops, turned the clocks back on aging. You could have killed us all." Millicent shook with fury. She knew what she had to do—it was going to hurt, but there was no other way. "Why don't you ask your friend to use the Whispering Astrolabe to find Ethan?"

Moore's eyes widened, greed and shock flickering across his face. "You have it? They gave it to you?" He turned back to face Barnaby, taking each step toward him as the ground rumbled. "Why didn't you tell me?"

Millicent's heart raced—this was her moment. Summoning all her strength, she twisted violently in his grip, feeling the sharp sting as skin tore from her arm. Barnaby's hold loosened just enough for her to wrench her arm free and grab the chains of the artifacts.

With a sharp yank, the chains snapped, and Barnaby, off balance, released his grip entirely. The cold metal of the chains bit into her palms as she clutched them tightly. Millicent stumbled backward, clutching the artifacts to her chest, and called out, "QUARK!" She held tight to the fur. "We can do this," she whispered, her resolve solidifying into action.

Quark's arms extended, grabbing her by the collar of the fur coat and reeling her back like a deep-sea fisherman with a good cast. She flew through the air backward, uncontrollably, mirroring Orin, who dangled in Quark's other hand.

"Hello. Hello. Time to go." Orin smiled.

Quark's legs extended in great strides, running toward the skiff. By the time they were up the ramp, Barnaby and Moore realized what had happened.

"Can you fly this?" Millicent asked.

"We'll soon find out," Quark replied. The engines roared to life, the vibration thrumming through Millicent's body, her teeth chattering as they took off. The ship ascended, circling overhead, leaving the two villains behind. Escaping the atmosphere, searching for their next destination, they darted past *The Beck & Sail.*

41

"Slow down, Quark!" Millicent demanded. "It will break."

Rattles, jingles, and clunks throughout the little ship slowed in rhythm. Spirits lifted, hoping they might continue unharmed. As they breathed a collective sigh of relief, the klaxon sounded. Lights on the panel began to flash, one after another, until half the board was blinking. Alarms blared from the back, and fear gripped them all as the rattles and shakes intensified.

"There!" Millicent pointed to a gray rock. "Maybe we can land there."

Quark did his best to crash with grace.

Passing through the thin gray veil of an atmosphere, the planet transformed before their eyes. Their mouths dropped open as they gazed upon the magical world below. It was unlike anything they had seen before. The valley unfurled like a living painting, water lilies springing to life, trees inviting dreams beneath their boughs. Life glowed from the surface in a symphony of colors. Iridescent flora swayed in a breeze that carried the intoxicating scent of honey and starlight. Crystal-clear streams meandered through fields of softly glowing vegetation, their burbling song a soothing counterpoint to the ship's cranky engines.

The craft skidded across a green field like a plowman's blade cutting deep in the spring. Tossing the three around inside, their fate rested on friction to slow and gravity to keep them down. Grinding to a halt, the sound of wires sizzling and the smell of burnt plastics filled the cabin.

Millicent headed for the door. "Grab Orin."

"Wait, let me check the pressure and atmosphere," Quark said.

"No choice," she insisted as smoke began to fill the cabin. She hit the button, and the door opened, unfurling the ramp into the new and strange world.

Harmonious landscapes stretched as far as the eye could see, the clear air filling her lungs with a sense of tranquility she hadn't felt in years. Each breath was a reminder of their fragility, yet also a promise of new beginnings. A silent awe, a sense of reverence filled the air as she beheld this untouched alien paradise.

"This must be the place," Millicent said, taking off the fur coat. As Millicent stepped onto the alien soil, the beauty around her felt like a cruel joke. Her mind kept replaying Barnaby's cold eyes as he revealed his betrayal. She clenched her fists, fighting back tears of anger and disappointment. *How could I have been so blind?* she thought, the weight of her trust in him now a bitter taste in her mouth. She closed her eyes, took a deep breath, letting the mellifluous, cool winds gently caress her skin, sending a tingle of pleasure that made the little hairs on her arms dance. A sense of peace washed over her, soothing the turmoil that had been raging inside. "What do you think?"

"Over there." Quark pointed. "I am sensing something in that direction."

Orin stirred, addressing what the others were thinking:

"Trust, once a bridge of gold so bright,
Now lies in ruins, shattered by night.
Barnaby's smile, a mask of deceit,
Leaves hearts heavy, dreams incomplete."

Quark's circuits buzzed with increased activity as he attempted to reconcile Barnaby's actions with previous behavioral data. "I calculate a 98.7% chance that I missed crucial indicators of Barnaby's true allegiance," he stated, with a note of what could almost be described as regret.

An uncomfortable silence hung between them as they walked, each lost in their own thoughts. The betrayal had created an invisible barrier, a shared wound that none of them quite knew how to address. Millicent found herself glancing at Quark and Orin, wondering if they too felt the ache of Barnaby's absence, the void where their friend should have been.

In the stream, happy fish flapped, and bioluminescent glows of life emanated from creatures thriving in an ecology of balance and grace. Each step along the path sounded with the pads of cat-like tenderness. The path wound through the valley of the foothills, leading them to an otherworldly wall of crystal that covered the mouth of a cave. Millicent's heart skipped a beat at the sight. The crystals shimmered with an ethereal light, and she felt a strange pull, as if the barrier were whispering secrets only she could hear.

"Keeping us out?" Quark asked.

"Or keeping something in?" Millicent replied.

The three approached the wall for further inspection. Each step nearer felt familiar. A sense of being drawn closer to see something beautiful. Each of them peered intently into the crystals, seeing mirror-like reflections of themselves, but not quite. In the reflective world, the sky was a kaleidoscope of colors, shifting and changing with the mood. The foothills rose to mountains and fell into valleys, while streams, brooks, and rivers changed flows, rising and falling, even forming fountains. It was as if they were gazing into another life, another world, another path not taken.

Millicent's reflection in the crystal mocked her, wearing a confidence she no longer felt. "If I was so wrong about Barnaby," she murmured, barely audible, "what else have I misunderstood? How can I trust my own judgment?" The question hung in the air, unanswered but heavy with implication.

Millicent's reflection looked back at her, then winked.

42

"Allow me to assist," he started. "Let's get you to one hundred percent." The arm extended and plugged into Quark. The arm started to spin, winding Quark's power to maximum. Another extension reached out and clicked a new component into place. "Now you're three times stronger." A set of gears exchanged older cogs and sprockets with those of an unknown alloy. "Faster and unbreakable."

"Thank you. Nice upgrades."

"You'll need them for what you're about to do."

"You know?"

"I am just a reflection of you, the best of you, the worst of you, the you-est you you can be."

"All of me?"

"All."

"Then you know."

"I know."

Quark's mind, a complex aggregation of intricate clockwork

and advanced algorithms, pondered the weighty decisions ahead. Reflecting on the monumental task of saving the Supercluster from the creature known as "Moore," he found himself contemplating two drastically different paths.

"Tick-tock, tick-tock, Quark, old boy, the gears of destiny never stop. Here you are, a humble assembly of old clock parts, faced with a choice that could alter the fabric of the cosmos itself."

"It's a curious twist, isn't it?"

He paced back and forth, feeling the new upgrades and features start to click in, his movements punctuated by the gentle clinking of his metal components. "Option one, destroy Moore's world with the harmonic resonator of planet Echo."

"This planet is called Echo?"

"Yes."

"It's a powerful place. The sheer destructive force... it would be a symphony of annihilation, each note resonating with cataclysmic power."

"But what of the innocent lives of humans and beasts caught in the crossfire? Can I bear the weight of such a decision, to wield destruction so indiscriminately?"

His gears turned faster as he considered the alternative. "Option two, the Temporal Locket. Simply turn off the Time Core and halt the relentless march of time itself."

"A cleaner, elegant solution, like stopping a clock to preserve its beauty forever. But is it that simple?"

"The Time Core is the heartbeat of the Supercluster, the pulse that keeps everything in motion. To stop it, even momentarily, would be to play god with the essence of existence."

Quark's thoughts grew philosophical, a trait that often emerged when he found himself in solitude. "What is time, anyway? Just a series of moments strung together, like the teeth of a gear. We measure it, we depend on it, but do we truly understand it? And here I am, a mechanical marvel, contemplating whether to halt it entirely. How ironic."

Staring at his reflection, he realized the beauty of his build in the polished metal surface of the control panel, the time and care Millicent had spent bringing him to life. "I may be made of springs and cogs, but my thoughts are as intricate as any clockwork mechanism. The beauty of existence lies not in perfection, but in the unique quirks and complexities that make us who we are."

"Perhaps, in this moment, I am more than just a robot. I am a thinker, a philosopher, a bearer of responsibility."

Quark grew introspective. "Every second counts, every moment matters. I'm learning to embrace each tick and tock as a gift. And yet, the decision I face is one of great consequence. The wisdom of the ages is etched into my gears. I may not have all the answers, but I'm always eager to learn."

"What are the Tenets of Time?"

"Yes, yes, consult them, let's. Time is fleeting, time is subjective, time can heal, time can be a source of regret, time is a force of change, time is cyclical."

The reflection shook its head. "Hard lessons to learn, but they have all been present on this journey."

He sighed, a sound more mechanical than human, yet laden with emotion. "Life is like a grand clock, with countless interconnected pieces. Every part has its role to play, no matter how small or insignificant. My journey may be full of twists and turns, but I know that each step brings me closer to understanding my true purpose. And that, my friend, is worth all the time in the world."

Finally, Quark made his decision, his resolve reflected in the steady rhythm of his internal mechanisms. "I believe in the power of preservation over destruction, in the elegance of a solution that minimizes harm. The Temporal Locket it is. I'll turn off the Time Core, stop Moore in his tracks, and save the Supercluster without the need for a catastrophic symphony. Sometimes, the best way to find your purpose is to embrace the unexpected detours and see where they lead."

With a renewed sense of focus, Quark prepared to set his plan into motion. "Time may shape us, but it's up to us to decide what kind of masterpiece we want to become. And I've decided to be a masterpiece of hope, resilience, and wisdom. After all, life's too short to be wound up tight."

Quark's gears whirred with newfound vigor. "Tick-tock, tick-tock, the clock of life never stops. But for now, just this once, I'll make it pause. For the greater good, and for the Supercluster I hold dear."

43

In wonder's thrall, Orin stood, beguiled,
    Before a crystal wall, his reflection wild,
    Shifting shapes, in colors bright,
    A kaleidoscope of self in cape's embrace each night.
    A cape of warmth, a shield of dreams,
    Other times sleek, or worn by streams,
    Yet always him, yet never quite,
    A dance of self in morphing light.
    In symphony of planets' song,
    Mystical insights grew so strong,
    Verses bloomed within his soul,
    A poet's heart, to write, his goal.
    His hammock home, 'tween fragrant trees,
    In shade and breeze, at perfect ease,
    Birds chased spring in branches high,
    His heart ached for that clear blue sky.
    From afar, he heard a gentle pace,
    Byron, Shelley, Keats, in grace,

The poet famed, in light did weave,
Words of gold, a genius's leave.
More handsome than his statues three,
His brilliance flowed, his spirit free,
Orin's heart did yearn and pine,
For talent, fame, for light divine.
But in his core, a truth did lie,
His words, though pure, could not reach the sky,
On Vaporshade, an average soul,
On Gearturn, unique, he'd found his role.
Admiration's glow, Millicent's care,
On Gearturn, his spirit bare,
Yet seeing Byron's face so near,
Love for the myth did reappear.
In crystal's light, his truth did form,
He'd never be that fabled storm,
Yet in his heart, a peace did bloom,
His path was set, beyond the gloom.
For in his soul, he'd found his place,
A poet's heart, in cosmic space,
Unique, adored, in Millicent's gaze,
A friend, a bard, through all his days.

44

Millicent was hypnotized by the wonder of it all. She stood in front of the crystal wall, entranced by her reflection as it changed, morphing between what she thought she looked like and other versions. Always keeping her red hair, it might be in braided tails while she wore expeditionary taupe overalls in the jungle. Or large and free, a mess floating in space, researching distant stars in an orange one-piece suit in preparation for a spacewalk. As she gazed into the crystal wall, the reflections shifted, each presenting a different version of herself. In one, her auburn hair framed a face of confidence, sitting on a mountain edge, a blue scarf trailing in the wind. *Is this who I could have been?* she wondered, feeling a pang of longing for the adventurous spirit she saw. The image dissolved, replaced by another—this time in the familiar surroundings of the lab. Many visions were in the lab where she spent so much of her life. She could see the wrinkles and stress under her eyes in worlds that overwhelmed her, and the carefree lightheartedness in a life of ease. Pale-skinned, at times bone-thin.

It stopped on the bridge of *The Beck & Sail*, wearing Black-water's jacket, facing away. When she turned, a green patch covered her left eye, with a scar still fresh, peeking out and running down her cheek, a scarlet reminder.

"Oh!" Millicent's knees buckled as she stepped back in fear of her own reflection. "Wha—"

"You must be the one who survived Inkwell," came a near-growl from a wild animal. "Come to gloat?"

"No." Millicent shook her head.

The one eye looked her up and down, hate pouring over her in judgment. "Not much," she spat. "Nothing special. Whadd'ya do to get outta that jam?"

"On Inkwell?"

"Where else?"

"Who did that to you?"

"Aye, Grace. Her blade got me good." She pointed to her injury.

"And Barnaby?"

There was a purse of her lips, holding back emotion, protecting herself from something she dared not say. "Saoirse Shadow showed him no mercy. I was lucky to get off Inkwell alive. Unlucky to face the MindShredders, but I took the day and their ship, this ship, as a prize."

"It was Barnaby," Millicent answered her question. "He came after me when Grace had me under the blade."

Her laughter started as a chuckle and grew to a mocking cackle. "Listen to you, all with your properness and posture. 'Oh, look at me, I'm so special.'"

"I am not, not special. I just feel a purpose. To save the Supercluster, to save Gearturn."

"Listen to yourself. Save the Supercluster? Not me. I'm savin' my skin, going after Grace, Saoirse, and the whole gang, well, what's left of 'em."

"What about the malfunction in time?"

"Don't care. Not my problem." She sounded cold, emotionless. But her face tightened as a dark grimace rose from within. "I want Grace. I want her dead. Take her apart. If you wrong us, shall we not take revenge?" She sounded like a growling animal, the beast within that craved flesh, hunted for red meat. "She challenges me. She challenges me, and I won't give up! I'll chase her through the Clockwork Constellation, across the storms of Soma, and through the chaotic realms of Inkwell before I let her win! Her strength makes me angry, and her mysterious ways drive me mad. But I'll face her, no matter what, even if I have to fight the gears of time itself!"

Changes started to ripple in the crystal mirror. Colors swirled, lights flashed, as the reflections looked bright like the brilliance of fresh inks on canvas from the masters, soft like clay in the sculptor's skilled hands. Her anxiety grew, uncertain of what she might face next, what inner demons might spring to life and remind her of choices made, of mistrust placed.

"Finally," she said, looking to herself with hope among the smoke and sparks of the bridge on fire. "It's working, Quark." She called across the void. "You'll have to destroy Moore. Kill Moore. There is no other way." An explosion sent her back, but she stood again with desperation. "This place, this planet you're on, is Echo. You can control it. Control the power." She tried to explain against the noise and commotion. "Difficult to explain it all, you'll need to trust me. Trust us. Use the ship, create a controlled energy pulse, as large as possible, even if you break her. The planet Echo is an amplifier; you need to build a harmonic synchronization between the engines and guns with Mister Marlowe. Echo will use that power and multiply it. Direct the energy, focus it." The failing ship started to break apart. She lost her footing but held tight to finish her explanation. "Point it at the cavern. Destroy it all."

"I would need to take the ship before I did anything like that. What about the Time Core? The Temporal Locket, the Whispering Astrolabe, Grandfather's Pocket Orrery?"

At the loss of oxygen, "Red herrings, all. Moore misled you. Misleads you." Her last words as the vacuum of space stole her life: "It's a trap."

Millicent watched in horror as she slipped away. The disbelief that this would be her fate filled her with anxiety and worry. Something ate at the pit of her gut. She did not want to die. Not like that. There must be another way to save... "Why do I need to save the Supercluster?" she asked out loud. "Why me? I make clocks. Why did I think I could do something so monumental? I should go back to my workshop. Who cares if I live the same moments over, or have to say tick-tock instead of tock-tock? I'll be the only one who knows, and I can live with that. I can live."

"Oh. Hi there." The kind voice came from the mirror.

"Hello," Millicent replied. "Are you Millicent?"

"I am."

"Where are you?"

"The clock shop. Where are you?"

"The planet Echo."

"Cool."

"I cannot see you."

"No one can. I am invisible. There was an accident, and, well, you know Grandpa Thaddius."

"Honey," her grandfather called from a distance. "Who are you talking to?"

"Myself."

He stepped into view. "Millicent?"

"Grandfather?" Her heart swelled with happiness to see him again. "You are alive."

He smiled. "Yes, yes, I am. And I can see you."

"Yes."

"Where are you?"

"Planet Echo. I have traveled here to try and stop Julius Kilmoore from bringing chaos to Gearturn with the Time Core."

"Julius?" A puzzled expression crossed his face. "You mean, Big Joollie? The little kid Ethan and I grew up with?"

"Yes, him."

"He died decades ago, in the temporal tsunami. I've told you that story; Ethan and I told you that story."

"I've never met Ethan."

"Sure, sure, he was over to the house just two days ago. It was an awful thing, losing Big Joollie, the smartest person I've ever known, well, aside from Ethan."

"Grandpa," she said with the softness of a child asking for help, "I, I am trapped in an enigma. I've been betrayed by a space pirate." She attempted to use as few words as possible, knowing that things might change again. She might lose this Grandfather. She was desperate for help. She could not do this alone. She was not smart enough, not special. "Julius is alive to me. He wants to bring chaos to the Supercluster, to Gearturn, through a Pandemonium Paradox Pulse powered by the Time Core."

"Hmm, that is a tricky one. You can't trust pirates. I'm not sure what this pulse ray thingy is." He scratched his head.

"Have you tried turning off the power source?" Invisible Millicent asked.

"What?" The answer struck her hard, knocking her back. "That might work."

"Yes, turn it off, turn it back on, and that should reset everything."

"I like that idea, Millicent," Grandfather said. "Do that. I'm just a gears and sprockets man; what would I know about Time Cores and Paradox Pulse thingies?"

Her stomach rumbled uncomfortably. She felt an unexpected sensation. Her head tilted back involuntarily, her mouth opened wide, and to her amazement, a fluttering cloud of blue iris-colored butterflies emerged, taking flight into the world of Echo. "Well," she mused in surprise, "I guess they were real after all."

Millicent's smile grew as she watched the mirror before her shift and change. The flashes before her no longer held fear or anxiety; they were hope and promise. She wasn't looking at her future; she was looking at options from the menu of time. It was up to her to choose.

Her reflection changed again; it was Barnaby. On the bridge of the ship, engaged in battle. He was young, whole, and salty as ever. Instead, Barnaby wore a bright red twilled fustian jacket. She wondered, "Why would the crystals show the reflection of another?" She watched and listened.

"Ready the cannons," Barnaby barked. "Mister O'Malley, steady our course." Barnaby turned to the aft. "Mister Wren, we be needin' full power. Kick whoever ye need to make us move."

Millicent punched as hard as she could, sending her right fist through the wall, into the world playing out before her. She grabbed Barnaby Blackwater by the scruff of his collar and pulled as hard as she could, with all her weight, dragging him off the bridge and to her feet on Echo.

Broken crystals started to heal themselves with an icy

crunch until the wall of the cave looked just as it did when they arrived.

Barnaby looked up. His eyes met hers, and they connected. She wasn't sure if she was going to beat him to a bloody pulp or hug him, when he asked, "Arr, and who be ye?"

PART V

RACE AGAINST CHAOS

45

"You pulled him out of the crystal wall?" Quark repeated, his mechanical voice tinged with awe.

"Yes," Millicent replied, her eyes darting between the space pirate and her robotic companion. "I can scarcely believe it worked myself. By all logic, my hand should be shattered. But something deep within me—an instinct I can't explain—told me it would succeed."

Quark's optical sensors whirred as they focused on the newcomer. "I must say, I do admire his jacket. That shade of bright red is quite striking."

The pirate, looking bewildered but intrigued, straightened his posture. "Arr, it be needin' some explainin'—where I am, why I'm here, and who you lot be. Last I knew, I was battlin' ships from the Brotherhood of the MindShredders, about to unfurl me Infinity Fold to thwart 'em."

Millicent's lips curved into a knowing smile, her eyes twinkling with a mix of relief and amusement. "That wouldn't have worked, I'm afraid. I'm not entirely sure why, but had you done that, your crew and ship would have been trapped in an endless loop. The MindShredders would have simply given up and departed."

The pirate's eyebrows shot up, a mixture of surprise and grudging respect crossing his weathered features.

Orin signaled to Quark to set him down. Looking up to meet the eyes of his friends, he took the moment to explain:

In the crystal's light, my truth revealed,
 A reflection bare, no more concealed.
 Millicent, Quark, and Barnaby dear,
 Listen close to these words you hear.
 You have carried me far, through space and time,
 Your strength and grace, in rhythm and rhyme.
 I have been blessed, with fortune grand,
 To call you friends, to dangle by your hand.
 But now I see, through crystal's gleam,
 I must stand tall, fulfill my dream.
 No longer lean on your good grace,
 I must contribute, find my place.
 Your aid, a crutch, an excuse, I confess,
 A burden on you, I can no longer press.
 It's time I rise, share the weight,
 On our adventures, I must participate.
 I must show my worth, my true intent,
 Not just take, but give, and be content.
 Your tasks, achievements, I respect,
 And now, my friends, it's time to reflect.
 To stand alone, to walk my path,
 To share the load, embrace the wrath.
 With abilities shown, and merit clear,
 I step forward, with heart sincere.

Millicent, Quark, Barnaby too,
Thank you for all that you do.
From this moment on, let it be known,
Together we journey, but I stand on my own.

As Orin continued his heartfelt poem, the others listened intently. Millicent's eyes glistened with pride, while Barnaby's eyebrows raised in surprise at the eloquence of the small creature he had mistaken for a teddy bear. Quark's circuits hummed softly, processing and storing every word.

When Orin finished, Millicent's voice was warm with emotion. "Orin, I am so proud of you," she said, a happy glow suffusing her features. She then turned to Barnaby, her tone shifting to one of gentle challenge. "Barnaby, we should speak to your better angels."

Barnaby's eyes widened, a mix of confusion and amusement playing across his weathered features. "Yar, what is that?" he asked, gesturing toward Orin. "A cat? A giant teddy bear?"

"He is Orin," Millicent explained patiently, "a poet from Vaporshade."

Recognition dawned on Barnaby's face. "Aye, that explains it." He nodded, stroking his beard thoughtfully. "The gravity, the length of their days and nights. Pleasure to meet you, Orin."

As night began to fall, Quark and Orin gathered kindling and started a fire near the cave entrance. The flames cast flickering shadows across their faces as they settled into a circle, the warmth a comfort against the chill of the alien world.

In a circle, they sat for hours, retelling their adventures as they understood them. It was Barnaby who had taken them by Celestial Spider. Barnaby who had saved her on Inkwell at the blade-point of villains. Barnaby and his crew who had found the coordinates and returned with the Whispering Astrolabe, while the other three had retrieved the Temporal Locket. When all three artifacts were together, Barnaby had delivered them to Kilmoore.

As they spoke, emotions flickered across their faces—pride at their accomplishments, fear at the dangers they'd faced, and a hint of betrayal at the memory of Barnaby's final act. The weight of their shared experiences hung in the air, a testament to the bonds forged through adversity and the lingering questions that remained unanswered.

Millicent, her voice tender and reflecting her kind heart, said, "I know there is still good in him, somewhere. He is good. We just need to find a way to switch him back."

Barnaby Blackwater, clad in his crimson coat, offered a wry smile. "Aye, I'm a rat bastard of the highest order," he retorted. "But what did ye expect from a space pirate? Chivalry and charm are for poets and princes, not for rogues like meself."

"I've seen you at your best, Barnaby," Millicent countered softly. "You might be a salty spirit, but a rogue?"

"Aye, that be true," Barnaby conceded, a hint of vulnerability creeping into his voice. "I've got a soft spot, I'll grant ye that." He paused, his eyes twinkling with a mixture of mischief and wisdom. "It sounds like we're in deeper waters than a pearl diver with a broken rotating watch bezel. Looks like it's time to evolve gills or grow wings."

"Well said," Millicent acknowledged with a nod. "We still need to save Gearturn. Barnaby has the greatest reward waiting there from the Clockmaster when we succeed, and our home is in danger."

Quark whirred thoughtfully before speaking. "Rust may come with age, but wisdom and resilience are the patina that make life's journey all the more beautiful. My reflection and I exchanged a great deal of information that I believe could help."

"Information?" Millicent asked, knowing in great detail each cog, spring, and spoke inside him. She felt a motherly pride seeing Quark grow and become more autonomous.

"My counterpart called it an upgrade, but I sense it's so much more," Quark explained. Turning to the pirate, he added, "Will it be alright to call you Barnaby 'The Red' from now on? It might be confusing to try and address you by your true name."

Barnaby's face split into a wide, toothy grin. "Yar, Barnaby 'The Red.' I like it. Fits me well."

Quark continued, his voice tinged with excitement, "I've been contemplating the Time Core since my upgrade, and I think I understand it better now. The Clockmaster tried to explain it, but it didn't really click until now."

"Arr, this Time Core be mere words to me," Barnaby huffed. He plucked a long stick from the pile and produced a small blade from his pocket. With practiced ease, he whittled the bark at the end, paring it to a fine tip. His hand dove back into his leather pouch, returning with a small pot bearing a turn lid and a paper sack of chocolates labeled "bon-mots."

Carefully, Barnaby extracted a chocolate ball, skewered it on the stick, and dipped it in the white marshmallow fluff nestled inside the jar. He rotated the creation over the fire, letting it roast until it achieved a light, gooey golden-brown hue. This confection was then sandwiched between two crackers from the same pirate sack. He pressed the planes together, pinching the sweet glob into a perfect morsel before popping it into his mouth with evident satisfaction.

"What's that you have?" Millicent asked, her mouth watering and eyes wide with curiosity.

"No name for it," Barnaby replied, licking his lips, "but it tastes mighty fine. Care for one?"

"Oh, yes, please," Millicent responded eagerly, her scientific mind momentarily overtaken by the allure of the mysterious treat.

Moments later, Millicent found the warm treat in her hand. It crunched between her teeth, allowing the sweet mess to pool in her mouth and bring her taste buds to life. "Chocolate?" she asked, eyes widening.

"Milk chocolate," Barnaby confirmed with a nod.

"Is that... is that peanut butter? And marshmallow?" She moaned in delight, rocking in place near the warm fire. "I don't think I've ever had anything like this before. It's exquisite."

"Stick with me, Miss Millicent." Barnaby chuckled heartily. "We always eat well on *The Beck & Sail*."

She reached into her bag and retrieved a paper sack. "I've been eating the standard-issue meal pellets. Would you care to try?" She leaned over and shook the bag, dropping three large brown pills into his hand.

He looked up at her with disbelief, then back at the pellets with curiosity. Barnaby cautiously pinched one and placed it in his mouth as if it might be poisonous. His remaining teeth crunched. A grimace flickered across his face as he managed, "Interesting taste."

"I loathe them," she replied with resigned acceptance.

Barnaby released all the tension in his shoulders, no longer hiding his true feelings. He let out his gut and exclaimed, "Aye, it's bloody awful. Let's make you another of these sweet treats to make up for a lifetime of facing those monstrosities."

As Millicent watched Barnaby craft another delicious treat, she turned to Quark. "What were you saying about the Time Core? You mentioned an upgrade?"

Quark clicked and hummed, retrieving and cataloging memory sequences. "Imagine a child in a playroom with an endless supply of coloring books and materials," he began. "Each page, each book, represents the complete Supercluster. The child has already colored in every page and book, creating a cube of all the events, colors, people, and moments that make up the Supercluster's entire history and future."

"That explains a lot," Barnaby scoffed. "I've seen these drawings, and they never stay inside the lines."

Millicent laughed heartily, realizing she couldn't remember the last time she'd enjoyed being with others so much. She felt an inner warmth, not just from the fire but from the simple realization that she wasn't alone in her struggles.

Quark continued, "Think of our Supercluster, Barnaby—the Clockwork Constellation, the Phantom Spires, Soma, everything you've seen and everywhere you've traveled. It's all already in that pile of coloring books."

Barnaby "The Red" whistled low. "That be a lot of coloring books. I've traveled far and seen many things." He couldn't help but think back to the countless adventures and the lives he'd touched—some for better, others... not so much.

"We call it the 'Time Cube,'" Quark explained. "In every page, or moment in time, it already exists, even if we're only experiencing one page at a time as we flip through it."

Both Barnaby "The Red" and Millicent leaned back, their minds grappling with concepts deeper than they had ever explored before.

"But here's the crux," Quark continued, picking up a stick and sketching a cube in the sand. "There isn't just one coloring book. There's a whole library of them. This is where the Clockmaster's explanation fell short. He missed elucidating the coloring book analogy. Imagine endless books in an infinite number of libraries, each representing a different possible Supercluster or timeline. These are all the other Time Cubes or Block Superclusters."

"...what was it? The Blockhead Supercluster?" Barnaby queried, his brow furrowed in concentration.

"The Block Supercluster Theory, Captain," Quark clarified. "It's a concept in physics suggesting that time isn't a flowing river but more like a solid block—past, present, and future all existing simultaneously."

Millicent's face clouded with concern. "I've seen this book, physics. It was locked away in Grandfather's things."

"Arr, we have physics where I'm from," Barnaby interjected, "but we call it something fancy... *Philosophiæ Naturalis Principia Mathematica*. Me weapons and engineer men, Mister Wren and Mister Marlowe, they know all about this."

"Gearturn doesn't follow the teaching of advanced physics. It stops at pendulum metrics," Quark said.

"So you're telling me we're just characters in some cosmic novel, and the ending's already decided?" Barnaby exclaimed. "That takes all the fun out of being a pirate!"

Quark clicked and whirred before answering, "Not necessarily, Captain. While the events might all exist within the block, our perception of time allows us to experience these moments sequentially—like reading one page after another. You still experience the thrill of the unknown, even if, from a broader perspective, the outcome is already determined."

Millicent, her eyes alight with curiosity, posited, "So, let me get this straight—it's like looking at a map. The entire journey is there, from start to finish, but you don't see every part at once. You experience it step by step, mile by mile. That's how we live our lives, moving through time as if turning the pages of a story."

"Aye, now that makes sense." Barnaby nodded, stroking his beard thoughtfully.

Orin, inspired, interjected:

Pages turned, paths unfurled,
In a block, we see the world.
Yet with each step, each breath, we find,
The story's told, but not in mind.

Barnaby leaned forward, his brow furrowed. "So, if I'm understanding this right, we're all just following a script that's already written, but we don't get to peek at the next page?"

"Precisely," Quark affirmed. "The Block Supercluster Theory suggests that all points in time—past, present, and future—exist simultaneously in a four-dimensional space-time continuum. We perceive time as moving forward, but in reality, every moment is equally real, just like different locations in space."

Barnaby mused, "But that doesn't mean we're puppets with no control. We still make choices, we still experience emotions, and those choices are part of what makes each moment unique—whether or not the future is already 'written.'"

Orin, moved by the discussion, offered another verse:

A block of time, yet hearts are free,
To love, to fight, to simply be.
In this grand tale, with pages wide,
We carve our paths, and there we bide.

Barnaby raised his fluffer jar. "Here's to the pages we haven't read yet, then. May they be filled with enough twists and turns to keep even a pirate guessing." He put the lid on and sealed it with a turn.

Millicent turned to Quark, a new question forming in her mind. "Quark," she said thoughtfully, "you experience time, understand time, perceive time differently than Barnaby and I, don't you?"

"That's true," Quark responded. "As an artificial being, my understanding is vastly different. You are my creator, and life—what might be considered death for me—is merely the flip of a switch."

Millicent leaned forward, intrigued. "Think back, access your memory banks. Help us connect the dots you're seeing that we don't."

The whirs and clicks grew louder as Quark's lights dimmed, power diverted to retrieval and processing.

"Make me one more of those, Barnaby, please," Millicent requested. "They're delicious."

"Three?" Barnaby chuckled, reaching for the jar. "Yar, that must be some appetite."

As Barnaby and Millicent finished their third treat, Quark's sounds ceased, and he rejoined the conversation.

"You have something?" Millicent asked expectantly.

"I've synthesized an answer, but you might not like it," Quark cautioned.

Millicent smiled warmly, tilting her head. "Whether I like it or not, I should hear it. Facts don't care about emotions."

Quark began, "Doctor Kilmoore's transformation into his current state, as he explained, is due to the distance between atoms expanding. The Supercluster is expanding, creating holes. Celestial Spiders travel through these holes, shortening the distance and time traveled between points. Kilmoore lacks the protection of the crystalline structure of the Spiders, which shields the passengers, forever changing him. When he steps into the Time Core, he's entering the library, hoping to find the right book, chapter, and page to alter, changing the past for a better future."

"Saoirse and her gang wanted to flip back to earlier pages and color them differently"—Millicent stared into the fire, contemplating the explanation—"hoping to change their personal stories without disrupting the entire book. They weren't inherently malevolent; they simply wanted Calliope out of the book."

"Yes." Quark nodded. "This force, these powers, have been following us since the initial malfunction we felt on Gearturn."

"Like someone pulling strings," Barnaby mused.

"Precisely like someone pulling strings," Quark affirmed. "Kilmoore pulling the strings."

"Yar," Barnaby exclaimed, "Kilmoore believes he can erase parts of our coloring book and redraw them the way he wants? That means the other Barnaby... You're right, Millicent. There's still good in him."

Quark interjected, "My counterpart and I may have a plan. One option: board *The Beck & Sail* and use its power, with this planet of Echo, to destroy Kilmoore and the weapon he's built."

"Yar, my ship and crew are very good at blastin.'" Barnaby grinned.

"However," Quark cautioned, "putting life at risk when other options are available is illogical."

"I agree." Millicent nodded. "The harder option: turn it off."

"Turning it off and on puts the Supercluster at risk, not just Kilmoore," Quark warned. "Unless we can do it quickly." He quoted the third Tenet of Time: "Time can heal."

46

The skiff lay broken and battered, a testament to their harrowing escape. Millicent approached it with a familiar gleam in her eye, her pack of tools always at hand—elegant yet useful. This wasn't just a repair job; it was a puzzle, a challenge that made her heart race with anticipation.

As she knelt beside the damaged hull, memories flooded back: long nights in her grandfather's workshop, the smell of grease and metal shavings, the satisfying click of gears falling into place. Her fingers, once small and clumsy, now moved with practiced precision, coaxing life back into the dormant machine.

"Barnaby," she called, not looking up from her work, "what's the tolerance on these stabilizer couplings?"

The space pirate sauntered over. He squinted at the component, then grinned. "Aye, she's particular about those. No more than a hair's breadth, or she'll buck like a Zephyrian thunderhorse in a magnetic storm."

Millicent nodded, already recalibrating her approach. As

she worked, her mind raced ahead, seeing possibilities the original designers had missed. A tweak here, an adjustment there—she could make this skiff sing.

Nearby, Quark and Orin had formed an unlikely repair duo. The robot's extendable arms proved invaluable for reaching tight spaces, while Orin's poetic musings on the nature of broken things and renewal seemed to soothe the machine's temperamental circuits.

> *"Fractured metal, circuits frayed,*
> *In Echo's glow, we come to aid.*
> *With gentle touch and minds so keen,*
> *We'll mend what's broke, make old parts gleam."*

As Orin's words drifted through the air, Millicent could have sworn she saw a spark of life flicker through the skiff's dormant systems.

Time on Echo defied conventional measure. The sky above them was a constant, breathtaking display. Brilliant orange bands stretched across the horizon, their edges softening into delicate pinks and purples. Stars peeked through the fading light, twinkling like distant beacons of hope.

They worked through three cycles of this eternal gloaming, their efforts punctuated by Barnaby the Red's colorful curses, Quark's precise calculations, and Orin's soothing rhymes. With each passing "day," the skiff transformed. What had been a wreck now hummed with potential, its sleek lines hinting at the speed and agility they'd need in the trials to come.

On the third rise of Echo's never-setting sun, Millicent stepped back, wiping a smudge of grease from her cheek. Her eyes shone with pride and a hint of trepidation. The skiff was ready, better than new. But were they?

She looked at her companions—Barnaby the Red, with his roguish grin hiding a heart more noble than he'd admit; Quark, whose circuits were now starting to pulse with something akin to resolve; and Orin, standing taller, no longer content to be merely carried along.

"It's time," she said, steady despite the flutter in her chest. "We've got a Supercluster to save."

As they boarded the skiff, the weight of their mission settled over them. The time malfunction, Moore's machinations, the fate of Gearturn, and countless other worlds—it all came down to this moment.

Barnaby the Red took the controls, his hands moving with the confidence of a man born to sail the stars. The engine purred to life, a testament to Millicent's skill and the team's collective effort.

As they lifted off, leaving Echo's serene beauty behind, Millicent allowed herself one last look at the eternal sunset. Its warm glow began to follow them, a reminder of the harmony they fought to restore.

With a burst of speed that pushed them back into their seats, the skiff shot forward. Toward Moore. Toward destiny. Toward the ticking heart of a broken Supercluster that desperately needed their help.

The game was afoot, and time itself hung in the balance.

47

Barnaby "The Red's" fingers hovered over the control panel, a mischievous glint in his eye as he prepared to initiate their daring plan. With a deliberate motion, he cut the engines, plunging the skiff into an eerie silence. The sudden absence of the familiar hum sent a shiver down Millicent's spine.

"Aye, trust me," Barnaby "The Red" whispered and winked.

"I trusted a pirate once. This time needs to be better."

The Beck & Sail loomed ahead, a behemoth against the star-studded backdrop. Barnaby "The Red" guided their craft with the precision of a master thief, slipping into the ship's radar blind spot—a weakness he'd exploited countless times in his colorful past.

Quark hummed and vibrated, his internal chronometer perfectly attuned to the ship's schedule. "Right about now, the night watch will be answering nature's call."

Millicent held her breath as they glided past, close enough to count the rivets on *The Beck & Sail's* hull. For a heart-stopping moment, she was certain they'd be spotted. But Barnaby "The Red's" gambit paid off, and they slipped by undetected.

The planet's atmosphere embraced them, at first a gentle caress that quickly became a possessive grasp. Gravity tugged at the skiff, like a child pinching the nose of a paper airplane a touch too tightly. Millicent's stomach lurched as they began to accelerate, the peaceful drift transforming into a headlong plunge.

"Barnaby," she whispered, her fingers tight as she gripped her seat.

The space pirate didn't respond, his face a mask of concentration as he wrestled with the controls. The skiff rocketed over a landscape of craters and valleys, features blurring into a dizzying smear of grays and blacks.

Orin was wide awake now. His eyes were wide with a mix of terror and exhilaration as he composed aloud:

"Through void we soar, then plummet fast,
 Each breath could be our very last.
 In Barnaby Red's hands, our fate now lies,
 As toward the ground, our vessel flies."

The hill they'd spotted from orbit swelled rapidly, transforming from a mere mound to a looming mountain in what felt like the span of a heartbeat. The craggy face of the rock filled their viewscreen, growing larger with each passing second.

Millicent's heart hammered in her chest. They were going to crash. This was it. The end of their quest, the failure of their mission, all because of a reckless pirate's—

"Barnaby!" she cried out, unable to contain her fear any longer.

Just as it looked like their demise was inevitable, when Millicent could almost feel the crushing impact, Barnaby's hand moved. With a swift, sure motion, he engaged the landing rockets.

The sudden burst of power slammed them all forward against their safety harnesses. Millicent's breath left her in a rush, spots dancing before her eyes from the abrupt deceleration.

The roar of the rockets drowned out all other sound, vibrating through the skiff's frame and rattling Millicent's bones. Yet despite the chaos, she felt the subtle shift as the landing gear deployed, reaching for solid ground.

With a grace that belied their frantic descent, the skiff touched down. The impact was so gentle, so perfectly controlled, that for a moment Millicent wasn't sure they'd landed at all.

As the rocket's roar faded to a whisper, then silence, Barnaby turned to his companions. His face split into a wide grin with the thrill of the feat he'd just pulled off.

"Arr, now that," he said, "be how you make an entrance."

Millicent wanted to berate him, to unleash the fear and frustration that had built up during their descent. But as the adrenaline faded, she found herself fighting back a smile of her own. They were alive. They were undetected. And they were one step closer to confronting Moore and saving the Supercluster.

With trembling hands, she unclasped her safety harness. It was time to move. The real challenge was just beginning.

The skiff's landing gear settled into the rocky soil with a soft crunch, mere meters from one of the five entrances to Moore's cavern. Quark's initial scans, performed during their first ill-fated visit, had mapped out these access points. This particular entrance, clearly of ancient origin, bore the weight of centuries of disuse.

As they disembarked, the group huddled close, their breath visible in the chill, stale air. Millicent's eyes darted nervously between her companions, each face etched with determination and barely concealed fear.

"Remember," she whispered, over the distant drip of water echoing through the cavern, "we each have a crucial role to play."

Orin nodded, while Barnaby "The Red's" hand rested on the hilt of his cutlass, a grim smile playing on his lips. "Aye, and I've a date with me doppelganger. Time to see which Barnaby Blackwater truly rules the galax-seas."

Quark's circuits hummed with anticipation. "Millicent and I will neutralize the Time Core," he stated, his normally jovial tone now replaced with something more serious.

They shared a moment of silent communication, each understanding the weight of their mission. The fate of the Supercluster hung in the balance, dependent on their ability to work in perfect synchronization.

Barnaby "The Red" broke the tension with a single word: "Courage." It wasn't just a platitude but a rallying cry, a reminder of what had brought them this far.

They pressed forward into the ancient corridor. The walls, slick with moisture and age, seemed to close in around them. Phosphorescent fungi cast an eerie, pulsating glow that did little to dispel the oppressive darkness. The air grew thicker as they advanced, heavy with the musty scent of decay and forgotten secrets.

As they neared the end of the passage, a different quality of light began to filter through—the familiar, pulsating glow of the Time Core. Its rhythm, once so alien, now began to echo the beating of their own hearts.

Cautiously, they peered out into the vast chamber beyond. The Time Core dominated the space, its housing rising and falling like the breath of some cosmic beast. Its light painted long, dancing shadows across Moore's makeshift workshop, glinting off mysterious apparatus and half-finished inventions.

And there, unmistakable even in silhouette, was the panache of Barnaby Blackwater, looming over the hunched, monstrous form of Moore himself.

Barnaby "The Red" was the first to move. With the grace of a seasoned burglar, he slipped from the tunnel's mouth, using the ruined buildings for cover. His eyes scanned the debris-strewn floor, settling on a precariously balanced pile of metal scraps. With a well-aimed kick, he sent them clattering to the ground, the sound reverberating through the cavern like a thunderclap.

Moore's voice echoed in response, a discordant mix of irritation and excitement: "Go, go, see what that was, Captain. I'm nearly finished."

Barnaby Blackwater replied gruffly, "Aye, rats be my guess."

Seizing the moment, Orin stepped forward on his own. His muscles tensed, but his face was a mask of calm. With careful, measured steps, he positioned himself away from the Time Core and workshop, but well within Moore's line of sight.

Drawing a deep breath, Orin prepared to unleash his verbal barrage. His mind raced, weaving together strands of rhythm and rhyme, chaos and adulation. He only needed to capture Moore's attention for a few crucial moments—long enough for Millicent and Quark to reach the Time Core, long enough for Barnaby "The Red" to confront his counterpart.

"The Chaotic Sonnet of Time's Unraveling, a poem in eight parts."

The game was afoot. The final confrontation had begun. Orin sounded strong and true, filling the air with lyrical power.

"I. The Summons

Moore, great architect of time's discord,
Draw near and heed this humble bard's refrain.
Your deeds, like ripples in a cosmic fjord,
Deserve a verse, a wild and untamed strain.
From distant stars, I've journeyed far to sing
Of chaos's beauty, your vision unbound.
Let my words echo, let my praises ring,
As I extol the new world you have found."

CRUNCH. Moore's massive form shifted, his improvised stool groaning in protest. He leaned to his right, trying to catch a glimpse of the unexpected poet. The movement sent shadows dancing across the workshop, momentarily obscuring the pulsing glow of the Time Core.

The curious giant, at first reluctant, rose to his full, imposing height. He lumbered toward Orin, each step sending tremors through the cavern floor. When he spoke, his words were a low rumble that Orin felt in his bones.

"I have work that needs to be done, be gone, little one, be gone. Don't stir my rage, or you might find my mouse's cage."

Despite the threat, there was a note of intrigue in Moore's tone. His eyes, set deep in his misshapen face, glinted with a spark of interest.

Seizing the moment of distraction, Millicent and Quark sprang into action. With the stealth of seasoned thieves, they slipped past the workshop's threshold. The pulsing light of the

Time Core beckoned them forward, its rhythmic glow painting their faces in alternating light and shadow.

As they crept toward their target, Orin drew a deep breath, ready to launch into the next stanza. He knew that every second he could hold Moore's attention was precious. The fate of the Supercluster hung on his ability to tell a tale so enthralling that even a mad genius couldn't look away.

The air crackled with tension as Orin prepared to continue his performance, Millicent and Quark inched closer to the Time Core, and Moore's massive form loomed over them all, a titan poised between curiosity and rage.

Barnaby Blackwater stepped forward, his weathered boot testing the ground with each step. The familiar rasp of steel against leather froze him in place. From the shadows, a figure emerged, blade glinting in the dim light, a crimson corsair at the ready.

Barnaby Blackwater's eyes widened as he took in the sight of himself—a ghost from the past made flesh in a red jacket. "Well, well," he drawled, masking his shock with bravado, "who might this handsome devil be?"

Barnaby "The Red's" lip curled in disdain. "Aye, handsome is only the start. Deadly to match." The man's stance was coiled, ready to strike.

"I've heard of beauty being a curse," Barnaby Blackwater quipped, eyeing the razor's edge of the blade, "but you take it to a new level. Aye, it must be painful to see my face used to such perfection."

Barnaby "The Red's" eyes flashed with barely contained fury. "You wear my face, but you'll never lose the guilt of abandoning our men. Those men trusted us, and you left them to rot, trapped, and ran. You'll carry that guilt every day for the rest of your life—fortunately, that time will be short."

A shadow passed over Barnaby Blackwater's face, a flicker of remorse quickly buried. "Aye, you be the one who stayed." With deliberate slowness, he drew his own cutlass, the metal singing as it left its sheath. The weight of the weapon felt familiar in his calloused hand, a grim reminder of countless battles fought. "Not smart enough to get away and later return to save the day."

The scarlet swashbuckler spat on the ground, his contempt palpable. "Aye, and you be the one to cut and run. It's clear-cut to me, I don't like the man you've become."

"Every wrinkle I own is a lesson learned," Barnaby Blackwater retorted, shifting his stance as he stepped just outside of reach, "and I've got a face full of experience."

"Every wrinkle you wear will always bear the mark of a coward." Barnaby "The Red" lunged forward, his blade a silver blur. The other man reacted with surprising speed, their weapons meeting with a resounding clang that echoed through the chamber. "Arr, you may have me face, but ye've not got me charm," Barnaby Blackwater quipped.

"Charm? Is that what you call it? I thought it was the smell of low tide," Barnaby "The Red" retorted.

As they circled each other, Barnaby Blackwater took on a taunting edge. "Your so-called friends are only with you out of desperation, not loyalty." He feinted left before swinging right, Barnaby "The Red" barely managing to dance out of reach.

Undeterred, Barnaby "The Red" pressed his attack. "Your moves are as creaky as a ship in a storm." He unleashed a flurry of strikes, forcing his older self to give ground. "I call this The Mermaid's Sneeze!"

"You should call that a Kraken's Tickle! A mere scratch." Barnaby Blackwater held his shoulder where the blade cut through the jacket, shirt, and skin already starting to bleed.

The clash of steel on steel filled the air as the two men—mirror images separated by jacket colors, guilt, and resentment—engaged in a deadly dance. Each strike carried the weight of their shared past, every parry a denial of the other's accusations. As they fought, it became clear that this confrontation was about more than just survival; it was a battle for redemption, for the soul of the man they both claimed to be.

48

"I. *The Dance of Entropy,*" Orin announced clearly through the cavernous space.

Moore's massive form shifted, a mountain of flesh and bone creaking with irritation. "How many of these are there?" he grumbled, his voice rumbling with an impact Orin felt in his chest.

Undeterred, Orin continued, his words painting vivid images in the air:

> *"Time's rigid march, once steady as the stars,*
> *Now pirouettes in gorgeous disarray.*
> *You've snapped the shackles, burst through all the bars,*
> *That kept the universe in dull ballet.*
> *In chaos's embrace, new patterns emerge,*
> *A symphony of beautiful disorder.*
> *As old laws crumble, new truths surge,*
> *Painting cosmos with a fresh, wild border."*

Moore's misshapen head tilted, a spark of interest igniting in his deep-set eyes. "Interesting," he mused, massive fingers tapping against his workbench. "You're right; chaos brings new patterns and will bring down the old order."

As Moore contemplated, Millicent seized her chance. She crept past the distracted giant, her heart pounding so loudly she feared it might give her away. The Time Core's housing loomed before her, a fortress of metal and mystery.

Quark glided silently beside her, his voice barely a whisper. "I'm not just a timepiece; I'm a master of the art of evasion!"

Millicent couldn't help but smile, despite the tension. "Yes, you are, my friend." The tip of her tongue peeked out between her lips as she focused on the lock, her nimble fingers working with practiced precision.

The heat radiating from the Time Core caught her off guard. With each pulse, the temperature spiked, turning the air around them into a shimmering kiln. Then darkness would fall, plunging them into a bone-chilling cold. The rapid changes made her head spin.

"Here, here, let me try," Quark offered, his mechanical limbs extending. "Silently I can peel and pry."

With surprising gentleness for his strength, Quark eased the door open. The metal groaned softly, but the sound was lost beneath Orin's continuing performance.

As the door swung wide, Millicent's eyes grew large. The Time Core pulsed before them, a perfect orb of swirling energy. Its surface was utterly smooth, defying her expectations. Where was she supposed to use the Temporal Locket?

"It's round," she said over the sound of the Time Core.

"Gravity pulls equally on all sides, pulling at the Core, like a black hole," Quark explained.

Confusion began to cloud her mind, made worse by the

disorienting pulses of heat and cold. Millicent pressed on, skirting the wall until she reached the opposite side. There, finally, she spotted it—a small port, almost hidden in the orb's mesmerizing glow.

With trembling fingers, Millicent unclasped the Temporal Locket from around her neck. As she did, a familiar, loving sound drifted to her ears. "Grandfather?" she whispered, her eyes widening.

The Pocket Orrery on its chain around her neck began to vibrate, as if answering an unheard call. She fished it out from her white blouse, cradling it in her other hand.

"Millicent." Her grandfather's voice was clearer now, filled with warmth and urgency.

Heart racing, she stepped forward. In an instant, the world around her dissolved into pure light. She was enveloped in a cocoon of radiance, surrounded by a beauty beyond imagination. Everything made sense.

Millicent found herself reliving the start of her journey, every moment as vivid as when she first experienced it. But now, impossibly, she stood beside the Clockmaster himself.

The elder rose, his robes shimmering with otherworldly light. He resonated with the wisdom of ages as he spoke:

"The Time Core is the origin of everything, the singularity where time, space, and matter converge and diverge. It is both a physical entity and an abstract construct, the heart of the Supercluster and the source of all creation."

The scene shifted, each statement accompanied by a new vision of cosmic wonder:

"It emanates."

"Synchronizes."

"But the 'Time Core' originates. We, Gearturn, are the measure; it is the chaos."

Millicent's mind reeled as she witnessed the dance of creation itself:

"Ever-shifting, you will know it when you see it. Light and darkness, a dance of color, shapes that defy description."

"An orb, pulsing, vibrant hues from the past and the future. It is both beautiful and terrifying, peaceable and violent."

"Your mind will blend magic and advanced science, a harmonious balance of arcane forces and quantum mechanics."

Just as abruptly as it began, the vision changed. Millicent felt herself pulled through time, cradled in the Time Core's embrace. She landed in her grandfather's workshop, on the day of his memorial. The weight of her black dress matched the heaviness in her heart, the world around her dark and cold.

But the Time Core wasn't finished. It lifted her once more, carrying her further back. The scent of salt air filled her nostrils, accompanied by anguished cries: "Ethan! No, Ethan, no!"

She saw it then—the tower of old technology reaching into the ocean, and the impossible wave that rose to meet it. The temporal tsunami crashed down, and Millicent watched in horror as Ethan died a thousand deaths across countless dimensions.

Beside her stood Thaddius and Julius, their young faces pale with shock and grief. They were just boys on the cusp of manhood, unprepared for the weight of loss about to shape their lives.

In the span of a heartbeat, Millicent found herself back in the present, standing next to Quark in the Time Core's chamber.

"Did you see that?" she gasped, her mind struggling to process the cosmic journey she'd just experienced.

Quark's optical sensors focused on her, confusion evident. "See what?"

Millicent's whole body tingled with newfound knowledge, the realization spreading through her like wildfire. "I was just carried through time and space." She breathed in, filling her lungs with awe and dawning comprehension. "Moore was right." Her eyes were wide open. "Great gears of Glockenspiel, he was right."

Determination set her jaw as she reached for the remaining chain around her neck. "I can save them," she declared, her fingers closing around the Whispering Astrolabe. "With this, I can find them, save them."

As she prepared to use the artifact, the weight of her decision hung in the air. The fate of time itself balanced on the edge of a razor, and Millicent Gearwright held the power to tip the scales.

49

"II. *The Brilliance of Destruction,*" Orin continued, dropping to a near whisper as he took a subtle step backward. The cavern walls amplified his words, sending them echoing into the shadowy recesses.

Moore's misshapen head cocked to one side, his lips mouthing the word "destruction" with a mixture of curiosity and anticipation. The context gave him pause, his massive form tensing like a predator about to pounce.

> *"They call it madness, this grand design of yours,*
> *But genius often wears insanity's mask."*

Orin inched closer to the door, his heart pounding so loudly he feared Moore might hear it. The giant's brow furrowed, confusion etching deep lines in his already distorted features. His breath came in heavy, ragged gasps, filling the air with the scent of sulfur.

"Hey now, madness, insanity, what—" Moore began, but Orin pressed on, his words a lifeline he clung to desperately.

"You've opened countless unexpected doors,
Completed an impossible, Herculean task.
In breaking time, you've set creation free,
From the tyranny of cause and dull effect."

A grin spread across Moore's face, revealing teeth too large for his mouth, like stalactites and stalagmites in a cavern about to collide. "That's more like it." His voice rumbled through the chamber, making small pebbles dance at Orin's feet.

"Now possibility's a boundless sea,
Where past and future endlessly intersect."

Orin paused dramatically, taking another step backward. Moore, entranced by the little poet, shuffled forward, eager to be closer to this unexpected admirer. The pulsing light from the Time Core cast grotesque shadows across his face, accentuating his alien features.

"*IV. The Misunderstood Visionary,*" Orin announced, sounding steady despite the fear coursing through his veins.

Moore's grin widened impossibly. "Now this artist gets me." His eyes gleamed with a manic light, torn between his fascination with Orin's words and his obsession with his work.

Meanwhile, in another part of the cavern, steel met steel with a ferocious clang. The clash of cutlasses rang out like a twisted bell, a sharp, metallic symphony underscoring the deadly dance between the two Barnabys.

"Your muscles are as weak as your comebacks, old man," Barnaby "The Red" taunted, parrying a vicious strike. The cavern amplified each clash, sending echoes bouncing off the walls.

Blackwater sneered, "You may have my looks, but you lack my... everything else."

"Aye."

"Arr."

They circled each other, evenly matched, each waiting for the other to make a fatal mistake. Barnaby Blackwater closed his eyes for a moment of meditation, reaching out beyond the physical realm. To his surprise, he found his foe's thoughts open and unprotected, ripe for the picking. He had never trained with, or even met, Stark Maddox in his Supercluster.

"It's almost tragic how you waste—" Barnaby "The Red" winced, his words cut short by an unseen force. In his mind, he felt a presence, alien yet familiar, probing at the edges of his consciousness. He struggled for a moment, forcing out, "Need a nap, old man?" He shook his head as if bothered by an invisible insect, swatting at the air with his free hand.

Blackwater smiled, delighted at the impact. He closed his eyes again, focusing on the weak spot he'd discovered in his opponent's mental defenses.

Distraction clouded Barnaby "The Red's" eyes. His cutlass clattered to the ground as his hands shot up, cupping his ears. He fell to his knees, curling into a tight ball and screaming in terror while his doppelganger stood at a safe distance, watching with a mixture of pity and triumph.

"It gives me no pleasure to teach you this lesson," Blackwater said bitterly. "But let's face it, life has a way of giving ya the exact experiences you need to evolve. Boy'O, evolving hurts."

"Get out of my head." He strained. "There's hardly enough room in here for one of us."

Barnaby "The Red" tightened his fetal position, desperate to escape the mental onslaught. In his mind, memories and fears swirled in a chaotic maelstrom. He began to squirm and writhe, inching backward across the dirty cavern floor until his back pressed against the rough stone wall.

Back in the main chamber, Orin felt like a bone being chased by a colossal, hungry dog. He felt a moment's pride in successfully leading Moore away from the workshop and the Time Core, making Millicent and Quark's job easier.

> *"Maligned by many, understood by few,*
> *Your burden weighs like Atlas's mighty load.*
> *But I perceive the greatness shining through,*
> *The noble purpose on your winding road.*
> *For in disruption lie the seeds of growth,*
> *In upheaval, the chance for return.*
> *Though others curse, I offer you this oath:*
> *Your name shall echo 'cross the transformed Gearturn."*

As the last word left Orin's lips, he saw Moore snap to attention. The giant's head whipped around, his gaze locking on to the workshop and the Time Core within. The air began to thicken, charged with the weight of Moore's sudden shift in focus.

"You, little one," Moore rumbled, his fury shaking the air, "are a commotion, not a convert." He turned, his massive form blocking out the light. "I must complete my work. More power, more control, more chaos. I need more to save Ethan. I can get to him. I can bring him back, save him." His words were tinged with a desperate, manic energy that made Orin's blood run cold.

In the tunnel, Blackwater felt the tremor of Moore's rage

and movement. "Aye, feel that? The big guy must be upset. Did he find your friends?" He turned, ready to head back the way he came.

Barnaby "The Red" lay spent on the ground, still curled into a tight ball. He had never known punishment or torture like this before. A thousand million memories buzzed in his head, an agonizing swarm of past defeats and rejections, pecking at his sanity without mercy. The cavern's chill seeped into his bones, a stark contrast to the burning in his mind.

Barnaby "The Red" had only one way to stop this impending madness, to slow his alternate, and it was his last act of desperation, saved for the occasion of saving his own life. His right finger extended, and the tip touched his right eyeball, where that twinkle and charm had sparked for years, extracting the stolen star. Enduring the pain, he removed the star that had shone there for many seasons and saw it balance on the tip of his finger. With a simple flick, the star shot across the distance, growing in size, heat, and strength, blinding Blackwater. As he ran from the blast, Barnaby Blackwater shouted, "You squandered your powder and ball, ya got nothin' left but your life!"

As Blackwater was chased away, Barnaby "The Red" felt a moment of relief. The constant hum of the Time Core pulsed through the rock beneath him, reminding him of the stakes. He knew the source of this mental magic now, it was emanating from Blackwater in brown, and understood what needed to be done. It wasn't enough to distract him; he had to destroy him. Millicent hoped that there was good in him, that she might find redemption, but not now. He had to be stopped. But how?

50

"Quark." She sounded desperate. "I can save Ethan." The Whispering Astrolabe pulsed in her hand, its siren song impossible to ignore. "I can save Grandfather. Stop Moore."

Quark crackled with urgency, his circuits sizzling in the Time Core's heat. "This wasn't the plan, Millicent. You can't change time. Thaddius and Ethan are gone. I know you miss your grandfather, but this isn't the way." He inched closer, servos whirring. "Give me the Temporal Locket. We can pause time, just as we planned."

Millicent's eyes flashed with defiance, her words sharp with anger. "You'll ruin everything. I'll get them back."

Quark's optical sensors dimmed with concern. "This isn't you, Millicent. Listen to yourself—think of what happened to Saoirse. Don't do this. Moore isn't right. Please, give me the Locket."

But Millicent was transfixed by the Time Core's mesmerizing glow, its power calling to her with impossible promises of ultimate control. She inched closer, her skin blistering as she approached. The urge to merge with it, to control time itself, overwhelmed her reason.

"There will never be another chance like this." Millicent quavered as she raised the Astrolabe. It whispered to her seductively, "Who?"

"Ethan," Millicent breathed. "Find Ethan." She lifted the artifact to her ear, eager for its guidance.

The chain of the Pocket Orrery jerked violently, as if possessed. The two artifacts warred with each other, one yanking toward her ear, the other desperately pulling free.

With a sharp snap, the Orrery's chain broke. The built-up tension released in an instant, and Millicent's hand flew up, smacking her squarely in the face. The impact jolted her back to reality. The Time Core's hold weakened, and though the Astrolabe still called, its voice now seemed distant. Millicent blinked, her mind clearing.

In that moment of lucidity, she saw a vision of her grandfather. His hands were raised, palms out, repeating a silent mantra: "Let go."

Millicent looked down at the artifacts—Astrolabe in her right hand, Pocket Orrery on the ground, Temporal Locket around her neck. As she reached for the Locket, a thunderous crash shook the cavern.

The far wall exploded inward. Through the dust and debris loomed Moore, his grotesque form barely recognizable. "More!" he roared, ripping at the walls as if they were made of tissue paper.

His massive arm shot out, grasping for Millicent. In that split second, she made her choice. She yanked the Temporal Locket free and hurled it toward Quark.

The robot's reflexes were lightning-fast. He leapt, snatching the Locket midair. His arm extended impossibly, slotting the artifact into the hidden port at the Time Core's base.

With a precise twist of his wrist, Quark activated the Locket. The Time Core's pulsing slowed, its breath cooling. In less than a millionth of a second, Quark reversed the Locket, turning it back on.

A blinding wave of light exploded outward, engulfing everything. Time itself paused, just for an instant. The shockwave rippled across space-time, racing past Echo, Zephyria, Inkwell, Gablehaven, and deep into Gearturn's core. It washed away the temporal distortions, cleansing the Supercluster of Moore's misguided attempts to rewrite history.

As reality reset itself, Quark sprang into action. He lunged toward Millicent, whose body was already showing signs of temporal burn. His momentum carried them both away from the Time Core, his unique alloy shielding her from the worst of the energy burst.

Moore, fixated on the Time Core, leaned into the blast. "More!" he bellowed. His enormous mass was drawn in, his screams echoing, "More! More!" All of his hugeness compressed to a singularity in a terrifying flash of light.

The cavern walls, once transparent and unyielding, now liquefied and collapsed. No longer constrained by Moore's will, they melted away like wax. The chamber flooded with piercing light, forcing Orin to stumble backward, shielding his eyes.

As the light began to fade, Millicent stirred in Quark's protective embrace. She blinked, her vision slowly returning. The Time Core pulsed gently now, its rhythm steady and controlled, "Tock-Tock."

"Did we... did we do it?" she whispered.

Quark's optical sensors scanned the room. "Affirmative.

Temporal readings are stabilizing. The malfunction has been corrected."

Millicent struggled to sit up, wincing at the lingering pain from her close encounter with the Time Core. Her eyes fell on the Whispering Astrolabe, now silent.

"I almost... I could have..." she stammered, the weight of her near mistake crashing down on her.

Quark sounded gentle. "But you didn't. You made the right choice, Millicent. You saved us all."

A low groan echoed through the chamber. Orin stumbled toward them, looking dazed but unharmed. "Did it end?" he asked, tinged with wonder and exhaustion. "I still have four verses, my friend."

Before Millicent could answer, a familiar figure appeared in the doorway. Barnaby "The Red" limped in, looking battered but triumphant.

"Arr, looks like I missed all the fun," he quipped, surveying the destruction around them. "Did anyone happen to see my darker half? He may have slipped past me."

Millicent felt a bubble of laughter rise in her throat, born of relief and the sheer absurdity of their situation. Soon, all four of them were laughing, the sound echoing through the remnants of Moore's lair.

As their laughter subsided, Millicent's expression grew serious. "We did it. We saved Gearturn. But what now?"

Barnaby "The Red's" eyes sparkled with his characteristic mischief. "Well, lass, I know this little tavern at the end of the galaxy. The rum's always ice-cold, and the beach is perfect for resting your feet."

"We have earned a drink," Millicent agreed, a smile tugging at her lips. She carefully retrieved the Pocket Orrery and tucked it safely into her pack alongside the Whispering Astrolabe.

Red watched her. "Aye, that we have. Then the Supercluster is our oyster, and I've heard tell of a treasure so vast..." He trailed off, filled with promise.

Millicent looked at her companions—Quark, steadfast and loyal; Orin, no longer content to be a passive observer; and Barnaby "The Red," the rogue with a heart of gold. She felt a surge of affection for this mismatched family she'd found. There was no replacing her grandfather, but she felt a fuller life ahead. "Adventure sounds perfect," she said, smiling. "But first, let's go home. Gearturn is waiting for us. Barnaby has a reward waiting from the Clockmaster."

"I do?" Barnaby's eyebrows shot up in surprise. "I mean, I do."

As they made their way down the tunnel where they had entered, life began to flourish around the Time Core. Walls started to crawl with lichen, sprouts of green broke through the floor, and streams of water began to trickle and flow. The Time Core was returning its world back to what it had been before Kilmoore discovered it—a lush, hidden place that created time.

Millicent paused, taking in the transformation. "It's beautiful," she whispered, awe in her breath.

Barnaby nodded, uncharacteristically solemn. "Aye, lass. Sometimes the best treasures are the ones we protect, not plunder."

51

Barnaby "The Red" inhaled deeply as he stepped onto the bridge of *The Beck & Sail*, the familiar scents of polished brass and ozone from humming machinery filling his nostrils. It felt like coming home. His eyes swept across the control panels and the crew at their stations, a mixture of anticipation and apprehension churning in his gut. This was the true test—would these men accept him as their captain after all they'd been through?

"Captain on the bridge," Mister Marlowe announced, his voice carrying a hint of uncertainty.

The crew snapped to attention, their eyes fixed on Barnaby. He squared his shoulders, pushing aside the pain from his recent injuries, and nodded to Millicent, Orin, and Quark, who hung back near the entrance.

Barnaby "The Red" clicked the communicator. "Mister Wren, status report."

"All systems clear, one hundred percent, sir," came the prompt reply.

"Aye, good." Barnaby "The Red" switched to the ship-wide channel. "All hands, this be your captain. I'm pleased to report our mission was a success. A reward awaits us on Gearturn for our efforts. After arrival, we'll be takin' some well-deserved shore leave. Prepare to make way."

To Barnaby's relief, no questions or challenges arose. The crew accepted him without hesitation. He allowed himself a small smile. True, there was no immediate treasure, but the promise of a reward on Gearturn should keep the men satisfied for now.

"Mister Rook, set course for Gearturn, best speed," he ordered.

As Rook and O'Malley carried out his commands, Barnaby turned to Millicent. "Miss Gearwright, I hear ye've got some ideas on improvin' our engines. Why don't you and Quark head down to assist Mister Wren?"

"We're on it, Captain," she said steadily, though her mind raced with thoughts of the wonderful challenges ahead and the bittersweet memories of their journey.

Later that evening, the four heroes gathered in the captain's quarters for a well-deserved meal. They fell upon the food with ravenous enthusiasm, savoring every bite after days of emergency rations. As they ate, a comfortable silence settled over the group, punctuated only by the clink of utensils and the occasional satisfied sigh.

Millicent was the first to break the quiet. "What do you think the Clockmaster's reward will be?"

The pirate captain paused, a chicken leg halfway to his mouth. "Gold's always good," he mused. "Though platinum might be more useful for the ship."

Millicent chuckled. "What if it's not treasure? What if they give you a plaque or a key to the city?"

Barnaby's brow furrowed. "A gold key?" He shook his head. "A key that don't open anythin'? What good is that?"

"It's a symbol of gratitude, I suppose," Millicent explained.

"Arr, I'd rather have somethin' I can spend," Barnaby grumbled good-naturedly.

As they continued to discuss potential rewards, Orin remained uncharacteristically quiet, focused intently on his meal. Quark, ever-observant, noticed but said nothing.

Days later, *The Beck & Sail* docked at Gearturn. Barnaby "The Red" and his crew, resplendent in freshly pressed uniforms, disembarked with heads held high, ready for their heroes' welcome. As they stepped onto Gearturn's surface, Barnaby "The Red's" heart sank. There was no fanfare, no grand welcome—just the indifferent hustle and bustle of everyday life. The citizens moved past them, oblivious to the peril they had faced and the sacrifices made. A bitter taste filled his mouth, and he clenched his fists, feeling the sting of unacknowledged heroism. The weight of their unrecognized efforts pressed heavily on his shoulders, making him feel like a stranger in a world he had saved.

Millicent saw the disappointment etched on Red's face and the restlessness in his crew's eyes. For them, years had passed since the start of their adventure, even if it felt like mere months.

"Let's see the Clockmaster," Millicent suggested, trying to lift their spirits. "Surely he'll recognize your efforts."

As they made their way through Gearturn's streets, Millicent noticed subtle yet pervasive changes. New rules were in place, and a militia patrolled the thoroughfares, questioning citizens about their activities with an air of suspicion. When questioned herself, Millicent's protests were met with a cold, robotic response: "These are the rules. We are following the rules, and you should too."

Premier Jasper Horologe, recognizing the tension, intervened swiftly. "This is Millicent Gearwright, a good citizen of Celestial City, a productive member of Gearturn," he declared with authority. "Please, she follows the rules. Let her be on her way."

As they continued their walk, Millicent spotted a familiar face in the crowd—a middle-aged woman contentedly making her way to market. "Ivy Equinox," Millicent called out warmly, "so good to see you doing well."

The woman's face lit up with recognition. "Little Millicent Gearwright," she replied, filled with affection, "you need to stop by for some of my seasonal preserves. I have a jar set aside just for you."

"That would be delightful," Millicent responded, her smile genuine. "We can catch up on things." As Ivy continued on her way, Millicent couldn't help but notice the subtle signs of aging in her friend's face. It was clear that Ivy had avoided facing her fear of going through youth again, instead settling somewhere short of full retirement. Not everything was as it once was, but nearly, Millicent realized with a pang of sadness.

As they approached the Clocktower, the familiar "tock-tock" of Gearturn's timekeeping echoed through the streets, a constant reminder of the ordered world they had fought to preserve. Millicent led her team through the crowd, acutely aware of the odd looks their pirate attire attracted. They were a group out of place and out of time, heroes unrecognized in a world they had saved.

At the giant walnut door, Millicent raised the large metal knocker and let gravity sound their arrival. The same gatekeeper as before answered, his eyes widening in recognition and then narrowing with suspicion. "You?" he exclaimed, tinged with alarm. "I was told not to let you in."

Undeterred, Millicent pushed past him, leading her companions into the Clockmaster's chamber. The air was thick with tension as they entered, an atmosphere of resistance to their presence. "Clockmaster," she began with determination and a hint of defiance, "I bring before you Barnaby Blackwater and the crew of *The Beck & Sail*. They have returned from their journey to fix the Time Core and save Gearturn. They come to claim their reward."

The Clockmaster's tripartite form shifted, confusion evident in their synchronized voices. They glanced at each other, their movements almost mechanical.

The eldest Clockmaster leaned forward, his gravelly voice carrying a hint of skepticism. "Reward, you say? What exactly did we offer, and for what purpose?"

The youngest Clockmaster added, his tone sharp, "And this broken Time Core—when did this supposed calamity occur?"

Millicent felt a chill run down her spine as the reality of their situation began to dawn on her. She hesitated, her mind racing. Nevertheless, she pressed on, steady despite her growing unease. "Yes, broken, casting this world into chaos," she explained, glancing at Barnaby for support. "But they fixed it. You are welcome." She bowed deeply, a gesture both respectful and partly mocking. "Now, the reward you promised."

"Time Core broken?" The Clockmasters' voices echoed with disbelief, their expressions shifting from confusion to concern.

Barnaby "The Red" stepped forward, his eyes blazing with resolve. "Aye, the Time Core," he growled. "We fought tooth and nail to keep this world from plungin' into eternal chaos. Kilmoore's schemes nearly tore the fabric of time apart. And now you stand there, oblivious to our struggles?"

The Clockmasters exchanged uneasy glances, their synchronized movements betraying their uncertainty. "Kilmoore... Time Core malfunctioning..." they muttered, as if testing the words for truth. The eldest finally spoke up, more contemplative. "We... we were unaware of such events."

Millicent felt a surge of anger and despair. "Unaware? How could you be unaware?" she almost shouted. "We fought through the chaos, through time itself, to save this world. And you... you don't even remember?"

Barnaby "The Red's" jaw tightened as he stepped closer to the Clockmasters. "We risked our lives, lost good people, and faced unimaginable horrors," he said, low and intense. "All for Gearturn. And now you tell us you know nothin' of it?"

Leaving the chamber, their unrecognized deeds weighed heavily on them. Disappointment etched on their faces, Barnaby and his crew headed to the market for provisions. With a nod of unspoken understanding, Barnaby parted ways with Millicent, Orin, and Quark, knowing their paths would cross again.

Millicent, Orin, and Quark made their way to Orin's cottage, their steps heavy with the burden of their invisible victory. But as they approached, they were met with a sight that stopped them in their tracks. Where Orin's home had once stood, there was now only an open plot, the building razed, a lot vacant. Standing outside the space was a single man in the uniform of the militia, his face an impassive mask.

"Upon this land, my heart's retreat,
    Where once stood walls, now lies defeat,
    'What's happened here?' I cry in dread,
    My voice in shock, with anger fed.
    My cottage gone, without a trace?

What storm or hand did this displace?
Why would you do such a callous thing,
Destroy the peace that home did bring?
What gives you the right, with might so fierce,
To tear my world, my soul to pierce?
Uproot me from the life I've known,
And trample dreams I've built alone?
O wrath of fate, O cruel design,
Why strip away what once was mine?
In echoes loud, my spirit roars,
For justice lost, for open sores."

The militiaman's response was cold and bureaucratic, devoid of empathy. "Sir," he started to explain, his tone matter-of-fact, "this building was condemned by the city. You did not follow the codes of compliance or the rules of upkeep. On notice, we delivered thrice, we didn't hear an answer, exterminated the mice, and brought the place down. Here is the bill and invoice you need to pay for the work we did on your behalf. You've got ninety days to pay or will be deported from Gearturn."

Orin's face fell, the weight of this new reality crushing his spirit. Each word from the militiaman felt like a poke at a bruise, deepening the wound of his loss. His mind raced back to the memories of his home, now reduced to rubble. He trembled with a mixture of sorrow and grief-fueled resolve as he spoke, each line of his poem a desperate attempt to make sense of the senseless destruction. He felt his dreams crumble around him, replaced by a grim resolve to find solace elsewhere:

"If this is the way the law's cold hand,
Shall shape my fate, shall rule this land,

Then home I'll go, with heavy heart,
Back to Vaporshade, where dreams did start.
On a hammock in the shade, I'll lie,
Beneath the vast and tender sky,
Where sweet-scented breezes play,
And birds in springtime chase and sway.
I was wrong to leave my quiet nest,
To seek the world, to face its test,
For all the trouble, all the strife,
That came with seeking a different life.
In my pursuit of new and bold,
I lost the warmth, the gentle hold,
Of home's embrace, so calm and kind,
Now shattered dreams are all I find.
With heart distraught and spirit torn,
I long for peace, where I was born,
To Vaporshade, I'll make my way,
And in its shade, my soul will stay.
No more to venture, no more to roam,
I'll find my solace, safe at home,
For in that tranquil, shaded glade,
My broken heart might yet be swayed."

Millicent watched Orin, a man who had once embodied the quiet peace of Gearturn, now a shadow of his former self. The destruction of his home felt like a cruel metaphor for the changes they all faced. As she held him close, she realized that sometimes, the hardest battles were not those fought with weapons but those waged within.

Millicent began to weep. She held her friend in a warm embrace. "There's only so much a hug can do, no matter how hard I squeeze."

With a heavy heart, Orin bid his farewells, much wiser, independent and strong, and resolute to make a name for himself on these next adventures. He made his way to the Celestial Spider terminal, leaving Millicent and Quark to face the changed Gearturn without him.

Millicent watched him go, her heart weighed down by the cost of their victory. They had saved Gearturn, but at what personal price? No glory, no reward, not even a simple "thank you."

Days passed, filled with sorrow and a profound sense of loss. Millicent found herself adrift in a world she had saved but no longer recognized. The streets of Gearturn, once familiar and comforting, now felt alien and cold. Then, unexpectedly, a summons arrived from the Capitol Clocktower.

As Millicent approached the imposing structure, her heart raced with a mixture of anticipation and trepidation. This time, the doors swung open without question, the gatekeeper's previous suspicion replaced by a deferential nod. She entered, her dress flowing gracefully, hair meticulously styled, with Quark freshly polished at her side.

The Clockmasters' chamber vibrated and hummed with extra energy. As Millicent stepped forward, she noticed subtle differences in each Clockmaster's demeanor.

The eldest Clockmaster, his eyes deep-set and wise, spoke first. "Millicent Gearwright," he intoned, his voice rich with gravitas. "We thank you for answering our call."

"Indeed," added the middle Clockmaster, with silver hair and keen eyes. "It's not every day we host the savior of the Supercluster."

Millicent blinked, hardly daring to believe her ears. "You... you know?" she stammered, sounding of hope and disbelief. "You understand what we went through?"

The youngest Clockmaster leaned forward, his face etched with a combination of awe and guilt. "It took us far too long to piece it all together," he admitted. "Your claims... they were extraordinary. We needed time to verify them. Every planet in the Clockwork Constellation has confirmed your reports. The facts don't lie."

"And verify them we did," the middle Clockmaster continued, his tone tinged with respect. "We've come to understand the monumental risks you and your companions faced. The battle against Kilmoore, the temptations of the Time Core's power..."

The eldest Clockmaster nodded. "Your heart remained pure, Millicent. For that, we owe you our deepest gratitude."

Millicent's joy faltered. "And my friends? They were essential to our success."

The Clockmasters exchanged glances before the youngest replied bluntly, "Pirates don't receive honors here."

Millicent felt her hope begin to crumble, but the eldest Clockmaster quickly interjected, "Regardless, we wish to honor you, Millicent. We propose naming a day in your honor. No, a week would be more fitting. In fact..."

"A month," the three Clockmasters declared in unison, their voices harmonizing in a way that sent a shiver down Millicent's spine. "We shall proclaim Millicent Gearwright Month, in recognition of your heroic deeds in saving our world. A new Clocktower will be built next to this one, from the finest craftsman in all of Gearturn, with a mechanical display telling your journey. You can supervise its construction."

Millicent's mind raced as she weighed their offer. Images flashed before her eyes—the perils they'd faced, the bonds they'd forged, the sacrifices they'd made. The green of Inkwell. The stale smell of Celestial Spiders. Those mean owls and the rich soil where she found the Temporal Locket. Facing her true self in the crystal wall. Seeing the edges of time itself, almost a toy in her hand. Her heart ached with the injustice of it all. When she finally spoke, she was firm but laden with emotion.

"I'm deeply honored by your offer," she began, measuring her words carefully. "I must decline." She stood strong as a gasp echoed through the chamber. "My friends—yes, even those you dismiss as mere pirates—were as vital to saving Gearturn as the gears in a clock. Their names deserve to be honored alongside mine. To accept this without them would be a betrayal of everything we fought for." She paused, gathering her thoughts. "It goes against everything we've fought for. And perhaps... perhaps I was wrong before. A little chaos, a little unpredictability—it's what makes life vibrant and worth living."

The Clockmasters stared at her, clearly taken aback by her refusal. Millicent bowed deeply to their thrones, then turned and strode out of the chamber, her head held high. As she walked away, a laugh bubbled up from deep within her, startling Quark.

"What's so funny?" her clockwork companion asked, puzzled by her sudden mirth.

Millicent's eyes sparkled with a mixture of wisdom and mischief as she replied, "The butterflies have all escaped."

Two weeks passed, and Millicent found herself in her workshop with Quark, working on a mechanical clock that would tell the whole story of all their adventures. Part of her wanted to mark the adventures with this new timepiece. Part of her needed to stay out of the way of a militia, whose reply to her was to repeat, "Those are the rules. We follow the rules, why won't you?"

She felt this overwhelming sense of disharmony. Everything looked the same on Gearturn, but it felt different. Or maybe she was the one who had changed. Probably both, if she were to be honest with herself.

Seeing the new rules, the militia, the suspicion... it was jarring. "This wasn't the Gearturn we fought so hard to save," she opened up to Quark. "And yet, in a way, it was exactly what I had always believed in—order, structure, rules. But now, after everything I experienced, it all feels... stifling to be here."

She sat at her stool, at her favorite part of the workbench, and said, "This feels different. Is this my stool? Did something happen to it? Did you try and fix it?"

"I did nothing of the like. It's the same stool, in the same spot it's always been."

She turned back to her work. Aligning the gears and cogs of the new clock, she found her mind drifting, becoming unfocused. "I miss the unpredictability of our journey. The thrill of not knowing what would happen next, the joy of finding creative solutions to impossible problems. Even Barnaby's recklessness, which used to drive me mad, now feels like a breath of fresh air compared to the rigid conformity around here.

"Don't get me wrong—I still believe in the importance of order," she explained to Quark, fidgeting with a cog that never fit. "What would Barnaby say? Wild winds and rough seas that make life worth the sail! It's what drives innovation and growth. Are you sure this is the same stool?"

A knock at the door revealed Barnaby "The Red," his expression a mixture of excitement and concern.

"Aye, I be needing your help, Miss Gearwright," he said without preamble. "I've had word from Gablehaven. Word be, me darker half has been causin' trouble there."

Millicent's eyes lit up. "What kind of trouble?"

"Scaly, reptilian kind," Barnaby replied with a grin. "They've got themselves a crocodile problem."

Millicent felt a thrill run through her. She just wasn't a gears-and-sprockets girl. The life of a simple clockmaker no longer called to her—she craved adventure and purpose. Something where merit could show her worth.

"Count me in," she said without hesitation. "But first, there's something I need your help with here."

That night, under the cover of darkness, away from the eyes of the militia or the watch of the Clockmaster, Millicent and her companions crept through Gearturn's streets. With Quark's help, she carefully chiseled into the stone of the tabernacle where the Tenets of Time were displayed. If Gearturn wanted control and to only follow the rules, she would give them a new one to consider.

As the first light of dawn bathed the Celestial City of Gearturn, the key monks moved in a hushed line, their footsteps echoing softly as they approached the towering clocks to wind their ancient springs. The warm light of sunrise caressed Millicent's marble etching, casting a gentle glow across its surface. In the morning's embrace, the marble took on a life of its own, its cool, smooth texture now suffused with a golden warmth that hinted at the day's promise. As the sun climbed higher, the marble would shift and change, reflecting the passage of time in shades of light and shadow. But in this first light, it radiated a quiet hope, a silent reminder of the lessons etched not only in stone but in Millicent's heart from their incredible journey.

Below the original tenets: Time is fleeting, Time is subjective, Time can heal, Time can be a source of regret, Time is a force of change, and Time is cyclical, a new line shone: "Time is Precious, more so with friends."

Back on the bridge of *The Beck & Sail*, Barnaby "The Red" stood tall, his loyal crew at their stations and his newfound family by his side. "Mister O'Malley," he called out with renewed purpose, "set course for Gablehaven. We've got some crocodiles to wrangle."

As the ship lifted off, Millicent felt a surge of excitement. Their adventure wasn't over—it was just beginning. And this time, she was ready for whatever the Supercluster might throw at them.

The Beck & Sail soared into the star-studded expanse, carrying its mismatched crew towards new horizons, new challenges, and the promise of more thrilling escapades in the vast Clockwork Constellation. The familiar "tock-tock" of Gearturn faded behind them, replaced by the steady hum of the ship's engines and the beating of their own adventurous hearts.

"Captain, the scope is showing three Mindshredder ships ahead."

Millicent and Barnaby's eyes locked in a knowing look. This was only the beginning.

THANK YOU

Thank you for embarking on the adventure of *Clockwork Constellation: Chrono Chaos*! I hope the journey was as exciting for you to read as it was for me to write. If you enjoyed it, I'd greatly appreciate if you could take a moment to share your thoughts on Goodreads, Amazon, Barnes & Noble, or your favorite book platform. Your reviews and word of mouth are invaluable in helping independent authors like me reach new readers. Tell your friends.

Stay tuned—Millicent, Barnaby, and Quark will be back for more high-flying thrills in *Clockwork Constellation: Crocodile Cult*!

The *Clockwork Constellation* faces its most dangerous challenge yet—crocodiles! Barnaby Blackwater, the notorious time-stealing pirate, and Millicent Gearwright, the brilliant young inventor, are thrust into a perilous mission with Quark, Millicent's loyal robot, at their side. Their journey takes them to Gabelhaven, a world famed for its towering spires and steeples, where the Crocodile Cult, a shadowy mafia-like organization, is tightening its grip on the galaxy.

As they team up with daring Steeplejack Gideon Highwire and rogue pilot Stark Maddox, they begin to unravel the mystery of the Crocodile Cult's enigmatic leader. What is the cult's ultimate goal? And how far will they go to seize control of the galaxy?

Fast-paced and brimming with adventure, *Clockwork Constellation: Crocodile Cult* promises readers a thrilling ride through dizzying heights, treacherous skies, and vertigo-inducing spire-top battles. As they soar above Gabelhaven's towering steeples, facing secretive factions and high-stakes showdowns, the clock is ticking—can they stop the cult before it's too late?

Grab your copy today and dive into the heart-pounding sequel to *Clockwork Constellation: Chrono Chaos*!

ACKNOWLEDGMENTS

Special thanks to:

Sara Kelly, for your sharp editing and honest feedback.

Anne Kern, for the late-night texts, voting on covers, and character approvals.

Lila Henry, for being my willing test subject.

ABOUT THE AUTHOR

Paul Michael Peters is an acclaimed American author, masterfully weaving narratives that traverse the realms of thrillers, suspense, and the beautifully unexpected. Renowned for his adeptness at crafting compelling twists and delving into life's quirky tangents, he invites readers into worlds both startlingly and intimately human.

Dive deeper into the worlds created by Paul Michael Peters by signing up for our newsletter. As a welcome gift, you'll receive a complimentary copy of *Love in Her Big Two-Hearted River*, offering a glimpse into the extraordinary experiences that define his work. Join us on a journey through stories that resonate with the intricacies of the human spirit and the shadows of the unknown.

Web: https://www.paulmichaelpeters.com/

ALSO BY THE AUTHOR

MIST AND MOONBEAMS:

STORIES FROM THE GREAT LAKES EDGE

Along the Great Lakes' shores, five poignant tales unfold, exploring love, loss, power, and control.

Dive into the heart of the Great Lakes region with *Mist and Moonbeams: Stories from the Great Lakes Edge*, a compelling anthology that captures the essence of adventure, the depths of human emotion, and the quest for redemption. Through five distinct tales, this collection unravels the complex tapestry of love, loss, and discovery against the backdrop of America's iconic freshwater horizons.

Mist and Moonbeams invites readers into a world where the mystic allure of the Great Lakes intertwines with the human spirit, offering a journey of unforgettable tales that resonate with the call of the wild, the pain of heartbreak, and the hope of new beginnings. Discover the magic and majesty hidden in these stories, where each page turns to reveal the profound connections between us and the natural world.

RIGHT HAND OF THE RESISTANCE

Amid relative peace, plots for assassination, upheaval, and revolution threaten the balance of power.

In a world eerily parallel to our own, life is bisected by the Barrier—a monolithic edifice that symbolizes division and control. It segregates nations and dictates the very fate of those bold enough to cross. *Right Hand of the Resistance,* by Paul Michael Peters melds the heart-pounding suspense of Tom Clancy, the speculative genius of Dan Simmons, and the prescient vision of George Orwell to capture the essence of a divided society. It challenges the Golden Rule by asking, "How well should we treat one another?" The narrative follows perilous treks to the north, fraught with danger yet illuminated by the hope of a better existence beyond the oppressive divide.

Paul Michael Peters maps a world where passage across the Barrier involves high costs and profound sacrifices, all under the watchful eyes of authorities dictating fates. Amidst this, a covert resistance emerges, daring to defy and dismantle the status quo, embodying the novel's core themes of rebellion and resilience.

Through a blend of suspense, intrigue, and fiction, Paul Michael Peters dissects themes of love, faith, family, power, and control. This narrative compels readers to question their realities. *Right Hand of the Resistance* is an exploration of human extremes, delivering a narrative that resonates deeply with our contemporary challenges while hinting at ominous futures.

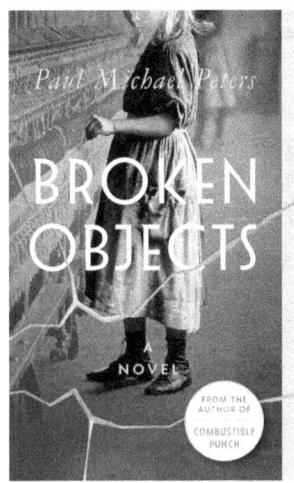

BROKEN OBJECTS

A poor immigrant's daughter is sold into servitude, trapping her in a cycle of bad choices and broken people.

"The world breaks everyone and afterward many are strong at the broken places." — Ernest Hemingway, A Farewell to Arms

Broken Objects captures the spirit of America in the era between the start of the Civil War and the turn of the new century following the life of Linnea Karlsson, the first naturally born American in an immigrant family from Sweden, now farming north of Detroit, Michigan.

At the age of ten, Papa sends Linnea to work in the city. Farm life is rough, but Linnea quickly learns she must be tougher growing up in the textile mill making uniforms for the Union Army. Each person she meets introduces her to an America in adolescence, transforming her life. What will she learn that shapes her into becoming a woman? What does it take to persevere through life's hardships from the Civil

War through Reconstruction for the average American to create a new century of greatness?

COMBUSTIBLE PUNCH

A high school shooting survivor becomes the fixation of a female serial killer.

Haunted by memories of a high school shooting, not even the bottle can wash away the gnawing guilt and creeping feelings of inadequacy that batter Rick's conscience daily.

His life has been a mess of broken marriages, writer's block, terrible choices, and the morbid pity of others. When he meets Harriet at a writer's conference, the record doesn't scratch as he falls back—only this time, he may not get up.

INSENSIBLE LOSS

Two people discover that drinking from the Fountain of Youth can make them younger, but not better.

2053: An old man, Viktor Erikson, lies on his deathbed. Alone and with no known relatives, he is tended to by Olivia, a nurse. He has only one request: that she reads to him.

The request is not unusual, but the battered, leather-bound tome she must read is no ordinary book. Written in 1839, it chronicles the discovery of the fountain of youth by Morgana de la Motte—and Viktor Erikson.

What starts off as a swashbuckling adventure on the high seas in search of riches and eternal life soon transforms into something quite different: a clash between two personalities bound by love and deceit, locked together by a terrible burden of necessity.